Inheritance

Fallon O'Neill

This is a work of fiction. Names, characters, places, and incidents are products of the author's imagination or are used fictitiously and are not to be construed as real. Any resemblance to actual events, locations, organizations, or persons, living or dead, is entirely coincidental.

World Castle Publishing, LLC
Pensacola, Florida

Hardback ISBN: 9798891264908
Paperback ISBN: 9798891264915
eBook ISBN: 9798891264748
First Edition World Castle Publishing, LLC, February 15, 2026
http://www.worldcastlepublishing.com

Cover: Nix Whittaker
Editor: Karen Fuller

PROLOGUE

It is a dark age, a bloody age, an age of pike and shot. It is an age of devastation, an apocalypse born of man. And yet, amidst the fire, pestilence, and death, it too is a time of high art and fledgling science, of testaments to man's reason and the tragedy of his promise.

In the wake of enlightenment, schism and uncertainty sweep the abbey and manor alike, ushering in the question of faith and doctrine yet to be written. With the Word of God and grievous miracle in the common tongue, man is cursed with a great and terrible freedom—the gospel of the self. With the way to heaven in one's hand, hell vomits forth a hate unrivaled.

Come the clarion call, brother turns against brother in tides of torrential carnage. Mortars fire with thunderous booms across acres of carrion and scatter the crows. The Ecclesiarchy stands as a hollow edifice of piety and prestige, its indulgences spent on gilded works and greased palms, belfries tolling only to sound the alarm. The farms and fields are trampled and robbed to the lowest root. Swaths of parishes are razed by desperate brigands, the innocent hanged from gibbets for sport, the very soil sodomized by suffering. Even the Imperial Cities, with their bastion walls and lecture halls, are not exempt from the horror, their decadence but a veil over cesspits of revolt and violent agitation—feeding the worms of the earth.

In such an age, is it the destiny of mankind to suffer a world of perdition? Is it the Hand of God that conducts the Music of the Spheres, binding us to these atrocities? Or is there something else—the will to act, beyond the book or the preacher? At least, it is true that sin not only stains our hands, but those of

our fathers and forebears.
Those who laid the foundation of ruin.

CHAPTER ONE

The mists thickened. Swirling in dampness, they enveloped the upland moor, as if conspiring to blot out the sun. Sequestered in the relative safety of the stagecoach, Rufus lifted the curtain with slender fingers, eyes fixed upon the brooding mountains. Gaunt trees loomed on either side of the Old Road, and brooks cleaved their way through the hills, bleeding into loathsome mires where leeches swam in sullen waters. Distant peals of thunder filled the valley. His only companion was the silhouette of the driver. Stone and soil shuddered under the wheel, and yet, the coach lumbered on its due course.

Something snapped. Whether branch or spoke, Rufus could not say.

"Sir," he called, "would you kindly slow down a bit? Are we in such a hurry?"

"That we are," the driver said. "You'll thank me when we reach the hamlet. Only a fool travels the Old Road at night."

Rufus unscrewed his pewter flask and took a shot of whiskey. His face was pale and betrayed his sickly nature. Though he fancied himself a member of the peerage, his hair was disheveled and oily. Dressed in a violet vest and black trousers, Rufus sported brass buttoned cuffs and would not dare leave home without his tailcoat—a weather-worn shield against that which addled his humors. Even now, he reread the letter, trying to make sense of it all.

Urgent. I have a job for you. Return home to the family estate.
Baron Matthias Grünewald

A sudden shift in the road summoned a wave of nausea. What was he to make of this? What manner of job? What was so urgent? Regardless, the seal was unmistakably of House Grünewald with its arboreal heraldry. Rufus had not seen the estate since childhood and only remembered it vaguely, though its surrounding acres had clearly seen better days.

"You're a long way from the city, lad," said the driver. "Who are you, really?"

"Does it matter?" Something about the driver unsettled Rufus. Maybe it was the way he stared over his shoulder, or how his lips were peeled in a grin, but if this was a local's way of conversation, then Rufus preferred silence. "I am the grandson of the baron, for what it's worth."

"What?" the driver scoffed. "Now that you mention it, I can see the resemblance. I wouldn't go flaunting that around, though. Just a bit of friendly advice."

"I assure you, this is hardly my idea of a holiday."

"On business?"

"Something of the sort."

Rufus took another sip from his flask. A fortnight had passed since he had left the comfort of his loft. He missed his feather pillows and garret window overlooking the theater district, where he frequented the cafes, drank with playwrights, and flirted with barmaids. It was hardly sustainable. With tabs unpaid and goodbyes unsaid, Rufus had answered the letter. Desperation had gotten the better of him, and so, he found himself on the Old Road.

Suddenly, a wheel shattered as the shriek of horses filled Rufus's ears. Before he could grasp the door, the coach swerved and toppled, and he fell prone against the wall. Winded, he gasped for air and heaved himself upright, pushing past the bludgeoning pain in his back as he crawled out of the wreckage. Moments bled together in a montage of misery as Rufus salvaged his luggage.

Such were his priorities. The coach had stumbled into a pothole. It was not until after Rufus had gathered his belongings that he realized something—the driver was nowhere to be seen. Even the horses had vanished into the woods.

Silence stung the air.

Rufus's heart sank into his chest. Dread cast a pall upon his thoughts. He found himself in a particularly dense stretch of woodland. Skeletal branches clawed at the setting sun, and a faint mewling reached his ears. Slowly, he opened a trunk and drew his blackthorn shillelagh—head hollowed and filled with lead, imported from Skellige. It was the only practical thing he had brought. The Old Road lay before him, and so, step by step, he began the trek to Altstadt.

"Nothing for it," he muttered.

Rufus attempted to tread lightly, but the creak of his wheeled trunks betrayed any notion of stealth. The clouds darkened as a cold breeze whisked piles of dead leaves. Passing by shallow graves and thick, gnarled trees, Rufus propped his coat's collar, if only to ease his own lingering fear. Then came the rain, pattering in torrents against roots and foliage. Before long, his clothes were soaked and his thighs began to chafe. In the wake of the silver hour, Rufus spied a palisade of sharpened logs blocking the roadway. A pair of broad-shouldered figures emerged from the mists. Clad in slashed doublets and voluminous breeches, armed with matchlock pistols and halberds, they sported a range of colors and luscious beards—landsknechts, so-called "servants of the land," by the look of them.

"Halt," the taller one shouted. "In the name of law, there is a toll. Pay up or face justice."

Rufus halted in his tracks. "Ah, yes, of course." He reached for his coin purse, only to find a meager handful of brass pennies. "Uh," he managed, "may I ask what the toll is?"

"Depends," said the other. "You look pretty well off."

Rufus brushed his wet bangs out of his eyes. "I wouldn't go that far, but my grandfather is the baron you serve." He offered the damp letter from his pocket. "I assure you, it's authentic."

"Yeah," scoffed the shorter of the two, "you get the friends and family discount."

Rufus watched the men reach for their pistols. He raised his hands and stepped back. "Easy, gentlemen," he said. "What's the toll, exactly?"

"For you?" One of the brutes eyed his luggage. "Half."

"Pardon?"

"Half of whatever you've got."

Rufus bit his lip but was not one to argue. He kicked open a truck and bid the "guards" to take their pick. As they rummaged through his belongings, Rufus crossed his arms and mustered the courage to speak up. "How do you know the baron?"

"Oh," said the tall one, "we're part of the 'local militia,' if you take my meaning."

"I'm afraid I don't."

The landsknecht tipped his feathered hat with a sneer. "Make no mistake, we're the best of what you could've encountered out here. And we're going easy on you."

"How thoughtful...."

After parting with his silk shirts, a spare coat, and more than a few bottles of brandy, Rufus conceded with a sigh. "Now, may I pass?"

"I'll tell you what," said the tallest. "Since we're on our way back, how about we escort you to town?" He grinned, revealing a gap in his yellowed teeth. "Free of charge."

Rufus raised a thin eyebrow, unsure as to what to make of this. Given his luck so far, they would likely shank him and dump his corpse in a ditch. Then again, there was something off about this country—an eerie forbearance that defied explanation.

Though he hardly took stock in local legends, Rufus had

his suspicions that things far worse than bandits dwelled in the gathering dark.

"I accept your offer," he said. "May I have your names?"

"No."

Rufus and his escort left the barricade behind. Night had befallen the Grünewald, though not a star shone in the sky. The darkness was thick and unnatural, as if wafting from the earth in a miasma. Roughly a mile down the road, one of the bandits raised an oil lamp, shedding scant light upon the trees and muddy trail. The other drew a long knife with care. Rufus clutched his shillelagh, gripping its heavy head, trusting neither of the mercenaries—a moan carried from off the road, belonging to no known beast and too warped to be human. His thoughts were flooded with images of ill-defined creatures, defying natural science and the taxonomy of learned men. From the edge of sight, he spied a shadow in the forest, only for it to vanish as soon as it appeared. At first, Rufus thought it was a trick of the light, but the color had drained from his captors' faces. Then he looked down. Rufus cupped a hand over his mouth. There lay a carcass of woodland game, perhaps a fawn. Judging by the sliced wounds and entrails, whatever had eviscerated the creature took its time, relishing in an agonizing kill, reflecting a brutality that no animal possessed. The guards crept around the carrion, eying the shadows for any sign of danger.

Nothing emerged. No one dared to speak.

Rufus weighed his options. The lamp would undoubtedly attract whatever lurked in the dark—he could flee blindly into the woods, taking his chances. Then again, he hadn't the faintest idea of how many leagues were left, and should he be caught, whether by bandits or the thing, death wouldn't be far behind. With a deep, shuddering breath, Rufus carried on.

Eventually, he spied lights beyond the forest, flickering from tall silhouettes, recognizing them as village dwellings.

"Altstadt?" he whispered.

His escorts nodded in silence. As they emerged from the Grünewald, Rufus was greeted by rows of wheat upon the outskirts—wheelbarrows and threshing flails were left strewn by mills and granaries, acres guarded by scarecrows in cruciform poses with heads of rotting turnips. A low granite wall separated these fields from the hamlet proper, where half-timbered houses loomed with slender gables and glowing windows. The gates were reduced to a few planks on rusty hinges, as if subjected to countless fires and raids. Not a soul lingered in the open street. Rising from the marketplace was the clock tower of the Rathaus, though the nearest establishment of note was the Hofbräuhaus—a coaching inn wafting with the smell of sausage and fresh bread by the west gate. Rufus assumed that would have been his destination regardless.

"We're safe here, no?" he asked.

"Safe as you'd expect," said the taller, "but yes." He heaved his payment over his broad shoulder and waved. "Take care, now."

Left with a single trunk, Rufus rid himself of the bandits with a grimace. Though hardly at ease, he opened the swollen door to the taproom, welcoming the warmth of the hearth. Under rafters and candled chandeliers, wooden tables and seats sat low in the dimness, and above the fireplace rested a poorly taxidermied head of a boar. A few huddled men took refuge at the bar, swigging swill as the night wore on. The ceiling moaned under the weight of its second-story business, salacious as it was, and the clink of bottles filled the air.

Rufus pulled up a seat only to be met with silent stares.

"Ah," he said, "I'll take a…drink."

The innkeeper, a burly middle-aged man sporting an artisanal mustache, nodded and poured a draft into a stein. Rufus shifted its contents with studious intent. It was flat. Stomaching the lukewarm brew, he pined for a bourbon but doubted the bar offered such luxury.

Forcing a smile, he offered a gloved hand in mock politeness.

"Hello," he said, "I'm—"

"We know," said the innkeeper. "Grandson of Matthias Grünewald. Heir apparent to the estate and its surrounds." He went back to polishing the glasses. "Welcome home, such as it is."

"Heir?" Rufus asked. "Well, a technicality, I suppose."

"What brings you to this godforsaken place?" asked a one-eyed patron.

"A letter, and work. Apparently, the baron has a job offer."

The locals murmured in low laughter. The innkeeper leaned on the counter, locking eyes with Rufus. "Just how much did your grandfather explain to you?"

"Not much, I'm afraid," he managed.

"Well, I'm not privy to say," the innkeeper shrugged, "only that you'd best stay indoors."

Keeping to his beer, Rufus wondered what the tight-lipped locals meant by such warnings. "I'll say this much. The journey here was…unnerving."

The innkeeper smirked. "Surprised you made it, to be honest."

"I don't suppose anyone can introduce me to the baron at this hour," Rufus said. "No matter. There's always tomorrow."

The innkeeper took a deep breath. "About that."

"What's the fuss? If I don't know any better, I'd say he's—"

The door swung open, and another local staggered into the inn. Balding and bespectacled, he groped his way to the bar, dressed in a thick, black coat and lambskin boots. Rufus inched back as the oddly well-to-do drunk raised a pair of wrinkled fingers, as if to wordlessly order a double. The innkeeper nodded in familiar understanding, pouring him a generous shot of the Hofbräu's finest rotgut.

"Gottfried," the innkeeper said. "He's arrived."

"Really now?" He raised his weary head. "The master's blood and kin?"

The innkeeper nodded in Rufus's direction. "So it would seem."

It took him a moment to understand the implications of the exchange, but Rufus soon caught on. "A pleasure to make your acquaintance," he said with a nod. "Are you the burgomeister of this town? A servant of the household?"

Gottfried downed his shot like a python on a dying rat. "Yes, I am." His eyes gleamed with inebriated resignation. "You are the spitting image of the master. God rest his soul."

"Excuse me?"

Gottfried turned to eye the innkeeper. "How much did you tell him?"

"Figured you'd want to do the honors."

"I beg your pardon," Rufus said, cheeks flushing with indignation, "b-but no one has explained so much as anything. I understand that you folk prefer to keep to yourselves, but if my grandfather is dead, I'd like to know how and why!" Though he felt many things, grief was not among them. He recalled nothing save the shade of an old man, obscured by the fog of distant memory. Truth be told, Rufus did not know him in the slightest. "What is the meaning of this?"

Gottfried uttered a sad laugh. "Come, I'll enlighten you of your ancestor's folly. Turn in your luggage and join me at the town hall. We keep the stronger stuff there at any rate."

The burgomeister slid a few thalers across the countertop. Laying a hand against Rufus's back, Gottfried ushered his ward down to Main Street. Houses and shops were locked for the night, many wholly abandoned, windows boarded and shut.

Near the Abbey of Saint Hildegarde, Rufus passed by rows of gray headstones, where the earth was damp and soft. Climbing the shallow steps towards the Rathaus, he fixed his eyes upon the clock tower—its strange dials and zodiacal rings, which shimmered with stained glass, encircled by wooden grotesques.

Bleak as it was, Altstadt was not without gothic sophistication.

"When was this town founded?" Rufus asked.

"Oh," Gottfried said, "difficult to say. Between fire, plague, and war, Altstadt has been destroyed more than once, and yet, folk always manage to resettle in the shadow of Schloss Fleischburg." Upon the threshold, he rummaged through his pockets and dug out a ring of iron keys. "House Grünewald has long presided over the hamlet and its surroundings."

With a click and creak, Gottfried unlocked the heavy doors and bid Rufus to follow him inside. Past the rows of wooden benches and columns sat a black curtained stage crowned with a slender podium. Flanked by staircases to the surrounding balcony, a handful of doors led to a variety of archives, most dilapidated by neglect. Oil paintings were framed about the walls—moody landscapes and portraits of long-dead magistrates. Musty and faded, the Rathaus was a shade of civility—a trove of records and ledgers that had not seen council in generations. Gottfried raised an oil lamp and led the way up the stairs to his own office, which housed a fine mahogany desk, brown hangings, and shelves of antique books.

The smell of dust and liquor permeated the air.

"Would you care for a vintage?" Gottfried opened a bottle with a thunk and poured himself a generous snifter of brandy. "Very good year. Almost as old as I am."

Rufus accepted the offer with as much grace as he could muster.

"Let's begin with the legalities," the burgomeister said,

rummaging through drawers of documents. "Ah, here we are." He laid a contract and a pen on the tabletop. "Sign here, please."

"Why?"

Gottfried gazed at the heir from over his spectacles. "The baron's left you, Altstadt, along with all his possessions. The estate and its environs are yours now."

Rufus read the contract carefully. Most of it was self-explanatory or superfluous, but a few phrases, such as "personal responsibility for any injury—physical, mental, or fiscal—that befalls the party in question," and "I hereby claim my birthright and pray that God have mercy upon my immortal soul," raised more than a few questions. He tapped his pen on the desk. The endeavor was absurd, and yet, what had he to return to? Crippling debt and an eviction notice? This was his only escape from poverty—a new beginning, though a far cry from the life of a socialite. With a deep breath and nothing to lose, he scrawled a shaky signature. Crimson ink bled into the parchment. Morbid certainty gripped Rufus's heart, and the implications of what he had signed swept over him like a gale. He reached for a snifter and took a drink—the liquor burned his throat yet carried a certain sweetness.

"Tell me," he asked, "what happened to my grandfather?"

"The baron was...eccentric," Gottfried began, "even by the standards of rural gentry. He kept himself locked away in the castle. Indeed, I was one of the very few to see him often." He eyed a particularly grim portrait above the fireplace. "He had a keen interest in occultism. Such passion drove him deep into study as he sought to master a power underneath the estate."

"And what is this power?"

An uncanny draft wafted through the open window, stirring cobwebs and motes of dust, as if the slightest mention disturbed an entity pervading the Grünewald.

Gottfried sipped his brandy, seemingly unfazed. "Centuries

ago, Schloss Fleischburg was built upon a fissure in the hill from which foul-smelling fumes escaped. So deep that no light could reach the bottom. Evil portents and sightings have been reported in the region since the earliest records, but it wasn't until recently that such phenomena were explored. Your grandfather rallied a troupe of convicts to explore the Pit, promising them freedom in exchange for this simple task. When the first was lowered into the darkness, he was told to shout out should he encounter any trouble." He finished his glass with a gulp. "Within seconds, there was a shriek, and the prisoner begged to be let up, raving and crying. He was driven insane by the experience and locked in the Narrenturm—the Fool's Tower. Of course, the other prisoners refused to participate in the expedition thereafter. Word spread and, by imperial decree, a chapel was consecrated over the Pit to prevent whatever lurked down there from clawing its way to the surface. Inner fortifications were constructed in haste, facing into the courtyard. However, this did nothing to stop your grandfather's meddling."

"What then?" Rufus asked.

"You can imagine that he didn't take kindly to such precautions. He delved deeper in secret and, eventually, descended into the Pit himself. It's been months since. Before he left, however, your grandfather sent out a letter to his next of kin. To ensure the estate would be governed properly, should something happen to him down there in the dark."

Rufus caught his leg trembling as he lifted a brandy to his lips. Though disturbed, he clutched his kneecap and mustered his reason. "Did you find a corpse?"

Gottfried did not reply.

Rufus refrained from scoffing. Surely, he was not expected to believe this. Eerie as this country was, whatever had killed his grandfather was of flesh and blood, assuming that he was truly dead. "Strange, to be sure," he said, "but I'm not one for ghost stories. I intend to administer an investigation. If only to put these superstitions to rest—"

The sound of shattering glass carried from down the hall, followed by a thud.

Rufus jolted out of his chair. "What was that?"

Gottfried rolled his eyes. "Mincemeat."

"I'm sorry?"

A four-legged shadow crept along the wall, and the lady of the manor revealed herself with a meow. She was massive, more of a sloth than a cat, and better fed than most of the townsfolk. Rolling on her side as if to demand scratches with an imperial stare, Mincemeat purred loudly, her thick double coat peppered with browns, grays, and blacks, mismatched eyes gleaming in the candlelight.

"Well, hello," Rufus said, relieved. "Aren't you a chunky one?"

Mincemeat recoiled at the heir's attempt to pet and swatted his hand lazily. Before Rufus could plead for companionship, she leapt with surprising agility midway up the bookshelf, content to glower at the unwelcome guest, ignorant of the wood groaning under her weight.

"I fear the baron has spoiled her," Gottfried said, words oozing with disdain. "Fat and slow in her dotage, I'm sure she misses the nightly morsels under the table."

Rufus eyed Mincemeat as she postured proudly, as if she were the true successor of the estate. Gottfried drummed his fingers against the table, regaining the heir's attention.

"At any rate," the burgomeister said, "you are proving quite agreeable." He refilled his own snifter with the last of the vintage. "More than I expected."

"Well, this is my estate," Rufus said. "How far is the castle?"

"Not thinking of venturing there yourself, are you?"

"I trust we have outriders?"

Gottfried gave a sardonic smirk. "Only the mercenaries hired by your grandfather to keep the townsfolk from revolting. Bandits and thieves all."

"That's what I feared. However, an expedition in broad daylight shouldn't prove too dangerous, should it?"

Gottfried sighed, deeply. "Get some rest, my lord. You certainly have work to do."

Rufus nodded and returned to the Hofbräuhaus, eager to rest. His quarters were fine enough—a modest bed with a thick quilt and plenty of pillows. He shut and barred the windows, not daring to test his luck. Pale slivers of moonlight pierced the mists, illuminating the broken battlements of Schloss Fleischburg, whose spires loomed stark in the wilderness. Then it dawned on him. There were no trade routes leading to or from Altstadt, nor military frontiers or points of strategic value. Why would a castle be constructed in this miserable stretch of a valley? It was a tactical anomaly. Unless the legends had a grain of truth to them. Regardless, sleep would prove a fickle beast. Rufus's thoughts wandered to the woods and unseen terrors, trying to rationalize what he had witnessed on the Old Road.

Something stirred in the darkness.

CHAPTER TWO

Rufus woke to muted rays of sunlight piercing the drawn curtains, causing him to moan and stir. He tossed off the blankets and reached for his morning shot of whiskey, forcing the "medicine" down with a cough—the aftertaste was smoother than laudanum. He stood slowly and cracked his spine. Dressed in the same clothes as yesterday, Rufus crept down the steps to the taproom, aged panels creaking underfoot. The bar was vacant, save for the proprietor who had seemingly spent all night polishing the same collection of glasses and steins.

"How'd it go last night?" the innkeeper asked.

"Well as it could've," Rufus said. "I've signed the contract."

The innkeeper snorted and shook his head. "Mustn't have much to come back to." He reached for a cask and poured a couple of beers. "Care for a sample?"

Rufus shrugged and took a sip. If last night's brew was anything to go by, it would wash itself down. He was pleasantly surprised. With sweet and slightly roasted notes, it carried a certain bitterness, reminiscent of a ripened brie and sour cherries.

"Just a tripel from Waldesrand," said the innkeeper.

Upon paying his tab, Rufus left for Main Street, greeted by daily life under a forlorn sky. Townsfolk went about their business, dressed in clothing typical of common folk—breeches, doublets, and the occasional beret or bonnet, mostly linen with bits of leather and salvaged finery. Sweeping porches and fetching water from the well, they eyed Rufus with suspicion, as if they had not seen an urbanite in years. Only the stonemason smiled as he chiseled a yet unnamed gravemarker, not far from the cemetery. Further up the street, the smell of spices and roasted meats lured

Rufus into the open green. Rows of costermongers served rural cuisine from pushcarts and open fires. Luncheon was of modest fare, consisting of bratwurst with stone-ground mustard—tough on the throat yet savory and spicy to taste.

Rufus paid the locals little heed, though they spoke in hushed whispers, ever in the monstrous shadow of Schloss Fleischburg, which loomed atop the wooded tor.

"Did you hear?"

"Yeah, another's gone missing."

"Whatever the baron woke's behind this, I'm sure."

"It's not natural, none of it."

At the hour's end, Rufus approached the Rathaus when its clock tower struck noon with bronze bells, reverberating across the square. Crows took flight from ledges as tiny windows creaked open, revealing a rotating display of shadowed figurines—pope and king, child, and commoner. Even the wooden gargoyles stirred, animated by little mechanisms, tilting their heads like curious hounds. Upon the last toll, Death swung its scythe in a *memento mori* and bid the mundanity of life to resume.

As if on cue, Gottfried opened the door and greeted him with a rigid grin.

"Ah," the burgomeister said, "to what do I owe the pleasure, my lord?"

"We've much to discuss. I'd like to learn more on the state of affairs, if you please."

"Of course, of course." Gottfried ushered him to his office, which was a bit brighter than Rufus had remembered. "As you know, Altstadt is a rural parish. We have very little in the way of trade, and most of what passes through is intercepted by highwaymen. Schloss Fleischburg and its grisly reputation are enough to deter most commerce."

"And how do we manage upkeep?" Rufus asked.

"Besides digging ourselves deeper into debt?" Gottfried

laughed, bitterly. "Most imports come from the lakeside hamlet of Innsbruck." He handed Rufus a pile of documents. "Income taxes under normal circumstances are one percent, though in times of particular hardship they can reach as high as three." He pointed at a particularly lengthy chart of brackets and inked numerals. "These are the records for the past five years. As you can see, our coffers aren't exactly brimming with gold."

Rufus's eyes widened at the figures. "We're flirting with destitution."

"That we are," Gottfried continued. "Most of your family fortune was exhausted by your grandfather's excavations. And there is, of course, his vast collection of trinkets and baubles in the castle proper. We could sell off an assortment of the oddities cached throughout the estate."

Rufus laid a thumb to his chin. "Salvage what we can to repay our debts."

"Shall I send out a word to the antiquarian?"

"Yes, appraisal will be in order."

Gottfried straightened his papers and tucked them away in a messy drawer. "Is there anything else you wish to ask, my lord?"

"I plan on setting out for the castle today."

"Oh? Not alone, I hope."

"No," Rufus said. "But I'd like an escort. I want you to post notices about the town. A 'substantial reward' will do, but a small party is needed."

"With all due respect," Gottfried said, "the townsfolk live in terror of Schloss Fleischburg. I sincerely doubt farmers and tailors will risk their lives for—"

"Then what do you suggest?"

Gottfried did not reply. The burgomeister picked and peeled at the quicks of his fingernails, beginning to bleed. Rufus knew better than to comment.

"You mentioned mercenaries?" he asked.

"Well, yes," Gottfried said with grave hesitation. "There are landsknechts who frequent the Hofbräu, unfortunately. Brutish and greedy. Hardly suitable for protection."

"I understand your concerns," Rufus said, "but can we afford to be choosy?"

"No, I suppose not."

"Thank you for your time, burgomeister."

With a swift nod, Rufus stood and saw himself out the door. Though scarcely half an hour had passed, the country seemed veiled in twilight—wind whispered through the barren trees as red leaves fluttered to earth in heaps of sickly foliage. He strode down Main Street to the west end of town, only to watch the people make way for a pair of familiar figures striding down the open way—dressed in patchworks of colors and codpieces of obvious compensation. With halberds propped over their shoulders and arquebuses at their sides, the landsknechts reeked of overconfidence. Rufus did not flinch at their approach.

The taller of the two gave a boisterous wave.

"Ah, the heir apparent," he said. "Do you find Altstadt to your liking?"

"It's certainly…rustic," Rufus replied. "Thank you for 'escorting' me to safety last night," his voice oozed with sarcasm, "in fact, as baron, I may have need of your services."

"So, you weren't lying after all," the taller one said. "Call me impressed, 'milord.' What is it that you had in mind?"

"Firstly, I'd like to talk about this over a drink."

"On your tab?"

"Not likely."

"Very well," the taller one laughed. "We'll play along. To the Hofbräu, then?"

Flanked by these miscreants, Rufus led the way to the coaching inn. He opened the door in a delicate manner, only for the landsknechts to barge in and drop their weapons with a deafening clatter. Rufus sheepishly signaled for three glasses and claimed a hearthside table.

"Now then—"

"Hold on." The taller one raised a hand. "How about some introductions first? I'm Leopold," he thumbed at his stout accomplice, "and this is my brother-in-arms, Hupert."

"Rufus."

"Pleasure to make your acquaintance. Again." Leopold leaned forward and shook his hand, grip firm and coarse. "So, what's this proposition of yours?"

"I need fighting men to escort me to Schloss Fleischburg," Rufus said. "Our mission would be to recover everything of value from its halls to be sold. If rumor is to be believed, there is…something down there. And I'm not exactly a soldier."

The mercenaries exchanged nervous glances. Leopold lifted a stein to his lips and took a swig of stale lager. "You mean something that drove grown men to madness? That's a tall order. Aren't your coffers dry? We charged your grandfather a pretty penny for our services."

"Haven't you been to the castle?"

"No. We're swords for hire, not the royal guard," Leopold said. "Besides, the Old Road is easy pickings for us. We've done jobs for the baron, true, but never met him in person."

"Yeah," Hupert added. "No one goes to the castle."

Rufus crossed his arms. "Schloss Fleischburg has no shortage of plunder. I'd be willing to part with a share of what we uncover. Say, as much as you can fit in your pockets?"

A glimmer of greed shone in Leopold's eyes as he drummed his fingers on the tabletop. "As much as we can carry without a horse. I'm going light on you."

"Fair enough."

"So," Leopold kicked up his feet on a spare stool, "when

do you want to set out?"

"After our drinks."

Leopold cracked his stein against the heir's snifter. "Prost! To a worthy haul."

Rufus swirled the contents of his chipped glass. "Indeed."

Within the hour, Rufus finished his business and paid his tab. Leopold and Hupert heaved halberds over their broad shoulders and led the way to the path beyond the Rathaus. Past the north gates, the company took to an uphill trail towards the castle. Black-barked trees pressed close to either side—even the grass was dead and dry underfoot, little more than patches of gamboge against desiccated soil. Slowly, the sights and sounds of Altstadt began to fade, until even the clock tower had vanished into the mists.

The landsknechts strode on as Rufus lagged, winded by the steep slope.

"What's wrong?" Leopold grinned. "Do we need to slow down?"

Rufus quickened his pace and swore under his breath, footfalls heavy against the dirt trail—perhaps too heavy. He was hardly accustomed to rough travel, oblivious to eyes in the woods. When the road began to widen, he sighed and raised his weary head.

Then he beheld their destination.

Schloss Fleischburg was a blight upon the valley, perched upon the edge of a great basalt cliff. It was squat and unremarkable with fortified masonry and teal tiled roofs, more of a prison than a keep. The iron-banded gates stood as indomitable doors that were designed to endure centuries of neglect. Constructed of four thick walls, the castle bore a certain malevolence. Everything about it was designed to intimidate. For these were the monstrous halls of Baron Matthias Grünewald, meant not to repel intruders but to contain something within.

"Charming bit of architecture, isn't it?" Leopold nudged the heir sharply.

Ill-timed humor aside, Rufus gazed in awe upon this bleak hold. The gates of Schloss Fleischburg stood slightly ajar, as if beckoning the company to test their mettle, promising them riches and ruin in equal measure. Yard by yard, the landsknechts advanced, halberds at the ready.

"Rufus," Hupert called. "Are you coming or what?"

"Y-yes, just catching my breath."

Through the front gates, Rufus and the landsknechts were greeted by the courtyard and silence. Fortified towers rose from old battlements like pillars of bone—windows gazing out as lightless eyes. Cloistered walkways lay in the shade of alcoves and bare columns, doors leading to wings of unknown chambers. Rufus took a few shaky steps, overwhelmed by the sheer scale. These were the halls of his lineage, though he felt no familiarity towards them. Constructed beside the gatehouse was a chapel braced with simple buttresses and a square turret.

Leopold pressed an ear against the panels and laid a finger to his lips.

Silence passed until the soldier pushed open the door. One by one, the company crossed the threshold into the chapel. Its walls and ribbed vaults were composed of mild stucco, and a series of faded frescos lined the niches, portraying scenes of *danse macabre*.

"How quaint," Rufus muttered to himself.

He was never fond of such imagery. In village pageants and courtly masquerades, folk dressed as corpses of varying walks of life, frolicking to a troubadour's song at the parish cemetery. The Great Pestilence was in living memory, and these festivities served to honor the grave that awaited all earthly things. A nasty prank had left Rufus with a livid scar on his ankle.

He shuddered, shoving his hands in his pockets.

These illustrations were not of mischievous ghosts, but fresh out of a mad monk's manuscript—an army of the dead, reaping the living as wheat in the open field.

"Eerie place," Leopold said, "but there's coin to be had."

Rupert nodded. "Check the alms box, will you?"

As his escorts passed the pews, Rufus approached the clothbound altar and noticed its candelabras—something was off in their placement. The landsknechts plucked coins from offering tablets and stuffed them into their codpieces and purses. Rufus rolled his eyes. When all was properly desecrated, he tipped the left pricket back and felt the floor tremble.

The altar slid back with a cloud of dust, revealing a stairwell descending into utter darkness. A faint ticking echoed from under the pulpit.

Leopold came to his side and peered into the passage. "What do you see?"

"Nothing," Rufus said. "Just a way down."

Slowly, the company crept down the steps in a single file. The smooth stone walls were bare of décor. Not a sconce lined the staircase. At last, they came to the upper foundations of Schloss Fleischburg—the brink of the abyss.

"Wait," Hupert said. "Do you hear that?"

The slow grind of stone carried from the way back. Rufus turned to the stairwell, eyes widening in terror. Before the company could bolt up the steps, the altar had locked in place—sealing them in the undercroft. Not a word was spoken.

Swallowing his panic, Rufus drew a sharpened letter opener. The landsknechts followed his lead. Hours had passed. Darkness enveloped the way forward. Rufus raised the lantern, barely illuminating the labyrinthine halls beneath Schloss Fleischburg. Step by step, he tried to soften his shallow breathing, lest he disturb whatever lurked in the dark. Leopold kept a firm hand on his shoulder, prodding the stagnant air with the point of his halberd. Hupert stuck to the rear, a matchlock loaded and aimed blindly at whatever awaited them.

"What is this place?" Rufus whispered to no one in particular.

Something trickled on his shoulder. Rufus spun around and brandished his letter opener, expecting a nameless predator to lurch down from the ceiling—no such thing emerged.

"What are you doing?" Leopold snarled. "Nearly gave me a heart attack."

"I thought I felt," Rufus began to explain, yet thought better of it. "Never mind...."

He recognized architecture from studies at the university—pilasters and columns of gothic orders, supporting high stone arches where the routes diverged. The ceilings sagged with the weight of the earth. The company felt their way along the ossuaries, cradling yellowed bones. On occasion, they would come to a stairwell promising to lead them ever deeper into the crypts. The floor shifted in Rufus's wake. He raised the lantern. The flagstones were splattered with sewage and sanguine fluid. At the end of the hall was an intersection split in two—presumably east and west. It was impossible to tell where they were in relation to an exit. Rufus eyed the flow in hopes of finding a culvert to the woods.

"Keep up," Leopold called from the bend. "We don't know how far these go."

With a shuddering breath, Rufus pressed on. Distant clatters and clangs echoed from behind locked doors and heaps of crumbled masonry, and dried blood streaked the near wall.

"A tad underwhelming," Hupert said, "I must admit—"

Metallic whining erupted from under the flagstones. Something sank under Hupert's heel—a pressure plate. Before he could so much as shout, a host of iron spikes sprang from slits in the floor and pierced his foot. Hobbling yet hardly unharmed, he collapsed loudly.

"Hupert!" Leopold's voice cracked. He ran to his comrade's side, who inched away from the slowing trap. "What happened? Are you alright?"

"Is it b-bad?" Hupert stuttered, ignorant to his own blood pooling onto the floor. "I...."

Though Rufus's face paled with sympathy, he stuck to the shadows, lantern aquiver in his grip. Something else stirred in the depths. His eyes darted about the far corners of the labyrinth—faint guttural whispers and the crunch of bones echoed from deeper halls. Leopold wrapped the gaping wound with a bandage and firm care, and handed Hupert a drought likely pilfered from the apothecary. With the empty bottle cast into a heap of rubble, he nodded, rapidly, as if the pain was beginning to numb. Leopold hoisted his comrade's arm over his shoulder and slowly came to Rufus's side. Limping down the corridor, they continued at a sluggish pace.

Leopold helped his wartime companion along the way until the corridor opened to yet another antechamber. "We can't keep trudging on like this. Let us rest."

"And let whatever horror descend?"

"The only horror is gangrene; should we keep this up."

Rufus knew that was a deflection of the true peril at hand. Leopold and Hupert clung to each other and slumped with fatigue. Shadows seemed to close ranks in a phalanx of blackness. The heir imagined forms of unseen terrors yet knew that an aimless march would get them killed just as well. "Then what do you suggest?" Rufus asked. "Camp here?"

"Certainly a start," Leopold said.

Rufus conceded with a sigh. They settled for the remains of a torture chamber, with displays of pliers and prongs, and half-mummified corpses hanging from their thumbs and stretched across the rack. He could almost hear the screams of the past.

Disturbed by the implication of his family's cruelty, Rufus approached the desk and uncovered a moldy diary.

On the baron's orders, I am to carry out the sentences of three convicts taken from the Imperial City of Chimay. Guilty of arson and immoral relations, they are to be put to work for his lordship's studies. As to what this entails, I am uncertain, but the baron frequents the dungeons to oversee their punishments. Much to my relief, this is not a reflection of my duties, rather of the baron's own curiosities. Namely, his interest in pain. He is writing a definitive work on the matter, but I cannot help but feel there's more. However, the baron appears to hold me in favor, for which I am grateful. I could not say the same for my predecessor.

Rufus shuddered, unsure as to what to make of this. As if in response to his own lingering fear, the skulls of the imprisoned seemed to stare at him. Meanwhile, Leopold foraged for dry wood to form a bonfire. Rufus lifted Hupert's leg upon a stool and tore off his boot. The soldier said nothing, face dripping with sweat. His lacerations had putrefied at an unnatural rate.

"Are you well?" Rufus asked.

"Oh," Hupert sighed, weakly, "fantastic…."

Leopold returned with an armful of planks and tossed them in a clattering pile. With the strike of flint and steel, he lit a fire, and the company huddled together around its meager flames. Rufus took a sip from his pewter flask—whiskey soothed his nerves. Leopold kept watch, leaning on his halberd, his back to the others as he peered into the fringe of firelight.

Frightened though he was, Rufus's eyelids were heavy and exhaustion got the better of him, if only to bask in a moment's rest. They were being watched. Drifting in and out of slumber, a silhouette lingered in the licking shadows of the fire, rippling along forked flames, looming as a man dressed in fine robes. Still as a corpse, the apparition stared at Rufus without eyes, and yet, there was something off about its height and posture.

Grasping weakly, Rufus gasped as the image vanished in a wisp of smoke.

"Grandfather?" he asked, weakly.

Rufus woke to silence—the campfire was exhausted, little more than a pile of ash and embers. Leopold eyed him oddly and shrugged, returning to his watch. Hupert was far worse for wear, feverish and struggling to stand, keeping a firm hand on his matchlock pistol.

"We'd better keep moving," Rufus said.

Leopold nodded and offered Hupert a hand. Despite the ceiling's height, the odor of woodsmoke was overpowering, and the air was a haze. Rufus kept his shillelagh close. Pebbles clattered in the corridor near the campsite, followed by the folly and creek of a crossbow.

"What was that—?"

An iron-tipped bolt flew out of the darkness and impaled Hupert through the chest—serrated with wicked barbs. He collapsed on his back and coughed a lungful of blood. Leopold knelt to his companion's side, trembling in shock that gave way to rage. Drawing his sword in a flash of steel, the landsknecht sprinted down the corridor and swung his blade in wild fury.

"W-wait!" Rufus cried and gave chase.

Whatever had slain Hupert had already gone.

Rufus kept his dagger close, desperate to fend off the lurkers waiting to strike. The corridors echoed with a chittering parody of speech. Something tackled the heir with a monstrous shriek. Pinning him to the ground was an emaciated corpse of a man—skin stretched tight over its frame, face drawn to a fleshy skull bearing rows of supernumerary teeth, erupting through its jaws. Dressed in scraps of leather, rags, and rusty mail, it clutched a longsword in its left hand—perhaps a conscript who died in battle generations ago, reanimated by foul magic.

The wight seethed and salivated, threatening to bite into his flesh. Rufus stretched his fingers and reached for his letter opener. In a fit of desperation, he stabbed the wight in the jugular. It staggered back and retched a lungful of rancid phlegm.

Rufus cupped a hand over his mouth, gagging at the stench and sights of white worms writhing in the pool of black bile. Hissing in a ravenous seizure, the wight lunged with sword at hand. Rufus dodged and stabbed, again and again, until it fell prone. To his horror, the knife did not cut through mere dead flesh but living tissue, not of man—crimson tentacles recoiled from open wounds as a serpentine form slithered and fled from the corpse.

The wight lay motionless.

On the fringe of sight, Leopold was caught in a melee with a horde of walking dead. Rufus was petrified. He watched on helplessly as the wights beat his companion into submission with cudgels and carved into his torso with blade and claw—feasting on his spilled innards. Within moments, Leopold's eyes rolled back, life ebbing from his mangled body.

Before Rufus knew it, he had sprinted blindly into the labyrinth. Slamming a door behind him, he hid behind a row of barrels and tried to salvage his wits.

The pursuers battered the door until it burst in a barrage of splinters and planks.

The slap of damp feet against stone inched ever nearer. There was an exchange of whimpers and rasps amongst the patrol until they abandoned their quarry. After what seemed an eternity, Rufus crept past the threshold and peered around the bend. The wights had gone as well as what remained of his companions. He raised the shattered lantern with a shaky hand and spied a wraith of daylight at a corridor's end, filtered through a wrought-iron portcullis.

Rufus crept through the bars and found himself in the Grünewald, surrounded by gaunt trees once more. Head pounding and hands shaking, a surge of nausea overcame him, and he retched into the brambles. He took to the poacher's trail, embarking for Altstadt, when he noticed a series of tracks leading to and from the sally port.

Rufus's heart sank deep into his chest. Wights were no strangers to the woods.

Regardless, the half-timbered houses of the hamlet welcomed Rufus with as much hospitality as was to be expected. He thrust open the doors to the Hofbräuhaus and took a seat at the bar. Gottfried was waiting for him and raised a glass with a mocking smile.

"Well," he asked, "how'd it go?"

CHAPTER THREE

In the following days, Rufus neither slept nor ate, harrowed by what he had encountered in Schloss Fleischburg. He spent long hours into the night poring over ledgers and records in the Rathaus, desperate to make sense of the horror beneath the estate, knowing well that he had traversed merely the edge of the abyss. Despite the richness of local folklore, Rufus found no certainty on the nature of this evil. It was not until the fourth day that he uncovered a bestiary—illuminated with calligraphy, brittle to the touch, written by clergy in centuries past.

Wiedergänger

Also known as revenants or revitalized cadavers, wiedergängers, as common folk so name them, are the dead that, whether by regrets of misspent life or daemonical possession, return to plague the world of men. Corporeal in nature, these walking corpses are driven by an insatiable bloodlust and feed on the flesh of the living. Though shorn of reason and intellect, the wiedergängers are able to wield arms and armor in a fashion and retain a predatory cunning akin to the wolf or the bear and hunt in packs; they infest villages and ill-use both men and beasts to carry out the will of greater evil. The defining traits of the wiedergänger are vestigial teeth, which erupt as tumors of the mandible. They are known to feed on their nearest relations and conceive through bite, as men bitten by the wiedergänger are to suffer a fever of the brain and share in its appetites. To cure the malady, one must purify the humors through leechcraft; if left untreated, the afflicted will surely die and rise again as one of the fiends.

Though Rufus put little faith in monastic texts, a shiver

ran down his spine. The illustrations in the margins of parchment were undoubtedly of the wights he had escaped from. If what the bestiary suggested was true, then "wiedergängers" were a blight upon his lands—an invasive evil to be exterminated. Reaching into the drawer of the desk, Rufus found a wheellock pistol, examining its hammer and pan. For a moment, he contemplated his own cowardice, how he left the landsknechts to die. Shame washed over his conscience, but in the end, he was alive.

That alone gave him comfort.

"What is wrong with this place?" he sighed.

Wearisome and overburdened, Rufus massaged the sides of his brow, uttering a moan of self-pity. He reached for the bottle and poured himself yet another shot. Wind whispered through the twilit windows—candlelight fluttered in its wake, and Rufus swore he saw a shift in the shadows. Cocking the pistol, he stepped to the door and listened intently—lumbering footsteps creaked up the stairs, slow and deliberate, punctuated by low murmurs.

There was a knock on the door.

"Enter," Rufus said, lowering his aim.

The heir was greeted by Gottfried, who held a silver platter of sliced apples and cheese. The burgomeister eyed the pistol with amusement and placed the tray on the desk, turning to shut the open window. The burgomeister shook his head and gave a nervous laugh.

"You remind me so much of him, you know."

Rufus opened his mouth, as if to speak—no words escaped his lips. He pondered how exactly to phrase his questions, as Gottfried was the closest thing to a friend he had. Mincemeat meowed and brushed against the heir's leg, if only to woo a morsel. The last thing Rufus wanted was to alienate himself further from the people of Altstadt, and yet, he needed answers.

"I don't suppose you can tell me of my grandfather,"

Rufus said.

He slid Mincemeat a slice of apple under the desk. She sniffed at the morsel and recoiled in disgust, preferring to yearn for cheese than to accept the paltry offering.

"That depends entirely on what you want to know," Gottfried said. "I'm not a man of science and know little of his studies." He adjusted his spectacles. "He was very secretive—"

"What can you tell me of his," Rufus paused, "affinity for torture."

Gottfried's smile had vanished. "I know little of such things."

Mincemeat took her leave, as if disgusted by them both.

"Apparently, the baron was keen on the study of pain. To say nothing of what tore my companions apart." Rufus stared at his confidant, sharply. "You're hiding something."

The burgomeister reached for his own snifter. "It's no secret that your grandfather was a man of morbid genius," he began. "One of his responsibilities was that of a prison warden. He kept criminals locked in the dungeons beneath the estate." He glanced at Rufus with glossy eyes. "I assure you. I had nothing to do with whatever happened in the cellars."

"Yet, clearly, you knew of his deeds."

"Deeds?" Gottfried paused, as if attempting to conquer his own defensiveness. "If I do tell you what I know, please, don't think less of me...."

Rufus did not reply. Gottfried thumbed the bookshelves for a clothbound volume of grisly nature, titled *Treatise on the Techniques of Interrogation and the Extraction of Truth, et al.* He flipped through the index, then to dissertations on the strappado and the breaking wheel, complete with instructions and illustrations of sickening detail. More disturbing even than these were the scrawling annotations in his grandfather's handwriting.

"Good lord," Rufus choked.

"The breaking wheel was the favored method of your household," Gottfried said. "With the onset of the Great Peasants' War, rebels were to be crushed from the 'bottom up,' from shinbone to shoulder, stopping before the neck, and the broken men woven between the spokes. They could be left to die for days." He pointed at a particular note. "Your grandfather had his 'enemies' displayed on masts on the road to the castle, as warnings to those who'd seek to challenge his authority. I had the courtesy of removing them before your arrival."

"How thoughtful of you…."

"Now, I must admit," Gottfried ignored the comment, "towards the end of his days, Matthias was a tad paranoid." He reached into a hidden compartment in the desk and withdrew several sheets of paper, and passed them for Rufus to read. "Here we are."

I hereby offer my services to Baron Matthias Grünewald. This contract will reign for three years of service when my freedom shall return to me. I also hereby defer all liability to the Baron of Grünewald in the event of incrimination for executing his orders under contract. Until these terms are fulfilled, my sword is his to command.

Leopold Schinder

Rufus eyed the burgomeister over the pages, watching as Gottfried shuffled about the bookshelves, as if searching for some elusive work to shed light on the sordid history of the Grünewald family. The heir thought it better not to bring attention to himself. Instead, he turned to the next volume and skimmed excerpts of his grandfather's diary in silence.

Commoners are rumormongers by nature, and the peasantry of Altstadt are no exception. I suppose that life spent in isolation only feeds the rustic imagination; however, secretive as I strive to be in my studies and experimentations, I find myself a figure in local legend. This is troubling, to say the least, given the pattern of unrest throughout the neighboring fiefdoms. In a time when iconoclasts and demonstrators put all manner of "deviant literature" to the torch, I find myself querying bands of landsknechts in hopes of defusing the spark of rebellion. Of all the replies, one fledgling captain seems to be the most appropriate sword for my cause. Born to a house of little renown, the youth is eager to earn his place among the peerage, though I have little intention of providing reference as baron of House Grünewald. If I am to reassert my rule, then I must invest in men skilled in the application of force.

Rufus slowly pieced together what Gottfried meant when he warned the heir of keeping such company. Leopold and Hupert were not merry men. They were killers who hid their sadism behind warm manners. The truth served to alleviate Rufus's guilt over their ends.

"This answers nothing." He sighed, straightening the papers. "How do such atrocities relate to the Thing in the Pit? Or the wights for that matter?"

Gottfried handed him a final text—a small leather handbook of alchemical studies. "This will provide insight on his motive, that much I know." His composure was breached by an unhinged grin. "I'm surprised you haven't inquired about your grandfather's age."

Rufus rolled his eyes, growing weary of endless research, and opened the book to a random page, unable to recognize the diagrams and rites of blood sacrifice.

"I don't understand…."

"Keep reading."

Rufus attempted to do so. Alongside the incantations written in common speech were translations of less identifiable origin, perhaps as scribed by learned men of Othello and Khand or the language of some secret cabal. Regardless, the scripture was faded, and more recent notes were slipped between the pages, amounting to a rough interpretation of their original meaning.

Known by some as vitae, "water of life" is the key to immortality; a bloodborne power awoken through fear and pain, a fifth humor in its own right, if only due to its unique potency. Its daily consumption as a tincture can extend one's life indefinitely. Mastery over life and death is not a trifling matter. Man is destined to die, whether he be king or commoner. However, as demonstrated by the wiedergänger, the mortal coil can be transcended. Such miracles prove the existence of a higher power. Whether God or daemon, I cannot say, but, as I study the Thing in the Pit, I wonder if there is truly a difference. At least, it is true that God is defined by His apathy to man's suffering and the horror of His own creation. In His silence lies a great and terrible freedom, despite the claims of the Holy See, and I seek to pursue my own ends. If man is touched by Him through terror, then I will extract the vitae of those less deserving of mercy. Indeed, I have a barony ripe with it.

Rufus shuddered and shut the book.

"This is insane," he said. "The baron was raising his people as swine to be slaughtered. To feed his own ambitions of what, eternal life?" Nausea reared its ugly head, threatening to wash over him in a case of the vapors. "I need to…." He pulled up a chair, running his fingers through his greasy hair, breathing shallow. "What lies beneath the estate?"

"Well," Gottfried said, "I don't suppose it's the fountain of youth as your grandfather hoped. One thing is clear. Whatever he uncovered still lives. And hungers."

Rufus laughed, darkly. "We're going to need a sharper sword."

As the evening wore on, Rufus wandered the streets of

Altstadt by his unhappy lonesome. Far from popular with the peasantry, he tried to ignore the whispers as they went about their affairs. Rufus did not blame them for their distrust. His family had brought upon them nothing but abuse. However, he kept the pistol close and never strayed from Main Street, for fear of being hanged from a gibbet in the square. Of all the truths he had uncovered, one thing disturbed Rufus most of all—he was the baron's descendant and not among the healthiest of men. Try as he might to dismiss notions of inherited madness, Rufus saw shadows where none existed and felt a constant gnawing at the back of his mind ever since his arrival. Loathing for his bloodline festered deeply, and its sins stained his soul.

"It's not my fault," he repeated in an unsteady mantra, "it's not my fault."

The townsfolk stared at him, tying knots in lengths of rope, and the gravedigger had dug more plots than the day before. Overcome with suspicion, Rufus quickened his pace to the Hofbräuhaus. Come five o'clock, he had retreated to the bar and ordered a double of whiskey without so much as a word. Nursing the shot, he found solace in the waking dream of drunkenness. Before he knew it, Rufus was already eying a number of working women huddled by the roaring hearth.

"No," he said to himself, staring through the innkeeper, "I am not one for such petty distractions."

"Doing well enough, milord? Take it, your excursion in the castle went south...."

"Word spreads fast in these parts," Rufus said, not realizing that he had already finished his fourth shot of the night, to say nothing of his day drinking.

"Small town."

"Well," Rufus said, "I don't suppose much can be done about my reputation." Those words were sharper than he meant. "That being said," he eyed the women by the scarlet sofa, "nor is there harm in seeking solace—"

"Oh, them?" the innkeeper laughed. "Didn't realize you liked girls."

"What?" Rufus sputtered.

"Not that there'd be anything wrong with that. Just, you know, with your voice and all, we thought you… might've been a bit queer."

Rufus slammed his pint on the countertop and splattered himself with a cloud of foam. "Don't be ridiculous. I'll have you know I had quite the count back in the day."

The women giggled at his faux pas, or so Rufus would like to believe.

"You're more than welcome to find out why," he blurted over his shoulder.

Drink after drink, Rufus brooded, perched upon the middle stool of the bar. Before he knew it, the wooden rafters began to swirl, and the laughter of patrons echoed in and out of his skull. The tarnished bar was cool against his cheek, and he scarcely heard his glass spill onto the floorboards—when a smooth, silky hand caressed the nape of his neck.

"Looking for a room?" she cooed.

Rufus managed a desperate grunt, feeling saliva pool under his lower lip, hardly a beacon of appeal. He groped about the bar and shoved himself upright, still seated.

"I am," he slurred, "drunk."

"I can see that."

Her flesh was lukewarm to the touch, yet her beauty was undeniable. With flowing locks of auburn hair and alabaster skin, her face was powdered, ever so slightly weathered. She was dressed in a deep, florid gown, emerald gossamer flashing in the hearthlight, which one of her standing was unlikely to afford, reminding Rufus of actresses who had rejected him with mocking laughter. Suspicion twisted deep in his thoughts, and yet, he found himself ensnared by her ambiguous gaze. There was a gleam in her hazel eyes, a will that somehow eclipsed her irises. Perhaps it was his own drunken stupor, yet her mystique was intoxicating.

If only he were half as articulate as his own thoughts.

"Oh, let me guess," Rufus choked, "you must think I have coffers overflowing somewhere in the estate. Which is true; however, I don't exactly have access to such wealth as to purchase your services." He stifled a hiccup. "Therefore, I doubt I can afford your company."

"Getting a little ahead of ourselves, aren't we?"

"I suppose so."

The woman pulled a seat beside him and swirled the contents of her glass—brandy, shimmering like amber in the firelight. She raised the snifter to her lips and took a delicate sip. Slowly, Rufus softened his gaze and smiled, and she grabbed his seat forcefully, pulling him close to her side. "Here," she said. "Give me your sleeves."

Intimidated yet aroused, Rufus did not know what to say, only to find her delicately rolling his cuffs and fastening his brass buttons, as if to make him proper. His cheeks flushed, and not due to drink. Few women had been so assertive in their affections, regardless of intent. The last thing Rufus recalled before heading upstairs was the scent of lilac perfume and her tongue swirling against his own—a momentary abatement from the macabre. Nude on the bed, Rufus massaged the back of his neck, and she wrapped her arms around his chest.

"What's your name?" he asked.

She kissed his ear, softly. "Does it matter?"

Rufus did not reply. Despite her pleasurable company, an unwelcome darkness pervaded the room, and shadows wove their webs beneath the candlelight.

"How long have you stayed in Altstadt?"

"Long enough," she replied.

"I suppose you're not one for idle conversation."

"What gave it away?"

Rufus bowed his head and donned his robe. Against his better judgment, he began to confide in his companion. "I don't suppose I may have...more of your time. Not in the physical sense." He handed her a palm's worth of thalers. "I need someone to talk to."

"About?"

"All of it," Rufus gazed out the latticed window, into the abyss of night. "With my office comes certain responsibilities, and I am learning things as I go, as it were. Among them is how to live, knowing that I profit from...this."

"Did you know your grandfather well?" she asked.

"No," Rufus said. "Truth be told, I barely remember Altstadt at all."

"That's probably for the best," she said.

Rufus's mind wandered to shadowed corners of speculation. "What do you know of him?" he asked, cautious in his tone and choice of words. "What can you tell me of his studies?"

The woman sighed. "I'm not privy to that, but the girls attended many of his soirées. He always kept the liquor flowing and paid handsomely for our services."

"Services?"

"I think you know what I mean."

Rufus swallowed his own revulsion. "Ah," he managed.

"If it's consolation, you're—"

"Thank you, but I think I'm going to vomit."

She laughed, buttoning her blouse, as if she had overstayed her welcome—when something pounded against the door, followed by a low, guttural moan.

"What the—!" she screamed.

The door collapsed from its hinges and slammed against the floorboards. A muscular silhouette lingered upon the threshold, wielding a bloody cleaver in its left hand. Before Rufus could reach for his pistol, the intruder tore him by the wrist and bent his arm backward, raising its blade with murderous intent. He struggled to no avail, grappled by the undead, its head split into a cavity overgrown with molars and broken fangs.

The wights had come for him once more.

Suddenly, there was a gunshot and a waft of acrid smoke.

The woman had fired at the intruder's skull, pistol aquiver in her grip. The wight moaned and staggered back, black blood oozing from the wound, and swung the cleaver wide, intent on butchering them both in a single stroke. Rufus tackled his companion aside and turned to the window—when a thought crossed his mind amidst panic. Wielding a wooden chair, he rushed at the wight with a desperate scream, pushing it through the window with a shattering blow.

The next thing he knew, the wight had tumbled out of the second story and landed with a sickening crunch, prone in the street.

"What the hell was that?" the woman gasped.

"One of my ancestor's sins," he said.

Rufus wrapped a belt around his robe and marched down the steps, only to be greeted by a gruesome sight. He cupped a hand over his mouth. The wight had made short work of the staff and patrons—butchered and mangled, limbs severed and strewn about the floor, tables and chairs toppled amidst splatters of blood. Something stirred behind the empty bar.

The innkeeper raised his balding head, eyes wide in horror. Rufus found himself propping the furniture back in place, lost in a dissociative stupor as he tried to make sense of the situation. What drove the wight to attack the Hofbräuhaus? Why was he being targeted by such evil? Was it the machinations of his grandfather? Or something else entirely?

"It came," the innkeeper stuttered, "from the cellar."

Mustering his wits through shock, Rufus took a candlestick and followed his host to the trapdoor. It was a tight fit. Beyond the racks and ricks of bottles and barrels, he was surrounded by walls of brick and hewn stone. A partly collapsed passage, little more than a narrow slit, delved deep into what Rufus feared were the vaults of Schloss Fleischburg. After shoving an iron-banded cask in a feeble attempt to seal the passage, he returned to the common room.

"Smugglers' tunnels," the innkeeper said. "Courtesy of the late baron."

"Why am I not surprised?" Rufus sighed.

The woman in green was waiting by the front door. Nothing needed to be said. Together, they crept around the coaching inn and searched for their assailant. The wight had gone.

"I am sorry," Rufus said.

"For what?"

"All of it. I don't know how to purge the evil in my blood, let alone if I can do much of…anything." He scarcely felt the tears trickling down his cheeks. "What must I do?"

The woman took him warmly by the hand. "You're not your grandfather." A moment's silence passed. She donned a wool hood and headed indoors. "It's Sophia, by the way."

"What?"

Rufus did not understand at first. He reached out in concern, but as if a phantom in her own right, she had already gone. Once more, the heir was alone in the bitter night.

Locked away in the Rathaus, Rufus lay his brow against the mahogany desk. Curtains were drawn over the windows to blot out the prying sun. Hungover and hardly rested, he held a leaky pen in one hand and a snifter in the other—a candid portrait of life as a baron. The door was ajar. Gottfried limped into the office with a lopsided grin, carrying a plate's worth of buttered flapjacks with Mincemeat at his heels. No doubt she wordlessly prayed for him to trip—then she could reap the benefits. Rufus raised his weary head and eyed the clock atop the mantlepiece. It was seven in the morning.

"Sleep well?" the burgomeister asked.

"Before or after the massacre?"

Gottfried placed the steaming meal before his master. "I heard you've met someone." He shot him a wink. "It seems you're getting along well enough with the locals."

"I don't remember paying," Rufus said.

"Well, you are the baron."

Rufus cut into the flapjacks with the edge of a fork, watching molten butter slip between the pancakes like edible gold. "Thank you," he took a bite, "these are…quite good."

"I'll notify the chef of your approval."

Mincemeat stared at the heir intently.

"Is there anything else of note?" he asked.

"Actually," Gottfried said, "a troupe of huntsmen managed to catch a wight last night—"

Rufus almost choked on his breakfast. "What?"

"They have the beast in shackles under the abbey."

"Did they kill it?"

"I'm not sure they had the means…."

Within the hour, Rufus pulled his waistcoat over his lean shoulders and headed to the grounds north of Main Street. In the shadow of Saint Baldwin's, Rufus reflected on the privilege of the clergy and whether they would endure that which savored the thought of defiling their cloisters. He dared not approach the steps, knowing he had no place in God's eyes, nor did he have tolerance for the dogmatic pretense of the masses.

The Hofbräu was the only church where he took

communion.

"They're keeping the thing in the undercroft," Gottfried said.

"Of course they are...."

Gottfried smirked, opening the bronze doors for his master. Rufus took a few steps upon the marble tiles, eying the colonettes and slender statues as he crossed the threshold. Heavenly figures, they seemed to eye him with divine judgment, faces carved into inscrutable expressions. He beheld a sad replica of the urban gothic—stained glass windows ripe with grime and neglect, muting what little light crept through the clerestories, and the hoarse chanting of a choir which sang upon the apse. Few folk bothered to attend the Morning Prayer—a testament to the futility of faith. Rufus followed the burgomeister's lead.

A friar in a crimson cowl greeted the guests with a solemn nod, bidding them to follow to the transept and descend the stairs. Down the steps, Rufus reached for his dagger out of instinct, only for Gottfried to grip his wrist, as if to wordlessly tell him to tread lightly. Past the colonnades which supported the low stone roof, Rufus tried to ignore the muffled moans of flagellants in bloodletting cells, and the sound of whips stripping skin from sinew. One cell in particular was shut tight, flanked by a squad of militiamen, and blessed with sacramental oils and lines of salt, as if to keep its ward from breaking free.

Something stirred within.

From out of the shadows, the abbot emerged with a rosary at hand. Crowned with a peppered tonsure, he was a gaunt man dressed in a habit of burgundy cloth, though not without bits of benedictine finery, such as the silver trimming of his robes. His face was as still as the grotesques lining the cloisters above, as if half-petrified by decades of divine silence.

"My lord," the abbot bowed ever so slightly, "thank you for your timely response."

Rufus nodded in kind. "I heard it was most urgent."

"Indeed, it is," the abbot said, turning to the last cell. "We've done all we can to restrain the thing, but I fear nothing can pacify it for long."

When Rufus approached, the militiamen did not step aside.

They were a meager lot, dressed in soiled tunics and gambesons, armed with spears and bludgeons forged from repurposed farming implements, as well as the odd stolen sword. The captain, a man of ruddy complexion with a bandage strapped across his brow, eyed Rufus with bitter distrust—well aware of his heritage.

"May I see the creature?" Rufus asked.

"Don't see the harm in it," the captain said, curtly.

The militiamen nodded to one another. The abbot drew a ring of iron keys and opened the cell door with caution. Rufus entered and eyed the prisoner from afar. Shackled to the wall, it was the same wight that had massacred the Hofbräu, veiled in unnatural darkness that no light could breach. Then it occurred to Rufus. Why was he summoned? What purpose did capturing the creature serve? Certainly, he couldn't let the thing roam free, and yet, what was he supposed to do? Suddenly, the door slammed shut—stirring the wight. He was trapped.

Uttering a guttural growl, the thing broke free of bondage and lunged for Rufus, its clammy hands outstretched as if to throttle him. On instinct, Rufus drew his dagger and swung up with a nervous stab, piercing its cold flesh. The wight did not so much as flinch.

"Stop!" Gottfried cried from outside the cell. "Get your hands off me!"

Against the struggle, Rufus was knocked against the wall. The wight thrashed him about the cell like a hound with a bone. He could've sworn that he'd broken a rib when its teeth raked against his shoulder in a rasping attempt to bite. Such was the wight's strength. Rufus screamed as broken fangs dug into his flesh and sanguine venom seeped into his veins.

Desperate to slip away from the wight's grip, Rufus slammed a knee into its sinewy torso, staggered upright, and burst through the door. The militiamen had beaten Gottfried into submission, and the abbot was nowhere to be seen. Even now, Rufus was overwhelmed by sickly sweats and pockmarked vision, barely able to hear the wight scrape its manacles against the walls—moments from murdering them all. What followed was a haze of carnage and terrified screams. The militiamen were not so fortunate as to escape the wight's attention. In their failed assassination, they were torn limb from limb in fits of unholy strength while Rufus lay limp on the floor, deaf to the sounds of slaughter. He scarcely felt Gottfried hoist him to his feet as they fled up the stairs towards the surface.

"It'll be alright, my lord," the burgomeister seemed to mouth.

Lost among the phantom silhouettes of the hamlet, Rufus's vision swirled with strange new vistas. In lieu of the streets of Altstadt, he wandered the sands of an antediluvian world, out of thought and time. Regardless of direction, he approached a structure rising from the far gray dunes—the black silhouette of a ziggurat. Even the wraith of Gottfried's guidance began to vanish in the wake of the vision. Step by step, Rufus wandered through the slender entry, passing rows of braziers lit with sickly green flame, and approached the monolith within.

Treading lightly, he saw the incinerated dead piled before the ebon stele, mystics and mentors, headless yet clutching skulls not their own—those who sought power and were deemed unworthy. Rufus outstretched a shaky hand and touched the cuneiform script and understood the rite. What needed to be done. Kneeling before the monolith, he took a skull topped with a tall candle and shut his eyes once more. He called out to the dark tapestry, to the lights which pierced its threadbare fabric—the burning stars. The candle was lit. In its flame, he saw the beginning and the end, the cradle and the grave. The last thing he felt was a total eclipse of the self, as if his soul had been split and began to multiply into a cosmic fetus waiting to be baptized in blood. The implications did not horrify him—rather, they provided a solace he hadn't felt since the womb.

Then the world went black.

CHAPTER FOUR

Rufus woke to sweat-drenched sheets and spinning rafters. Something furry and smelly was kneading his chest, as if trying to resuscitate him. He was too weak to move, barely able to breathe. Head throbbing, hands shaking, the heir tore off the blanket. Mincemeat skittered off her living perch in embarrassment and fled down the corridor, paws heavy against the floorboards. As the heir's sight cleared, Gottfried poured a cup of herbal tea by the bedside.

The burgomeister offered a saucer. "Awake at last."

Despite the fatigue, Rufus managed to formulate a few words. "What happened…?"

"How much do you remember?" Gottfried asked.

Moment by moment, Rufus's strength returned as he struggled to sit upright. "Not much after the ambush," he said, "just the struggle and…. How long was I asleep?"

"A week," Gottfried said.

Rufus cradled his skull. "What of the militia?"

"Escaped to the weald," Gottfried said. "No matter, they won't last long out there, between bounties and brigands." He dabbed the heir's forehead with a damp washcloth. "The wight also vanished into the forest. The hamlet has been rather uneventful in your absence."

"Good to hear it," Rufus sighed, deeply. "I didn't expect managing my family's estate to be so…dangerous." He staggered upright, only to give under the weight of fatigue. The burgomeister caught Rufus before he fell face-first onto the floor. "I'm alright," he lied.

"Easy," Gottfried said, sternly. "You took quite the beating at the abbey."

Rufus's eyes fell upon the burgomeister's bruises. "W-what about you?"

Gottfried smiled. "Oh, I'll be fine. You should get some rest."

Rufus climbed back into bed, partially against his own will, and Gottfried took his leave, shutting the door behind him. Hours blurred together, and Rufus shuddered as cold sweats took their course, and yet, he knew the truth. The pursuit of family redemption was petty at best. Gottfried was more than capable of administering the estate. Rufus was an idle youth roped into an ancestral scheme. If the horrors of the estate failed to kill him, the locals surely would.

"I have to get out of here," he muttered.

Mustering the remnants of his strength, Rufus crawled out of bed and reached for his shillelagh. He would need it to stand. Limping about the Hofbräuhaus, he scoffed at his own wretched state, and the floor moaned with every step. The ground floor was eerily vacant. Even the innkeeper seemed to have turned in for the night. Rufus made way to the stables in the hopes of finding a way back to civilization. A holster turned to face him, pitching hay into bales.

"Excuse me," Rufus managed. "Is there a coach leaving soon?"

The holster did not reply—blue in the face, Rufus wondered if he was born a mute. The heir examined the steeds, wondering if he had the strength to ride at all. He was a fool to consider and knew it well. Desperation overcame reason. He feebly tugged at a saddle, attempted to hoist his ailing body atop the horse—and stumbled into a heap of manure, crippled by aching pain. Eventually, Rufus managed to mount one of the nags, though he hardly remembered doing so. Hooves against cobblestones all but announced his departure. It was not until he saw a flash of green cloth in the lamplight that he paused.

A familiar woman had skirted into the neighboring alley.

"Sophia?" he wondered aloud.

Though tempted to follow, if only to ensure her safety, Rufus saw a silhouette leaning against the masonry wall, as if expecting her arrival—a customer. Gritting his teeth with envy yet unsurprised, the heir carried on with a stiff upper lip.

It wasn't the first time he'd been so easily forgotten.

Sagging under the weight of fatigue, Rufus felt the warmth of the hamlet fade, the darkness of the Grünewald seeping into sight. His eyes were fixed upon the moonlit road; alone, save for the chirr and chatter of verminous life, and the howl of wolves. Eventually, Rufus came across the toll gate where he had first met the landsknechts, its palisade still obstructing the Old Road. There was, however, a sidepath wide enough for travel by horseback. No sign or lantern served to guide him. If Rufus were to carry on, the wild awaited him.

"The next town can't be far off," he told himself.

Rufus's thoughts wandered to what he had left behind. Foul notions gnawed at the back of his mind, of leaving Altstadt to fend for itself—a death sentence in all but name. And yet, what could men do against the evil spawned from the dark corners of the earth? The journey did nothing to ease his anxieties. The moon evoked an eerie glow amidst autumnal canopies—vines hung as nooses, festooned over slender branches, and humidity pervaded the weald.

Strangest of all were the fungi that thrived in putrescence, blooming with spores among the fireflies, death caps sprouting out of earth and tree, and shallow graves dug in haste. There was method in the corruption, as if Rufus had wandered into a garden of decay. Bestial eyes gleamed out of the brambles. Even the horse was uneasy.

"There, there, girl," he patted her mane. "It'll be alright."

The trail seemed to spirit Rufus deeper into the weald, until spores and spiderwebs choked him, and the horse began to buck and snort. The forest danced madly with half-imagined lights and breathed with tides of subtle emotion. Rufus stared at his own hands, watching his fingers blur together. Whether a phantom of injuries or a symptom of madness, he did not know.

His steed came to a halt.

Voices carried on the air—womanly, wordless, perhaps an attempt to lure him off the path. As strength ebbed, Rufus dismounted his steed and approached a silhouette planted in the split in the road. It did not stir. Rattling reached his ears. A troubling effigy crept into vision—a wreath framed about a deer skull, splattered with dried blood, horns adorned with twigs, twine, and tiny bones. Against his better judgment, or perhaps on instinct, Rufus outstretched a trembling hand and caressed the effigy—when a shriek rang through his thoughts. He recoiled and collapsed, held captive by fear, and his horse whinnied and galloped into the night, leaving him prone. The birds and beasts had turned silent. Rufus tried to stand, but his sinew spasmed and strength failed him. The forest began to spin dully about his skull, and the world blurred to a dim orange glow. Something dragged him by the ankles into the deep and creeping darkness.

Rufus woke in a wooden cage, huddled and panting in the corner, and the smell of boiling broth filled his nostrils. A threesome of figures hovered over a cast-iron cauldron.

"Uh," Rufus grasped at the bars, "excuse me…."

They paid him no heed. Rufus's thoughts faded in and out of coherence as he reached through the cage. Wayward and weird, the sisters spoke the tongue of the land itself, every syllable reverberating in the heir's fractured mind.

The largest of the three, a brewess or beekeeper of sorts, raised a bloated hand and sprinkled a pinch of root into the stew. Spotted with bruises and gangrenous ulcers, swollen as if drowned, the middle sister was the first to acknowledge the captive heir.

"So," her voice was muffled by a wicker mask, "the princeling stirs yet."

"Aye," rasped the eldest, a woman wrapped in bandages and unhealed burns, her molten face shadowed by a scarlet shroud, "and a coward at that. Treading on ancient land to save his own skin, ignorant to the pact in his blood." She brandished a gnarled knife at her captive. "We do not take kindly to your wandering, princeling. Our land is not of man."

"Sorry," Rufus struggled, "I must've taken a wrong turn." He failed to stand, half-realizing how small the cage was. "If you'll pardon the intrusion, I'll be on my way."

"And where will he go, I wonder?" said the youngest and least grotesque, a virago with a wart-ridden face and hooked nose. Eyes swollen shut, as if asphyxiated by the noose tightened around her neck, she slammed a tenderizer against a heap of unknown flesh, mincing for the broth. "To sound the alarm and send in the mob?" She gritted her broken teeth. "Many have tried." She tugged at the rope dangling over her breasts, mockingly. "All have failed."

Rufus did not reply. Despite his terror, lucidity and a sense of malaise crept to the forefront of his mind. "Trust me, the estate has its hands full. And, if recent happenings are anything to go by, I'm more likely to be hanged from a gibbet. The peasants are, well…revolting."

The eldest gave a shrill laugh. "I'm almost inclined to believe you, princeling. Our garden has clearly gone to your head. Why should we believe you, the bastard of a bastard?"

"Because," Rufus said, "my only sin is ignorance."

"Ignorance of the horrors his blood hath wrought."

"I am not my grandfather." Silence befell the sisters, as if they were bewitched by the concept—that he was not responsible for the sins of his forebears. "But," Rufus looked away, "I digress. What exactly did he do to you, uh, finest of ladies?"

"Tricked us, he did," said the middle sister. "He drove us into the weald, rallying clergy and commoners alike. We were to be drowned, burned, and hanged. Awaiting a trial that never came, we endured the tortures of the Drudenhaus, for we knew of his ambition to tame the Thing in the Pit. Once, we were cunning women, respected and admired. He sought our wisdom and courted us under the Moon—we were but pawns to him. And now, he sends you to taunt us."

"But what a lover he was," cooed the youngest.

Rufus shuddered at the thought of his ancestor's debauchery with these crones, though he knew better than to comment. "I see," he said. "That must've been…very difficult."

"You lack his silver tongue," said the eldest, "that is undeniable."

"Sorry to disappoint."

"He is right to be afraid," the eldest continued, "though not of us. He fears the sins of the father, of the tainted throne he sits upon. The darkness that lurks in his own heart."

Those words struck Rufus deeper than he would ever admit. It was not guilt per se, as it was fear of his own potential. Out here, in the wilderness, the niceties of civilization meant little. In truth, he already had the strength and the means, and it was a temptation to make a beast of himself, to cast off the shackles of humanity, to become God. Should Rufus stray from the path, he would succumb to the madness that all men were capable of. To do so was to be free of being human, of the morality sung by muses and better angels.

As if in response to his epiphany, there was a shift in the moonlight.

"So it begins," said the middle sister. "The princeling has come to claim his birthright, his kingdom veiled in shadow. But the moon is not right yet," she whispered, "not tonight."

"Tonight?" Rufus asked.

"So inquisitive is he," mocked the youngest, fingers twitching over pulley and pivot. "Why, one would think him a man of the cloth." At that moment, she cranked a lever, and the cage was lifted sharply from the soil—with the hoist of a rope, it shifted and swayed over the boiling cauldron. "Tell us, princeling," she said. "Why do you deserve our mercy?"

Rufus considered his words carefully. A clever retort would undoubtedly amuse the sisters, but would not prolong his life. They valued honesty above all else, especially an epiphany under duress, but Rufus was shielded by nihilism, much to his own surprise.

"I don't," he lied.

The sisters erupted in a fit of laughter. "The broth will loosen the flesh from your bones, and your eyes will melt from their sockets." The cage plummeted towards the cauldron—it stopped inches before the black iron lip. "At least, they would've, should you have spoken a word differently. Besides," said the youngest, "you are too gamy to make good eating."

"Release the sacrifice," the middle sister bellowed.

From out of the woods came a host of groping dead—slaves to the sisters, to the malignancy of the weald. Deep red polypores and burgundy brackets grew from their flesh, skulls moldering hosts to mindless infection. And yet, Rufus saw thin forms writhing under their skins. The middle sister waved a fetid censor to lure the blind servants to the cage. Without grace or finesse, they lifted the bars and beckoned Rufus to disembark with uncanny manners.

"Who were they?" Rufus wondered aloud.

"Those who crossed us or failed to keep their word," said the youngest. "The rabble who sought fit to maim and mangle us. We merely returned the favor."

"And what of me?"

"You may go," said the middle sister, "if you swear but one thing." She lumbered before the heir, towering over him in girth alone. "You will neither return nor cross us. Regardless of what you see or hear. You will do what your ancestor did not and leave us to the Old Ways."

"In exchange," the eldest offered the palm of her hand, "we will foretell your fate."

The youngest nodded. "Gifted are we in haruspicy, ancient an art as it is." She stirred the cauldron with a ladle, as writhing intestines began to float in the broth. "Under the light of the Hidden Moon, all shall be revealed."

Though suspicious, Rufus knew better than to refuse. The infested surrounded him in a pagan circle, a mere command from tearing him limb from limb. Slowly, his strength returned, and he offered a shaky hand. "I will neither return nor cross you. Your affairs are your own."

A lukewarm gale rustled through the leaves, fanning the flames beneath the cauldron, as if the weald itself had been witness to the tying of the knot of fate.

"We have a contract," the sisters began to speak in grim unison, as if possessed by a will not entirely their own, by the moon herself. "Look into the cauldron."

Stifling his suspicions, Rufus peered into the entrails. Foul vapors flooded his senses. Slowly, the flesh began to ripple into the likeness of Altstadt, its half-timbered houses and slender gables, then to soft portraits of familiar faces, Gottfried and Sophia among them, disappointed yet hardly surprised—only to dissolve as quickly as they appeared. Though an impression of intestines, the message was clear to Rufus. Should he leave, no one would blame him. Then the flesh began to blacken. Screams of hamlet folk filled Rufus's ears. Altstadt did not burn—rather, it squirmed and contorted into a monstrous cancer, all-consuming and all-encompassing. The Thing in the Pit had broken free.

"No!" Rufus shrieked.

He collapsed on his back—dazed, reeling, on the border of madness. The sisters were silent in mourning. Rufus staggered to his feet, eyes wide in horror.

It was a vision, nothing more, yet so real in its finality.

"This is what will come to pass," said the sisters, "should you choose to flee."

The middle sister stood before him. "Though these sins are not your doing," she said, "to undo what he has done rests upon your shoulders alone. Only the son can redeem the father."

"That can't possibly...."

"Belief or disbelief lies with you, princeling. It will make no difference within a year's time. Go now. Do as you will. Take whatever path you choose. And do not look back."

Once more, the woods closed in, swallowing Rufus's sight as night turned to day. He staggered out of the Grünewald, stinking of sweat and nightsoil. Dawn had crept over the spires of Schloss Fleischburg, its rays piercing the mists like daggers of hope. His fatigue had vanished, and the hamlet lay before him. Step by step, Rufus returned to the cobbled streets, welcomed by the Hofbräu. The door opened seemingly on its own accord. The innkeeper seemed ignorant to the heir's absence. Gottfried, however, smiled knowingly.

Rufus wordlessly ordered a double, laughing to himself.

The innkeeper eyed him nervously. "Are you alright?"

"No." Rufus downed the shot with uncaring ease. "Absolutely not."

What he had witnessed was etched into his mind. The heir picked at the folds and cuticles of his nails, habitually peeling back bits of skin—until something wet and coarse stroked his ankle. Mincemeat licked him with uncharacteristic affection.

"I don't have any food," he said, smiling.

Mincemeat mewed, lightly, and lingered a moment longer.

Breakfast consisted of bread, sausage, and boiled eggs, which the heir washed down with ample beer. The innkeeper managed a smirk, as if he knew more than he let on.

"Surprised to see you back."

Rufus shrugged. "Just went out for a nightly stroll."

"I'm sure," the innkeeper's tone was tinged with sarcasm. "She was looking for you."

"More like my leftovers."

"I don't mean the cat."

It took Rufus a moment to catch on.

"I must admit," Gottfried added, "the harlot helped tend to your wounds. Tamed the worst of the fever. Strange remedies, those. The stuff of old wives' tales."

Rufus did not know what to say. It was true that he'd assumed the worst upon seeing her with another—that he'd been forsaken as a carnal plaything. He was happy to be proven wrong. He reached for his stein and lifted the lukewarm brew to his lips.

At that moment, Rufus felt his conviction renewed. Just as he signed the contract upon arrival at Altstadt, so too did he swear to never leave the estate until his work was complete. Not in pursuit of family redemption, rather because it was the "right" thing to do. And yet, Rufus knew he could not do this alone. He grabbed a stack of blank papers and a quill and began to write with all the inspiration he could muster.

Men-at-arms and mercenaries of the Empire,

It is with great humility that I request your participation in defense from an evil best left ambiguous at this time. The Barony of Grünewald is to establish an army – soldiers of any and all experience are welcome. There will be substantial rewards for assistance in ridding the land of violence and lawlessness, namely, in regard to expeditions to Schloss Fleischburg. Seek out employment at the hamlet of Altstadt by way of the Old Road. Travel expenses guaranteed. Funeral expenses and further benefits offered upon enlistment at the Hofbräuhaus.

Signed,

Baron Rufus Grünewald

"Gottfried," he said.

"Yes, my lord?"

"Send word to the Imperial Cities. I want fighting men. Men with nothing to live for. Veterans and vagrants. The estate won't clean itself up. We need an army."

"I see," Gottfried said, taken slightly aback. "And who will pay for this army?"

"Add it to the deficit."

Satisfied with his pitch, Rufus found it amusing how others would be dragged into these affairs much the same way as he. He imagined word spreading from inn to inn as unscrupulous men caught wind of the prospect of payment for cheap labor. Rallying to his cause, they would come to fight for glory and gold—and meet an untimely end as many had before them. The notion of shepherding these lost souls did not trouble Rufus as much as he would've liked or cared to admit. Instead, he thought of it as nothing more than good business—something to be paid for in blood. Regardless, he would sleep soundly that night.

CHAPTER FIVE

Rufus personally oversaw the application process, toiling over pamphlets and promises of "substantial rewards" to be dispersed to every corner of the Empire. Days of silence were to be expected, but after nearly two weeks, he was beginning to lose enthusiasm. Though distrustful of the locals, he permitted a well-regulated militia to continue its drills, if only to dampen further unrest. In truth, he knew they could do little against the wights and wiedergängers, let alone the Thing in the Pit. Rufus was content to lock himself in the Hofbräuhaus, snifter at hand, with Gottfried acting as envoy and errand boy for daily affairs.

"Don't look so dour," he told the heir. "Keep your expectations low and you'll never be disappointed. That's how I manage to keep my spirits intact."

Autumn days marched on, and Rufus realized that he had never fully unpacked his belongings—it was time he made himself at home. Following the deaths of Leopold and Hupert, Rufus had made it a point to recover his stolen luggage from the town constable. He opened the twin trunks and smiled sadly at reminders of life in the city of Chimay.

He found a framed sketch of the family in its prime, atop a number of folded waistcoats. It was a portrait of appearances. A nine-year-old Rufus forced a smile, father's hand gripping his shoulder sternly, mother holding his toddler sister—who died of plague later that year. It was at the funeral that Rufus met Matthias Grünewald for the first time.

Under a forlorn sky, the heir scarcely remembered what his grandfather looked like, but recalled his baritone voice, which commanded attention from all who heard it.

"I don't know what to say," the baron said, "or if I should say anything at all." He knelt low and held the heir's hand. "You're welcome to stay with me anytime, Rufus, should you—"

"Father, a word?"

Kindness slipped from the baron's face like a mask. Straightening his posture, Matthias turned to his son and daughter-in-law and humored their hushed concerns. Rufus did not understand then—in retrospect, it was undoubtedly for the best. Mother succumbed to grief as she took to the bottle, ignorant to the concerns of those closest to her. On the eve of her death, Rufus caught his father burning a collection of letters, invitations bearing the seal. He was told to go back to bed. It seemed Matthias would only make his appearance in moments of tragedy.

"I wish we could meet under better circumstances," he said, softly.

Rufus did not reply, content to watch the ravens atop the family crypt. Mother had been entombed beside his sister and others of the family who suffered premature death.

"Come," the baron said. "I have something for you."

The young heir's face lit up, if only a little.

"A small comfort, if nothing else." Matthias opened a leather case and delicately handed him a blackthorn cane. "I had it made just for you. Careful now. The handle is filled with lead. Quite the club in the wrong, or right, hands." He knelt and cupped the heir's shoulder. "It's called a shillelagh. Imported from the Isle of Skellige." His eyes shifted about the cemetery, as if on alert for prowling beasts. "Don't tell your father, but I think you're ready for it—"

"My lord?"

Rufus was torn back to Altstadt. Gottfried had interrupted his introspection, lingering at the threshold with Mincemeat at his side. The heir eyed the clock on the mantelpiece. He'd spent a good thirty minutes lost in thought. Rufus shut the trunk and stood sharply, wiping a lone tear from his eye, seeking to regain some semblance of perceived dignity.

"Are you alright?" the burgomeister asked.

"Yes. I'm just…pensive."

Among the other things Rufus had carried were rented manuscripts and letters of recommendation—mementos from his academic career. Come to think of it, he never knew how his tuition was paid, studying under the assumption that it came from his father's coffers. Quite the investment for a banker. The heir suspected that Matthias, though estranged from the family, always saw that his next of kin lived a comfortable existence. Whether a genuine attempt at love or the machinations of manipulation, Rufus could not say.

"I'm sorry," he tore himself free of reflection, "what was it you wanted?"

"They're here."

Word spread rapidly of not one but three coaches spotted on the Old Road. Rufus knew better than to get his hopes up, but Gottfried, deaf to his own advice, was enthusiastic at the prospect of anyone answering the call to arms. Come noon, rays of sunlight pierced the billowing sky, and a trio of black coaches emerged from the Grünewald, crossing into town and halting at the Hofbräuhaus—a host of armed miscreants disembarked, eager to examine their surroundings at the journey's end. Rufus watched from the second-story window with wide eyes.

"Well," Gottfried said, "don't just stand there. We'd best greet our guests."

Rufus came downstairs to the open bar. The innkeeper was seemingly overwhelmed by the crowd, who drank the local swill with varying degrees of enthusiasm.

"It'll be on the house," Rufus said. "Keep the liquor flowing." He eyed the mercenaries with keen interest, raising a glass to the nearest adventurer. "A pleasant journey, I hope?"

"Rather uneventful."

The heir nodded, silently examining the would-be recruit. He was young, too young perhaps, little more than an adolescent with his father's sword and vambraces.

"Well," Rufus said, "welcome to Altstadt." He raised his voice ever so slightly, as to garner the crowd's attention. "That goes for you all. Welcome." He forced a smile. "I trust you are familiar with the cause and why you are here? The nature of the available positions?"

Quiet befell the crowd, though a couple of sellswords remained occupied with their own conversation. Many eyes lay upon him. Though Rufus had the attention of those willing to listen, he couldn't help but twitch anxiously at the thought of public speaking, timid as he was.

"I assume you've all read the pamphlets?"

There was no response.

"Very well, then." Rufus shifted in place. "As you know," he began anew, "I am offering a substantial reward for any and all assistance in purging the estate of the perils which plague its grounds. This is left deliberately ambiguous, for evil takes many forms here in Altstadt—" He noticed a hand dart up from the crowd. "Yes," hope sprang in the heir's heart, "you there."

"Define 'substantial?'" someone asked.

There was a murmur of agreement amongst the audience.

"Ah," Rufus said, "I believe that is a question better answered by my treasurer." He beckoned for Gottfried to step forward and take his share of public interrogation. "If you please."

The burgomeister came to the heir's side. "As the young master has suggested, the exact reward varies from job to job, some being more perilous than others, but rest assured, four shillings and salvage rights for a delve. Six per bounty. To say little of the swine-folk."

Rufus shot him an aside glance but said nothing.

"They proliferate near Westerham," Gottfried winked, "a neighboring estate."

A handful of mercenaries had already stood to leave.

"As you can see," Rufus continued, "the estate is besieged by ample terrors. Brigands being but one of many. We have a handful of odd jobs posted by the Rathaus, chief of them being a series of expeditions into Schloss Fleischburg itself. Make no mistake—"

"Some of you may die," Gottfried added, "but the compensation will be unmatched. You will also have access to our facilities, including this finely appointed inn. Funeral expenses are guaranteed. And we will cover the cost of shipping your remains to your widows, if applicable."

Rufus sighed, deeply. "Does that answer your question?"

The soldier was nowhere to be seen, having left halfway through the explanation.

"Why all the concern?" someone laughed. "I've seen nothing horrific."

"Give it time," Rufus said. "But if it's the truth you want, then I'll divulge in full." Rolling his eyes, he stood atop a table like a ringmaster trying to corral an audience of restless children. "I, too, was skeptical of these woes upon my arrival," he said, "but, after seeing men ripped apart by the walking dead, I realized that I was…out of my depth. That's why I need you. Swords willing to fight for guilder and glory. Both of which I can promise in full. Now then," he raised a number of contracts, unfurling in his grip, "who will be so bold as to sign first?"

The crowd was more than halved by this delivery, but those who stayed were either grizzled veterans or youths with one foot in their graves—ten in total.

"Well," Gottfried smiled to himself, "I'd call that a successful pitch."

Rufus took a seat at the bar, dabbed a quill in an inkwell, and signed up the misfits in single file. One after the other, each as eccentric yet unremarkable as the rest, the heir indulged in small talk, meetings, and greetings.

Truth be told, he had forgotten their names upon enlistment.

"Next," Gottfried called.

It was not until a tall, brooding man, bitterly aged, came to the table that Rufus lifted his gaze from the roster. The stranger's face was veiled in shadow, dressed in a rich black doublet accented by deep violets and violent reds, with a rapier and pair of snaphances at his belt. His eyes gleamed from under the brim of a thrice-cornered hat tied with a scarlet sash. Darkness seemed to follow him, yet the hearth burned all the brighter, sharply contrasting with the ambivalence among the rest of the hirelings. He did not give his name.

"Ah," Rufus began, "hello."

"I have read your letters," said the stranger, "and have heard the tales."

"Excellent." Gottfried clasped his wrists, perhaps simply numb to any menace or notion of danger, mundane or otherwise. "And what's your story, pray tell?"

The stranger slid a pamphlet of his own onto the table—worn and wet, yet its ink untarnished. Printed in bold above the illustrations and accolades were the simple words.

WILHELM HEXENJÄGER
Witchfinder General of the Midlands

A chill ran down the heir's spine. Rufus had heard the tales of witch-hunters throughout the cantons and counties, of their ruthless techniques and penchant for torture. Not all were of the Holy See. Before the Great Schism, men who took the word of God as their own prowled the countryside as entrepreneurs of faith. Some were mere agitators, yet others were clerics who had forsaken the Ecclesiarchy in favor of their own convictions. They were men of action, unswayed by bribes or petty indulgences, and in that lay their danger. In divine protest, witch-hunters swore to burn out heresy no matter what form it took. Rufus's thoughts flashed with violent imagery—of blazing pyres, broken wills, and extreme prejudice, of the will to do great and terrible things in the name of righteousness.

"Well," Rufus said, "your reputation certainly precedes you."

"If you have nothing to hide, then fear not the flame."

"I'm sure many have heard that before."

Wilhelm spoke with slow deliberation. "Something dwells beneath the halls of Schloss Fleischburg. Something that drives men to madness. Your cause is just, but you know not what ails your lands." He glanced with suspicion at those huddled about the hearth. "Or your people."

"Wonderful. Now, if you'll sign here…."

With a sigh of restraint, Wilhelm feigned understanding and forced a smile. "I will sign no contract, as I have my own means to investigate these troubles. And you'd be loath to refuse my help, considering most of your recruits are dead men walking."

Rufus clammed up at the unwelcome truth.

"I will, however," Wilhem continued, "require your cooperation, should you accept my offer. Namely, for you to accompany me on these expeditions."

"Excuse me?" Rufus scoffed.

"Come, let us walk."

Rufus obeyed with grave reluctance. As the afternoon sun crept over the mountainous horizon, the townsfolk had all but vanished, having locked their doors and shut their windows.

"If I may," Rufus said, "your bedside manner leaves a bit to be desired."

Wilhelm eyed the heir sharply, his gaze cutting through him like a blade. "With all due respect, you have your duty and office, and I have mine." He turned his attention to the spires of Schloss Fleischburg, clutching holster and hilt with vim and vigor. "Few will, or can, appreciate the magnitude of your hardships. Tomorrow," he said, "we will chart the vaults and slay whatever we encounter. All the while delving towards the root of evil. Of course, we will need a small party of recruits as well. You mentioned the undead in the lower halls?"

"Wiedergängers," Rufus said. "Unless my research fails me."

"Those who walk again." Wilhelm paused and pondered. "I see. Do you know how they came to be? If plague or war had struck the land? Disaster can often stir the restless soul."

"I do not know, but Altstadt is no stranger to either," Rufus said, hesitating to divulge the truth. "I have my suspicions that my grandfather was something of a necromancer."

Wilhelm raised a thin eyebrow. "Do you have a record of these heresies?"

"Oh, all too many."

Escorting the witch-hunter to the Rathaus, Rufus watched on as Wilhelm pored over the library of ledgers and tax documents by candlelight, while the burgomeister lingered in the hall and Mincemeat glowered at the unwelcome guest from her bookshelf perch.

"It seems the baron's excavations were quite a venture," Wilhelm said. "Most expensive. Nearly every asset was exhausted to fuel this ambition. It's a wonder Altstadt is still standing."

"I'm more concerned with how you intend to combat the dead," Rufus said.

"It is true that the wiedergänger cannot bleed, as it has no humors save the venom in its veins. However, this also makes it susceptible to corrosion. Are you capable of providing that?"

"Not to my knowledge."

Gottfried crept into the office. "If I may, there is the Narrenturm."

"The what?" Rufus asked.

The Narrenturm was an hour's ride outside of Altstadt, situated on a beige stretch of moorland between the hamlet and the Grünewald's edge. Rising as a brick-and-mortar colosseum from the brush-choked dells, it was a fortress of fringe science, lined with rings of slit windows and crenelations, and crowned with a scarlet dome of shingled tiles. Before the entrance lay a garden of herbs and botanical curiosities, partitioned into plots and greenhouses, tended by silent orderlies in white and waxed robes.

"The Fool's Tower," Wilhelm said. "Yes. I am familiar."

"I had no idea such a place existed," Rufus dismounted his steed, "let alone as part of the estate." He eyed the lightning rods jutting from the rooftop. "We had buildings like this at the university. Observatories and lecture halls. Did my grandfather commission it as well?"

"No," Gottfried said, "and the Narrenturm lies outside your jurisdiction. It is owned by one Doctor Isidore Cronenberg. He has ties with House Grünewald yet did not answer to the late baron." He came to the heir's side. "From one eccentric to another, let me do the talking. The good doctor can be…cantankerous." He approached one of the gardeners. "Excuse me?"

The orderly raised his weary head without a word, eyes dull and vacant.

"We are here to see your master. It is most urgent."

The orderly nodded and turned to his superior, who turned to the overseer, so on and so forth, until the line reached the doorstep and a bell rang. After a moment's calm, the doors creaked open on their own accord, flooding the garden with the cries of madmen.

Rufus felt the color drain from his face.

Wilhelm eyed the orderlies with suspicion and made way to the darkened foyer. Together, the company was greeted by chessboard tiles, oil lamps, and irregular shadows. Echoing with incoherent babble, every corridor funneled the voices of lunatics throughout the asylum. Rufus covered his nose and mouth with a handkerchief, gagging at the odor of vomit and less identifiable fluids, when metallic whining reached his ears. The portcullis dividing the foyer from the panopticon lifted slowly, revealing a silhouette in a seat rolling to greet his guests.

"Well then," said a nasally voice, "it's not every day you come to visit, Gottfried." The silhouette clutched the arms of his wheelchair, twisting a pair of rotary handles, and emerged into the light. A knitted quilt was cast over his legs. He sported a pair of spectacles and was flanked by assistants in raven-beaked masks. "And this is the heir apparent?"

"We're looking for a Doctor Cronenberg." Rufus took a step forward. "Is he—?"

"Yes, yes," the doctor said, dismissively, "that would be me." He glowered from over his glasses. "Take it ill manners run in the family. Whatever brings you to the asylum?"

Gottfried nudged the heir. "We are in need of your expertise."

"Well, isn't that nice." Cronenberg pivoted his chair and wheeled to the burgomeister's side. "Let me guess, you and the witch-hunter," he jerked his head in Wilhelm's direction, "are planning to delve into the castle. Again." He smirked, darkly. "Slow learners, aren't we?"

Rufus raised a hand. "How did you—?"

"I'm not as senile as I look, your lordship," the doctor

snapped. "At any rate, if you're going after wights, you'll need something biting and acidic." He snapped his gloved fingers, bidding his assistants to escort them deeper into the asylum. "I'll get you fixed up."

Rufus was about to follow the doctor when he felt eyes upon him.

Glancing over his shoulder, he spied a woman in green staring down at him from the upper mezzanine, shadowed yet familiar.

"My lord," Gottfried called. "We mustn't linger."

Rufus shrugged and followed his lead. The laboratory was a museum of anatomical-pathological specimens. Shelves of medical curios—ranging from syphilitic skulls, jars of malformed fetuses and organs, to wax displays of horrific deformities—lined its tall stone walls. Chilled beneath the earthen moor, the chamber was somewhere between a morgue and an operating theater—an autopsy table sat in the middle of the room, surrounded by trays and racks of surgical equipment. Among the wonder cabinets, Cronenberg rummaged through the drawers and handed a host of tools to his assistants.

"Let's see," the doctor muttered, "there has to be something of use."

"You are versed in the ways of science," Wilhelm said. "I am curious as to your history with House Grünewald. I assume you supplied labor in exchange for weird findings?"

"You'd assume correctly." Cronenberg glanced over his shoulder. "We had dealings in the past and shared in knowledge of what lies beneath us." He raised a bonesaw, admiring the gleam of its teeth. "His studies were occultic. Mine are more empirical, but I can empathize with his ambition." Amidst the sachets of medicinal herbs and smelling salts was a collar of charges—tiny clay pots filled with gunpowder, iron nails, and ichor of corrosive properties. "Don't be fooled." He handed the bandolier to Wilhelm. "They can and will dissolve flesh and bone."

"Thank you," Gottfried said. "These will be invaluable against the wights."

Grateful as Rufus was for the unexpected aid, he couldn't help but feel uneasy regarding the circumstances. Why was the doctor so eager to help? What did he have to gain? Surely, Cronenberg would not part with such equipment freely, regardless of his history with House Grünewald. As if in response to the heir's discomfort, the doctor wheeled to his side.

"Oh," he grinned, "don't worry. I'll need something from you in turn."

"I had a hunch."

Cronenberg nodded. "If you're going after the undead, then I'd like a sample of flesh. A limb or two will be more than enough."

Wilhelm towered over the doctor. "And what, pray tell, would you use this sample for?"

"That's no concern of yours. Rest assured, my intentions are secular." Moments of silence stung the air as the doctor's patience ran thin. "If you don't like my offer, you're welcome to waltz into the ruins and test your luck. Now, if you'll excuse me, I'm a busy man."

"Very well," Rufus conceded with a sigh, "we will bring you a sample."

Wilhelm shot the heir a dire glance, but said nothing, and the doctor took leave to care for the lunatics rattling in their cages. Gottfried was seemingly pleased with the day's outcome and bade the company to return to their horses. Rufus lingered in the open moor, lost in thought. Stark against twilight, the broken battlements of Schloss Fleischburg shadowed the land, as if challenging the heir to test his mettle once more—he would answer in kind.

The season of slow nights for the Hofbräu had ended. Laughter and rancorous swearing filled the gambling hall, where new recruits threw dice against the rims of felted tables. Rufus smiled, watching as his men enjoyed a night of merriment before tomorrow's plunge. Wilhelm was confined to the corner, toiling over documents borrowed from the Rathaus. Against the heir's instinct to enjoy himself, he came to a rear table and joined the witch-hunter by the hearth.

"Find anything of note?" Rufus asked.

"Regrettably," Wilhelm admitted. "We're dealing with more than wights."

"What do you mean?"

Wilhelm slid the open tome across the table. "Read this."

Rufus skimmed the passage, its brittle pages delicate to the touch, threatening to crumble under his fingertips, as if the diary itself was centuries old. The most recent additions were slips of paper in between sheets of parchment, and undoubtedly bore the baron's penmanship.

Destitution and desperation often go hand in hand. It was during the height of my studies in reviving the dead that plague came to the estate. Much of the peasantry succumbed, and those unfortunate enough to survive were robbed of nearly everything they held dear. Grief can be a deadlier poison than even hate. One of my subjects, a miller who'd married young, had heard rumor of my practice and, having lost his wife and infant child to the pestilence, pleaded with me to revive his family. No small part of me was overjoyed at the prospect of animating the recently deceased – let alone with a willing participant.

We exhumed the mass grave and recovered the remains of the miller's family. No doubt he was disturbed by our desecration, but claimed to understand its necessity. For if we were to resurrect his loved ones, blacker deeds would have to be done. Under the gibbous moon, we offered blood sacrifices to the empyreal spheres and called upon the only god I knew would listen. The worms obeyed. However, our utterances were imperfect and the results disappointing. The cadavers groped and gibbered blindly as my serpentine servitors breathed a facsimile of life into their veins. I could not allow the rumor of this failure to spread among the hamlet folk.

The miller was not a simpleton. I believe a piece of him died that night, reaped by the implications of my sorcery. The botched wife and child writhed on the altar as mockeries of what was promised. He had seen too much. Paralyzed by despair, the miller realized too late as I sealed him in the catacombs, and yet, I detected a weird enthusiasm amongst the worms. Beyond the stone door, I heard him babble and haggle with the parasites, desperate to save his family – and himself. The bloodletting proved to be a worthy initiation, and he soon joined the ranks of the walking dead, a wiedergänger to be puppeteered by insidious will. There he would stay with his dearly beloved – forever.

"Just what are you suggesting?" Rufus snapped and shut the tome. "That my grandfather wasn't, or isn't, the only necromancer in those godforsaken halls?"

"Precisely," Wilhelm said. "Wiedergängers can be influenced by those able to manipulate the dark forces. I suspect there must be someone who commands their every movement."

"Then we must find the root of this evil and slay it," Rufus said.

Wilhelm nodded, slowly. "I concur," he said with hesitation, eyes fixed upon the drunken rabble, "but do you think these men are ready to confront such a force?"

Rufus did not reply, nor did he look at his men. He had seen the wights tear Leopold and Hupert limb from limb. The heir shuddered, rallying his own conviction if nothing else.

"I do," he lied.

"Then we set out tomorrow."

With nothing else to be said, Rufus returned to the bar, shuddering in the wake of ill revelations. A whiskey was in order. Downing the shot with a grimace, he massaged his brow with tired hands, eager to sleep after the exertions of a day's ride and public speaking. He saw a familiar figure out of the corner of his eye—the woman in green surrounded by potential customers. Envy washed over Rufus, cheeks flushed and red. Mustering his courage against a fleeting sense of etiquette, he approached Sophia and offered a sweaty hand.

"My lady," he said.

Sophia eyed him with amusement. "I'll see you gentlemen later," she addressed the leering men-at-arms. "Apparently, your financier has a proposition for me." She shifted down the stained sofa, bidding the heir to sit beside her. "Now you find time away from your duties?"

Rufus did just that.

"Sorry," he managed, "I've been busy."

"Rumor has it you tried to make a break for it. What happened?"

"What do you mean?"

"Why're you still here?"

Rufus clutched his empty glass and stared at the lopsided table. "Well," he said, "let's just say a woman's touch changed my mind." He stifled a grin, flattered by his own guile, until his eyes met with Sophia's, which reflected bitter disbelief.

"A coven," he admitted, "in the weald."

"Ah," she said, "you've met the Ladies of the Moon."

"You know—?"

"Of them." Sophia averted her gaze. "They've dwelled in the woods long before my time in Altstadt. Let's just say the country doesn't take kindly to women with minds of their own."

"Though it seemed my grandfather had no shortage of

lovers."

Sophia laughed. "Don't plan on letting that go, do you?"

Rufus smiled in kind. "Sorry." The hearth cast her in a flattering light, though the heir was flustered with uncertainty. He watched on as Wilhelm pushed past the mercenaries, most of whom would likely be hungover for tomorrow's expedition. "Listen," he reached for Sophia's thigh, "I'm going to the manor. Leading the company. And, well, I may not return."

"I know," Sophia said. "I have something for you." She reached into her cleavage and lifted a medallion bearing the bas-relief of the moon. She pressed it into the heir's hand.

"What is it?" he asked.

"Protection."

There was much Rufus wanted to say then. "Would you?" He tried to swallow the lump in his throat, clutching the medallion with white knuckles. "Would you have me tonight?"

Sophia leaned closely. "I'll give you a discount."

CHAPTER SIX

The following dawn, with loins sated and courage renewed, Rufus rallied his warriors of light upon the hamlet's fringe. Astride a black steed, clad in an ill-fitting cuirass engraved with fantastical imagery, he had prepared a rousing speech for the company while in Sophia's arms. Gottfried bore the standard of House Grünewald, its banner aflutter in the morning breeze.

"Arise," the heir recited his soliloquy, "arise, soldiers of fortune! Brothers and sisters in arms." He did not meet the tired stares of mercenaries slouched atop their nags. "Before us stand the gates to oblivion. There will be much blood spilt this day. Today of all days." Ignorant to their ambivalence, Rufus continued to pace before the company. "Redder than a welt. A wet welt. Burning with all the malignancy those halls have to offer. And we will overcome it. Ride now!" Ignoring the scabbard as it slipped from his belt loop, Rufus waved his ceremonial sword high in the gloaming. "Our wages await!"

The heir kicked his steed and tore up the trail to Schloss Fleischburg—until he came to its battlements and the memory of what awaited him cast a terrible shadow. Silence stung the air. The company was but a cantering shade in the distance, lingering upon the base of the cliff.

Wilhelm rode to his side, stifling a smirk. "Was that it?"

"Oh, shut up," Rufus snapped.

The heir dismounted and approached the open gates, sword at hand, shaking. When his troops had gathered in their lethargy, he led the way to the chapel—the entrance to the crypts.

Wilhelm raised a pitch-soaked torch and drew his own blade.

"Lead the way," he said.

Unseen eyes lay upon the company. Rufus glanced over his shoulder—his men shifted in place, nervously, as if beginning to realize that such tales were no exaggeration. Step by step, the heir descended the stairs into the lower vaults, retracing his route from so many moons ago.

"The sanctity of this place has been fouled," Wilhelm muttered.

"You don't say." Rufus rolled his eyes. "What is your plan then?"

"Delve into the dungeon," Wilhelm said, "slay the fiends we come across, carry our due payment to the surface, and pray that we elude the Necromancer."

Rufus felt the medallion's warmth under his silk shirt, as if Sophia touched his chest from afar. Something fierce burned in his heart—the will to protect his people and see the expedition a success. Clutching his sword's hilt, he led the plunge into darkness.

Rufus treaded lightly, careful not to step on the moldering bones strewn about the uneven flagstones, lest he lure the lurkers in the dark. Torchlight did little to pierce the pervading gloom—a wraith of radiance against the abyss. Down the halls, Rufus saw only spiders and rodents of unusual size. The walking dead had yet to detect his presence. Hours bled together until Rufus came to a set of stairs spiraling down the shaft of a well. He smiled, nervously, knowing that they had reached the threshold of another level. Dreary and wearisome, one of the mercenaries raised a torch and peered over the edge.

Even with light at hand, the company could not see the bottom.

"Is this the Pit?" Rufus asked no one in particular.

"Doubtful," Wilhelm said, "but evil lies below."

"I see," Rufus managed. "Forgive me. This is as far as I've

been."

The witch-hunter came to his side and cast his own torch into the depths, watching as it clattered off the heavy stone walls and into the unknown. Rufus took the lead, noticing the masonry shift with every step, transitioning from gothic sculpture to older stonework. When at last he came to the bottom of the well, Rufus felt a change in the air. He caressed the curving wall, crusted with a layer of dust and dampness, and wondered just how far these corridors went.

"We've reached the second level." His words echoed throughout the hollow antechamber. "Stay close and don't stray. I don't know what awaits us down here…."

"We've yet to see any sign of fortune," growled a mercenary.

"Aye," said another, "that much is plain."

Rufus rolled his eyes. "Rest assured, gentlemen, four shillings await you as promised for this delve. Now quit your whining and let's get a move on."

The heir was about to press on when a firm hand cupped his shoulder. Wilhelm raised a finger to his lips. Sure enough, monstrous whispers reverberated through the passage before them. With a deep, shuddering breath, Rufus took a defensive stance.

"What?" asked a recruit. "What is it—?"

A volley of serrated bolts flew out of the darkness, missing Rufus and the company by inches. They clattered against the floor, and the mercenaries drew steel. The slap of bare feet against stone filled the corridor, gathering speed, and a patrol of wights lunged into sight. Heart pounding, Rufus was the first to greet them with a desperate scream, swinging wide and wildly—a bone fist collided with his skull, knocking the heir flat on his back. He faded in and out of consciousness, and when he came to, the skirmish had already ended.

Wilhelm hoisted the heir to his stumbling feet.

"Do not rush in," the witch-hunter snapped. "The fiends do not bleed as men. Even if you slice off their limbs, they will still come after you." He stomped on one of the still-chittering skulls, smearing black blood and viscera against the heel of his boot, silencing the terror.

Rufus clutched his bleeding brow and failed to speak. The wights lay strewn about the corridor, clad in the armor of bygone eras, and yet, serpentine things slithered from the slain, little more than shadows, save for trails of slime, fleeting as the company's resolve. The living were present and accounted for, if shaken by what they had witnessed. Rufus was about to carry on when he noticed one of his own men staring pensively at those he'd lain to rest.

"Sir," Rufus called, "we'd best keep moving."

Towering, broad-shouldered, and clad in splint mail, the man-at-arms bore a bludgeon and kite shield with keen strength for his venerable age. He sported a groomed mustache and a black leather patch, perhaps having lost an eye in some unsung campaign.

"I know this livery," he said. "These men were part of Grünewald's standing army before the Great Peasants' War." He turned over a corpse and examined its arboreal heraldry. "Why bury them? Most who fell in battle were simply burned on the field."

Rufus mustered the will to speak past his pain. "What's your name, sir?"

"Radcliffe," he said, "and I'm no sir."

"Can you tell me anything else of the dead? How old are these cadavers, exactly?"

"At least a century," said the man-at-arms. "Before the duchies and cantons were united by the Empire, many houses relied on their own militias to 'keep the peace.' Today, those regiments compose the Imperial Army, and fief-lords use mercenaries to settle domestic matters. These 'men' served your house under oath. I recognize the coat of arms."

"How do you know all this?"

"My father served in the Ninth," Radcliffe said. "Under the late baron's command."

"Is that even possible?" Rufus asked. "My grandfather couldn't have been alive then." His words trailed off with his thoughts, remembering how the baron studied the means to transcend life and death through vitae—the fifth humor tied to the Thing in the Pit. "Unless...."

Radcliffe said no more, heaving his heavy shield, and joined Wilhelm at the vanguard. The witch-hunter and the man-at-arms exchanged whispers, much to Rufus's indignation.

"I assure you," he called, "anything you would mutter among yourselves, I will gladly listen to." He pointed at Radcliffe's chestplate. "Don't forget who fills your coffers—"

Radcliffe grabbed the heir by the finger, threatening to snap it effortlessly. "And don't forget who fights your battles. You're bloody toothless without us."

Wilhelm came between them. "Enough," he said, softly. "These petty squabbles will see us divided and vulnerable." He turned to the mercenaries who loitered and leaned against the wall. "You there," he addressed the miscreant in a deep green neckerchief—perhaps a grave robber, "check the east door. You," he turned to Radcliffe, "make sure they don't get gutted."

The man-at-arms nodded and obeyed.

"If I may," Rufus spoke up, "there is—"

"Here," Wilhelm reached into his pack and tossed the heir a bandolier, "wear this."

"Pardon?" Rufus examined the equipment, recognizing it as the collar of charges from the Narrenturm. "Oh," he caught on, "I see. You want me to play grenadier."

Wilhelm nodded. "Stick to the rear and use them sparingly. We need your intuition and expertise. How long did you say you've spent in Altstadt?"

"A little over a month."

"That's far longer than any of us. Come," Wilhelm ushered him to the east door, hushing his tone, "should one of us fall, the rest won't be far behind."

Rufus nodded in solemn agreement. The grave robber had picked the lock and leaned into the door—it opened with a loathsome creak. With a flick of flint and steel, Wilhelm lit another torch, peering into the darkened chamber. Nothing save stone and detritus awaited them. So they pressed on, room by room, hall by hall, until a tide of malaise threatened to flood Rufus's thoughts with half-imagined shadows as unnatural hunger gnawed in the back of his mind.

"Are you all right?" Wilhelm asked.

"No," Rufus admitted, "but we need to keep moving."

"There's something in the air," said the grave robber, as if sharing the heir's anxieties, leaning against the wall. "Almost like it's sucking the marrow from my bones."

"This is no different from the battlefield," Radcliffe said. "Stay vigilant and strong."

Wilhem nodded. "He's right. We can't afford to falter."

At the hour's end, the company stopped to rest briefly for a bit of landjaeger and hardtack—rations for the frontline. Radcliffe took the watch, leaning on his shield, though Rufus forbade them from lighting more than a few candles.

Tinderboxes were, after all, a commodity down in the dark.

"Any idea where we are?" asked the man-at-arms.

"In relation to what?" Rufus asked.

"You tell me."

"Heh," the heir took a sip from his flask, "fair enough."

Whiskey did little to curb the dread of the delve, but it was a distraction nonetheless. "Would you care for a drink?"

Radcliffe turned to the heir with an inscrutable expression. At first, Rufus thought he took offense, perhaps having sworn off the bottle, but the man-at-arms softened and took a swig.

"I apologize for my ill manners back there," Rufus said.

"I've dealt with worse on the front."

Rufus laughed, nervously. "I'd imagine so."

Radcliffe passed the flask. "Grunts and footmen often have arguments, but at the end of the day, all we have are our swords—and each other."

"Trite as it is, you're not wrong." Rufus crossed his arms and came to the fringe of candlelight, eying the shadows as they danced along the walls. One of the doors creaked shut on its own accord. Radcliffe stirred from his post. "Uh," the heir began, "that's...."

The man-at-arms raised a finger to his lips and raised his heavy maul. Together, they peered into the cellar and found a lockbox in the far corner. Radcliffe smirked and knelt before the chest, eager to loot its contents, but Rufus kept his distance. Something was wrong.

"Wait—!" As the man-at-arms lifted the lid, Rufus kicked the chest aside as a black-tipped dart flew into the ceiling, missing Radcliffe by inches. Inside lay a fistful of coins, due payment for such efforts. "Reward hard-earned," the heir said.

"Aye," Radcliffe pocketed his findings, "it'll do nicely." He shot the heir a smile of unspoken thanks. "Remind me to buy you a round when we get back."

So the company resumed their descent. Rufus led the way, when he saw a conspicuous crack in the wall. As the mercenaries carried on, the heir lingered, lit his own lantern, and peered inside. "Gentlemen," he called. "I think I've found something."

Whether a false wall or the work of terrible force, Rufus

did not know. Regardless, the fissure was wide enough to slip through. The chamber was cramped, little more than four walls, less than a yard apart. The desiccated corpse of some forgotten prisoner lay curled in the corner, clutching a well-creased paper in one hand. Light trickled through the iron grate far above, implying that the prisoner had been dropped into the oubliette, left to starve and succumb to his injuries. Rufus's fingers twitched as he reached for the paper.

To whoever finds me, know that I die free.

The heir smirked, knowing that such defiant resolve did little to ease the prisoner's suffering. Shocked by his own callousness, Rufus knelt and checked the corpse's pocket—finding a rusty key amidst ragged cloth. As to what it unlocked, he did not know. Regardless, a sickly warm aching emanated from the wound he received a month ago. Rufus shook his head, and the pain ebbed. Now was not the time to dwell on hypochondria and what could be.

"What did you find?" Wilhelm asked.

Rufus revealed his share of loot and pressed on. The company had halted, their course obstructed by a set of great bronze doors, cast with corpses and scenes of perdition.

He sensed a terrifying presence beyond the threshold.

"Hold," Wilhelm said, "there is an inscription upon the lintel."

"What does it say?" Radcliffe asked.

"I don't know."

"What do you mean?" Rufus asked, raising his lamp, able to read the text as clear as the common tongue. The font was twisted but hardly illegible.

"Halt, here lies," he paused, "the Empire of Death…."

The mercenaries did not reply or stir, eyes fixed upon

the heir in terrified awe, as if he had spoken some irrevocable blasphemy. Rufus did not know how to react.

"What? Can't you lot read?"

"Not cuneiform or…whatever the Devil that is."

Rufus felt the color vanish from his face. "I," he managed, "ah…."

The heir leaned against the door, only for it to slide open.

A bitter draft snuffed out torch and candle alike. The mercenaries drew their steel blindly, and yet, Rufus could make out the vague impression of an antechamber. Feeling his way along the rough stone walls, he drew his sword with deliberation—his other hand slipped into a niche and upon what felt like toughened leather.

"What the—?"

Wilhelm lit yet another torch, shedding light upon the walls of yellowed tibiae and rows upon rows of skulls. Rufus's hand graced a withered corpse dressed in simple gray robes, perhaps a monk of an unknown order long since laid to rest. He recoiled in disgust, wiping dust onto his trousers. The company had ventured into the catacombs, surrounded by the remains of thousands. Rufus wondered how many deaths were the doing of his ancestor.

"Mass graves?" Rufus asked.

"Must be from the pestilence," Wilhelm said.

"I hope you're right."

Rufus's eyes fell upon the ledger stones at his feet, though he did not read the names aloud. He came to the altar across the room. There stood the marble statue of a nine-eyed eel, coiled as a terrible serpent, flanked by candles, freshly lit, judging by the molten wax.

"What is that?" Radcliffe asked.

"I," Rufus paused, "don't know."

Whatever its origins, the statue bore a jawless maw

laced with ring upon ring of fangs, perhaps a lamprey or some daemonical variant. Rufus examined the idol with morbid interest, feeling a strange familiarity towards it. Then he remembered the serpents which emerged from each wight his company slew. Curiosity turned to dread. Coarse murmurs echoed from deep within. Step by step, Rufus led the way into the catacombs. Wilhelm remained by his side as the others lingered and looted—when the barrel of a gun pressed against the heir's spine.

"Do not take me for a fool," said the witch-hunter. "You have been bitten."

Sweat trickled down Rufus's brow. Anxiety fermented to panic, and he struggled to maintain composure. Though he scarcely knew the fate of the infected, it was true he had been the victim of a wight attack, spent over a week in recovery, and since suffered strange symptoms—which were growing worse of late. Despite this, he was still himself and would not suffer assault by a misguided zealot. Even now, the wound began to throb feverishly, as if to warn him of obvious peril. Something slithered past his boots. He glanced down as a swarm of jawless eels crept down the darkened passages, as if lured by the inhuman chanting. They were roughly a yard in length, writhing along the floor, leaving trails of slime and staring at Rufus with dead eyes. Wilhelm lowered his aim, as if conceding to the coming doom.

"Do not test me," he warned.

Side by side, they arrived at the heart of the catacombs. Rufus peered around a column of bone and beheld a congregation of serpents. An impossibly tall figure draped in a tattered hood and cloak, collared with rusted iron, raised its sagging arms in mock prayer. Muttering in a trance, it called upon every worm of the earth to slip under its cloak, in tribute to the grave. The figure slouched before a makeshift altar, surrounded by scattered piles of tomes—some open and annotated in blood, others shut and stained beyond recognition, pilfered from libraries across the

Empire. Resting upon the pulpit was an infant's skull crowned with a tall candle, lit with sickly green flame, a corpse-light, reminiscent of Rufus's vision from so many moons ago. Then it hit him—the tragedy of the miller from the baron's journals. Such was the poor soul's fate. What he'd become. Though robbed of reason and humanity, the miller sought to bring back those once dearest to him, even though he no longer understood why.

Rufus stepped back—a bone snapped under his heel.

The Necromancer raised its head, revealing a tanned face stretched and stitched to the seams of its hood. No eyes peered from beneath the gruesome mask, nor did it walk as a man, as if every movement was forced by flesh not its own. Despite its eldritch nature, the Necromancer hissed with seething anger, as if it were moments away from actualizing its undying love.

"Who," it rasped, "dares disturb us?"

For a moment, Wilhelm's eyes widened in terror. His pistol clattered to the floor.

It was the heir who stepped forward, if not entirely of his own volition.

"I am Rufus Grünewald," he said. "Rightful heir to Altstadt and its surrounds, and your kind is no longer welcome."

"The dead," it said, "will not suffer such insolence."

As the Necromancer stepped into the light, Rufus beheld its height in full and tentacles of musculature contorting under moth-eaten robes. The clamor and clatter of armed men echoed ever nearer as the heir's soldiers rallied to his defense.

The enemy was unfazed—indeed, if it knew fear at all.

"The flesh," it raised a fetid hand, "is willing."

Radcliffe raised his shield, only for his eyes to bulge out of his skull. Mouthing a scream, the man-at-arms dropped his maul with a clatter and clawed at his face, bleeding from every orifice. Before anyone could aid or so much as react, the soldier's bones ripped themselves free from their prison of flesh in a barrage of red sinew and steel.

Gore splattered Rufus's face. He stared in horror.

"And the bone," it twisted a wrist, "obeys."

With a terrified scream, Rufus lunged to deal a fatal blow. The Necromancer made no effort to dodge the impaling strike, cumbersome as it was, yet the heir's blade was caught in a tangle of necrotic tissue. Undying and unyielding, the Necromancer raised the back of its hand and swatted him across the chamber with unforeseen strength. Wilhelm salvaged his senses. The witch-hunter rushed to Rufus's side and sliced off the Necromancer's hand with a slash of his rapier. It did not bleed or cry out in pain—a swarm of tentacles lunged from the wound, striking like vipers from their nest, lashing against Wilhelm's arm in a bone-barbed scourge.

"Arise," it called.

Wiping the blood from his chin, Rufus staggered to his feet and wrenched his sword from the Necromancer's chest. It seemed ignorant to injury, raising a deathly fist to call upon the dark powers once again. Though the grave robber had flung a dagger into the enemy's throat, it remained undeterred. Familiar shadows lumbered down the hall to their master's side.

"Leopold?" Rufus managed. "Hupert?"

They were mangled mockeries of those who once served him. Leopold's stomach had been torn to a rancid cavern of ribs and entrails, though he still dragged his sword against the floor. Hupert slouched with a halberd at hand, the fatal bolt jutting from his chest. Both were host to nine-eyed eels suckled to their throats like babes to teats. It was clear Rufus then—these serpents, whatever they were, revitalized the dead as parasites, as puppeteers of the wights.

The Necromancer lingered, as if basking in their terror.

"We can't hold them," Wilhelm said, grasping his injured arm. "Not like this."

The witch-hunter led the retreat, falling back to the corridors, pursued by the dead. Rufus trailed the rear when the Necromancer outstretched a betentacled claw.

The heir tripped and fell with a crack—the host of clawing hands burst from the tiles, grabbing him by the ankles, rendering him prone. Leopold's blade came swinging down, narrowly missing the heir's neck, striking the floor. At that moment, Rufus remembered the bandolier strapped across his chest. In a fit of desperation, he lit a charge with a strike of flint and threw it at the fiend. There was a hissing flash and the acrid stench of acid against flesh. What remained of Leopold staggered as ichor ate away at dead skin and sinew, reducing the wight to a molten husk. With a violent swing of his own sword, Rufus sliced through the serpent as it attempted to detach from its host and flee.

"It's all right," Rufus shouted, "I've got one!"

Readying a second charge, the heir took aim and threw another charge at the Necromancer. Splashed with magnesium rain, it uttered a rasping shriek as its moth-eaten cowl dissolved rapidly. Twin gunshots filled the darkness, and a taste of grapeshot pierced Hupert's kneecaps, rendering the wight a helpless cadaver. Though most of the company had fled, Wilhelm returned to the heir's side. Tearing off its corroded robes, the Necromancer revealed its true, terrible form—an amalgam of corpses fused together by throbbing entrails, covered in clusters of pale serpents expelling their intestines to ensnare the host's musculature under a membrane of congealed mucus.

"You," it spoke as a crimson tentacle substituted its tongue, "incubate the same power."

"Don't listen to it," Wilhelm cried. "End this!"

Against all sense and reason, a question escaped Rufus's lips. "What are you?"

"We," it hissed, "are the Conqueror Worm."

At that moment, Rufus threw a third and final charge at the Necromancer—the serpents scattered as their host collapsed, its liquefied body spreading effortlessly like sand upon the tide. The heir sheathed his blade, and the parasites fled for cracks in the walls. One attempted to slip past Wilhelm, who stomped on its tail and ground his heel against its cartilage.

"Wait," Rufus said.

"They must be exterminated."

"Yes, but we promised Cronenberg a sample."

Wilhelm gritted his teeth in frustration. "You intend on keeping your word?"

"I have a feeling he'd prefer this over wight-flesh."

"True enough." Wilhelm sighed, "But do not forget," he stepped forward, "I know what you are. What lurks in your blood." He knelt and gripped the serpent by the throat, staring into its jawless mouth in disgust as it thrashed about. "You can carry the taint."

Rufus took a deep, shuddering breath, refraining from striking the witch-hunter across the face. "I am not my grandfather," he stuffed the serpent into a knapsack and tied the knot with sore fingers, "and, rest assured, I have done nothing wrong."

"See to it that you don't."

Such rage did not fade. If anything, it festered. Insults gave way to irrational hatred. The reputation of the Witchfinder General was not lost on Rufus. He could smell the smoke of blazing pyres and hear the screams of women condemned to suffer the flame—a fierce, agonizing heat rivaled only by the fever of his wound. Slapping his neck to silence the notion, Rufus retraced his steps to the stairwell, to the cellars and crypts, to the surface, and yet, the Necromancer's words haunted him with every step, writhing in his silent thoughts.

"The flesh is willing."
"You incubate the same power."
"We are the Conqueror Worm."

CHAPTER SEVEN

Altstadt held no fanfare for Rufus's return—little had changed in his absence. Dusk crept over the hills by the time he and Wilhelm took seats at the Hofbräuhaus. The two sat in bitter silence, keeping to stiff drinks in an attempt to numb the lingering horror they had witnessed. The heir tried to ignore his colleague's relentless stares, but the tension was insufferable.

"Relax," Rufus said. "I'm not going to eat you."

"That remains to be seen."

"Listen. It's true that I've been…bitten, but that doesn't make me one of them. I feel fine," he lied. "It's been over a month. If I were to succumb, I would've by now."

"Keep your voice low," Wilhelm hissed. "We don't know who may be listening."

"Oh, everyone knows. This is old news."

Wilhelm stared in utter shock. "And they suffer you as baron?"

"Guess I'm an improvement to my predecessor."

"A low bar indeed." The witch-hunter muttered into his drink. "Men less tolerant than I would see this land purged and put to the torch—"

"And I'm sure the deluge of blood spilled would go completely unnoticed by the Thing in the Pit," Rufus's words oozed with sarcasm. "Good thing you're not an idiot."

Wilhelm did not reply.

Rufus reached into his coin purse to pay for the next round, when he felt something writhe in his knapsack—remembering the serpent he'd captured in the catacombs.

Its gurgles were almost pitiable.

"Is your 'pet' still alive?" Wilhelm asked.

"Surprisingly." Rufus drew a couple of coins. A pall of sorrow washed over him. He remembered the soldier who would've shared in the round. "We've lost good men down there."

Wilhelm laid his tankard softly on the counter. "Radcliffe would've been a noble asset."

"We can't dwell on it, though," the heir told himself. "If we stop to lament every life lost, we'll go mad with grief. Altstadt needs capable men at the helm."

"Spoken like a witch-hunter."

Rufus couldn't help but guffaw at the truth. "Shut up, Wilhelm."

"Don't you two make the odd couple?" the innkeeper chuckled from behind the bar, polishing the same collection of steins and snifters. "Careful now, she might get jealous."

"She—?" Rufus was about to inquire, only to catch on and feel his cheeks flush with embarrassment. "Never mind that. I assure you, she's probably...busy with other clients."

"Uh-huh," the innkeeper said. "Nice necklace you've got there."

Rufus clutched the medallion out of nervous habit. "It was a gift."

"Oh, I know."

The innkeeper kept the whiskey flowing, and Rufus tried to ignore the terrors branded behind his eyes—the Necromancer and its hosts. Though the company had emerged triumphant against the wights and wiedergängers, Rufus could not shake the loss of good men. He hoped that Radcliffe would find peace among the slain, as a soldier on a front worth dying on.

Rufus raised his glass. "To Radcliffe."

Though he turned to toast Wilhelm, the witch-hunter had already gone. Once more, the heir was alone in the dark.

As the night wore on, Rufus eyed the idle recruits by red-felted tables, rolling dice over daily allowances. He smiled at their ignorance. The time would soon come when the heir would test their optimism and pit them against all the world's horrors. He wondered how many graves would be dug in the following weeks. Rufus slid the innkeeper a few pennies, about to leave for the Rathaus, when a woman in green approached. His heart began to quicken pace as he downed another shot.

"How'd it go?" Sophia asked.

Rufus laughed, darkly, resting his head in his palms.

"That well?"

"We slew the Necromancer. For what that's worth."

"Think you'd be happier—"

"No," Rufus snapped, "you weren't there. We barely made it back. We lost Radcliffe, and another went missing." He massaged his brow. "And that…thing."

Sophia stared at him in shock.

Rufus sighed, deeply. "Forgive me. I shouldn't have yelled."

She lay a soft hand on his shoulder. "You've been under a lot of stress."

"You might say that."

"Listen," she said. "There's something I want to show you."

Rufus raised his head. "Oh?"

Sophia took him by the hand and led him upstairs. At first, Rufus thought she was alluding to some sensual technique when they came to the balcony overlooking Main Street. The heir tread carefully around a gap in the wooden paneling and leaned against the railing. Below in the open green, craftsmen and carpenters erected posts for banners and colored lanterns, and garlands drooped under candlelit windows. A great wicker pyre was to be assembled before the Rathaus, and the familiar silhouette of Gottfried seemed to dictate these preparations.

"I don't understand," Rufus said. "What're they celebrating?"

"You."

"What?"

Sophia laughed. "Well, in part. Sorry, I couldn't resist. Every year, the abbey throws a festival on All Saints' Day. And, seeing your dedication to bettering our lives, the people planned to celebrate your return—well, if you returned. Folks from Westerham to Innsbruck will come. Besides, it'll be good for you to mingle with the other burgomeisters."

Rufus raised his head and beheld a splendid sight—the moon had swollen to an impossible degree, pregnant with light, drowning out the stars with radiance.

"You may not believe it," she reached for his hand, "but you have our gratitude."

Rufus should have been happy then—instead, guilt and sorrow eclipsed even the most humbling of gestures. Tears trickled down his cheeks. Overwhelmed with anxiety, the heir clutched the leaning rail, knowing he wasn't worthy of such praise.

He recoiled at Sophia's touch.

"I don't understand," he choked. "Why do you care for me? You know what evil my family has done. You've seen it firsthand. Besides, you must have other clients, and, well...."

"Is it really such a worry? That I sleep with other men? For coin?"

"Well, yes."

Sophia shook her head. "I suppose I'd be willing to part with my trade," she said. "If you'd be willing to take me as your mistress."

"I—what?"

Sophia caressed his cheek, ushering him to meet her gaze.

"And besides," she lifted the medallion from his chest, "you didn't object then."

"And I don't plan to now."

Before he could speak, Rufus's tongue slid against hers, tasting of citrus and fresh tobacco. Shuddering in her embrace, he felt delicate—fragile in her arms. Burrowing into her bosom, he basked in her warmth as the wind seemed to spiral around them. Even now, in the shadow of Schloss Fleischburg and whatever lurked in those halls, he felt something else transcended his fear—a moment of happiness.

The clock tower struck noon. Rays of sunlight pierced the billowing gray sky, shimmering against gentle rainfall as petrichor wafted from the damp cobbles of Main Street. When the bell ceased its tolling, folk resumed their happy business. Troubadours from neighboring duchies busked by the town gates, nomads drove colored wagons, eager to peddle salt, silk, and stranger things, and the Hofbräuhaus echoed with laughter and clinking tankards. Rufus bit into his bratwurst, lingering under the cover of a costermonger's tent to evade the rain. The scent of roasted meats filled his nostrils, though he still wasn't used to local cuisine, namely the mustard. Regardless, he watched as his people enjoyed themselves, as children ran through the alleys, chasing mutts, rolling hoops, and sticks.

"I've never thought I'd see this again," Gottfried came to the heir's side.

"What do you mean?" Rufus asked.

"Sunlight. Happiness. Hope."

Rufus smiled, sadly, but was grateful that the citizens of Altstadt were allowed a day's escape from the nightmare beneath their feet.

"I am glad," he said. "They deserve so much more."

"And I am grateful to have you here." Gottfried clasped the

heir's shoulder. "You had me quite worried when you fled into the Grünewald. I must ask," he paused, "why did you return?"

Rufus was about to confess regarding the Ladies of the Moon and his premonition of what would befall the hamlet should he fail in his duties, but thought better of it. Now was not the time to sour happiness with the truth. "I'm here now," he said. "That's what matters."

"Fair enough. Now then, the turnip carving contest awaits your verdict."

Rufus obeyed, if only out of obligation of office. Upon a long wooden table rested roughly a dozen swedes carved in a variety of grotesque forms and faces, candles lit within the shells, glistening bright against hollowed interiors. In an attempt to feign interest, Rufus patrolled the selection, squinting to discern what some were even supposed to be.

"Ah," he tapped a particularly rotten one with a finger, "I appreciate the effort."

"My lord," someone called, "if I may request your opinion."

"In a moment." Rufus waved with a forced smile.

Gottfried nudged him. "You're doing great."

"Thanks...."

Rufus approached the far side of the table, from where the voice had called, and was pleasantly surprised. The rutabaga had been sliced with artisanal skill and shaven with passion, but the subject matter, upon further investigation, troubled him deeply.

"Pray tell," he asked, "what is this...supposed to be?"

"Oh, a little something that appeared to me in dreams."

"I see," Rufus managed. The jack-o-lantern bore a disturbing effigy, reminiscent of the maw of a lamprey—of the nightmarish evils he had conquered not a night ago. "Quite vivid."

Rufus was about to appoint the winner with a gilded pin

when he heard the creak of wooden wheels inch ever nearer, remembering what he'd promised the good doctor.

"Baron Grünewald," Cronenberg called.

"Ah," Rufus said. "Not a moment too soon."

"Fancy seeing you in one piece." Cronenberg adjusted his spectacles with gloved hands, his wheelchair pushed by an attendant. "Did you manage to recover what I asked?"

"Yes and no, but I think you'll appreciate what I did manage to find," Rufus said. "Something far better than wight-flesh."

"Oh? Did you now? Consider me intrigued, your lordship."

"This way, if you please."

The Hofbräuhaus was flooded with drunkards and off-duty sellswords, much to the doctor's disdain. Rufus was quick to retrieve the satchel from his quarters and found his prize—missing. Screams carried from the tavern, and he rushed to confront the escaped specimen.

"It's alright," Cronenberg called from downstairs. "Everything's under control!"

When Rufus returned to the ground floor, he was pushed past the crowd gathered around the doctor and his attendant, the latter having captured the nine-eyed eel in a catch-noose.

"Ah," the heir waved, "let the good doctor do his work. Pay no heed. Back to your drinks." He approached Cronenberg with nervous caution. "Thank you."

"Thank me?" the doctor scoffed. "My boy, if this is what I think it is, then I should be thanking you!" He bid his attendant to bring the specimen to his level. "I've never seen a neunauge before. Alive. In such condition, well, short of the broken tail…."

"I'm glad you approve—"

"Well, don't just stand there," Cronenberg snapped at his attendant. "Get the cage!" With the serpent locked away like a precious canary, the doctor clutched it like a child coveting a golden egg in wonderment. "Come by the Narrenturm tomorrow," he said. "We'll have much to discuss. Now, if you'll excuse me, I have quite a bit of work to do."

Rufus sighed with relief as Cronenberg left the inn. Truth be told, the heir wasn't particularly fond of the doctor, and yet, if anyone could unlock the secrets of the estate by means of science, it was him. Rufus thought it odd how the peasantry once saw fit to hang him, but was grateful for the change of heart. He was almost willing to put the incident in the abbey aside and pave the road to happier days. Come twilight, the abbot led his procession of clergy from the cemetery to Main Street, waving censors of smoking incense and holding staves of benediction, reciting the scripture in a low chant. As the pious among the people offered alms and donations, Rufus saw it fit to approach the abbot.

"Father," he said.

The abbot smiled, uncomfortably. "Ah," he said, "Baron Grünewald. I am glad to see you in good health. How may I be of service?"

"I'd like a word. Regarding the late unpleasantries."

"I'm afraid you'll have to be more specific," the abbot said with a sigh, raising his crosier towards the cemetery. "Come. We'll talk where fewer will listen." Passing the rows of headstones, he approached a gothic mausoleum atop a rise. "I never got the chance to apologize for the revolt. Rest assured, I had nothing to do with the plot. Would I have known…."

"I appreciate that," Rufus said.

The abbot nodded, slowly. "You are a welcome change from your predecessor. Honestly, short of the family resemblance, it's difficult to believe you are Matthias's descendant."

"Trust me," Rufus said. "I struggle with the notion, too."

"I am, however, concerned by the company you keep."

"Mercenaries are perfectly under control."

"It is not them I fear, rather, the witch-hunter."

"Ah," Rufus paused, "Wilhelm's—"

"Dangerous. Men such as he reject the teachings in favor of their own zeal. Just as man devoured the fruit of knowledge, so too does Wilhelm take the Word of God for himself."

"He's not my first choice, but an asset in the delves. Besides, hasn't the Holy See twisted the Word of God for its own gain? Indulgences and inquisitions?"

"Tread carefully," the abbot kept his tone soft, "that is all."

Rufus nodded, about to take his leave, when the abbot raised a hand.

"How fares your wound?"

"Well enough."

"Then I will continue to pray for you."

Though Rufus knew the abbot meant well, something about his inflection made the heir deeply uncomfortable. As he returned to the festival, the heir pondered his next course of action. Altstadt seemed free of malaise, and yet, he knew it would not last. Today was going too well, as if evil was trying to lure him into a false sense of security.

"There you are." Gottfried emerged from the crowd. "Is all well?"

"More or less," Rufus said.

"Good, good. The burgomeisters have arrived."

Great black carriages had emerged from the Grünewald, pulled by handsome steeds, adorned with the livery of friendly estates. Aides and valets opened the doors, and out stumbled the lords. Westerham was a corpulent noble limping with a cane, a hairy hand cupped its bronze handle sculpted in the likeness of a boar, ankles swollen with gout. Innsbruck, on the other hand, was a gaunt magistrate of moist complexion, crowned with a cavalier hat and gull feathers. Rufus scoffed at their pompousness, wondering if the people viewed him in such a light.

"Ah," Westerham called, "Gottfried! What a pleasure to

see you again."

Innsbruck tipped his hat. "Indeed," he added, voice slick with phlegm. "It seems ages since you've hosted All Saints' Day here in Alstadt." He raised his long nose in Rufus's direction. "And this is the heir apparent, I presume? Welcome to the office."

"Pleasure to make your acquaintance." Rufus did not offer a hand, as Innsbruck's fingers glistened oddly in the twilight. "And you must see to the neighboring lands."

"That we do," Westerham said, sniffing the air like a truffle pig. "I see the banquet is well underway. We took the liberty of bringing our fair share." He clapped, and his servants emerged with spit-roasted pigs and a cornucopia of fixings. "My swineherds offer only their finest stalk."

"And I," Innsbruck raised a slender finger, "bring today's catch."

One of the household fishermen lifted a cloche and tore off the lid, revealing a tray of freshwater oysters, sliced lemon, and melting ice. Rufus's eyes widened—as a student, he hadn't had the luxury of such delicacies until now. Gottfried clasped his hands with a nod of thanks.

"This way, if you please," he said.

With a squirt of citrus, Rufus slid the morsel about his mouth, savoring its mineral richness. He sat at the head of the long banquet table with Gottfried by his side, flanked by strange peers. Westerham was a boisterous man with a surprisingly brash sense of humor and often alluded to his glory days on the field of battle. He was once a landsknecht able to retire with title and deed under vassalage to House Grünewald, which explained the oozing sore on his shin—one that wouldn't heal.

"You fought in the Great Peasants' War?"

"Yes," Westerham said, "your grandfather and I battled side by side against the rebellions, well, before peace let me grow soft." He raised a snifter with enthusiasm, splashing mead onto the soil. "Prost! I am glad to finally meet you. You have his eyes, you know."

Rufus forced a smile, unsure as to what to make of that. One of Innsbruck's servants took the liberty of opening a bottle of brandy and poured a round for the lords and their entourage.

"How does your estate fare?" Rufus asked.

The mood grew dour as the clouds darkened. The jolly color in Westerham's face began to fade as he forced a smile, lifting a bit of pork on a fork to his greasy lips.

"What do you mean?" he asked.

"Well," Rufus paused, choosing his words carefully, "it's no secret that Altstadt has endured its share of hardship. I'm doing my best to clean up the land, as it were, but I've heard, and know, little of the other hamlets down the Old Road." He reached for another oyster. "No harm in asking, I suppose."

Gottfried offered a toast to Innsbruck's bountiful catch, as if to distract the magistrate with flattery and good drink, knowing well the heir's agenda.

"I think I take your meaning," Westerham said, hesitantly. "Listen closely and do not tell a soul." He leaned towards Rufus. "Below the west borderlands, there is a maze of aqueducts that predate the founding of the barony. We dare not let our herds graze at night, for fear of beasts that walk as men. Swine-folk, if you will, have harassed my lands for some time."

"Swine-folk," Rufus repeated.

"Yes," Westerham looked away, "I know it must sound absurd, but—"

"After everything I've seen, pigmen seem almost preferable."

"And what, dare I ask, have you seen?"

Rufus and Westerham proved slow-burning friends, due to commiseration as lords of failing estates. Though the heir divulged in half-truths and first-hand accounts of necromancy, he was careful not to tarnish his grandfather's image, if only to save his own, petty as it was.

"Wiedergängers? Pardon if I start calling my pests, schweinemensch."

Rufus laughed harder than he should've at their mutual pretension.

"That being said," Westerham continued, "seeing as you have the gall to raise an army of your own, I am wondering if you'd be willing to part a fraction of your forces."

"May I ask why you haven't formed your own militia?" Rufus asked, though those words came out harsher than he meant. "Sorry, I don't mean to diminish your struggles."

"Let's just say," Westerham said, "I knew your grandfather well and, if your intentions are what I believe, then you'd do well to see the warrens for yourself."

That caught Rufus off guard. "And what are my intentions?"

Westerham shrugged. "You tell me."

Rufus withdrew from the conversation, eying Gottfried, who shot him a subtle thumbs-up. Disturbed by Westerham's intimate knowledge of his family, the heir helped himself to the platter of oysters, whose flavor seemed the only genuine thing in the estate.

"What about you, Innsbruck?" he asked.

"Oh," the magistrate said, "my lands are doing quite well. Catches such as these are dime a dozen. Our ice boxes will be well-stocked come winter."

"No hardships? No living dead?"

Before he could indulge Innsbruck's response, Rufus spied a pair of silhouettes on the edge of sight. A flash of green silk alerted him to the struggle in a neighboring alley.

"I thought I told you. You're not ready for so much excitement."

"I'm perfectly capable of taking care of myself," Sophia snapped.

Rufus peered down the alley and saw someone tug her arm. Rage flashing in his heart, he lurched out of his seat to rescue his newfound lover and saw a shadow against the far wall.

"Cronenberg?"

"What," the doctor snapped. "Pardon, your lordship, but this is my affair."

Rufus crossed his arms. "Is it now? Seems like you're harassing my mistress."

Cronenberg gazed from over his spectacles. "Your what?"

"It's true," Sophia came to the heir's side, "Rufus and I are…."

"Courting," he said.

"I see," Cronenberg scowled. "Well then, don't let me keep you."

With that, the doctor saw himself to the side streets. Rufus caught himself clenching his fists and breathed deeply, knowing that he'd be obligated to deal with Cronenberg tomorrow. And yet, something lurked in the back of his mind—a vague suspicion that could not be silenced.

"Sorry about that," Sophia did not look at him, "he's—"

"We'll talk about it later." Rufus offered a hand. "Care to join me?"

His mistress gave a reluctant smile. "Sure."

In twilight's wake, the feast and festival neared their end. Rufus washed down a last bite of pork loin with a shot of whiskey. Midway between nobility and the masses, he refilled Sophia's cup of cherried mead. Few words were spoken. Her etiquette was impeccable yet forced—even the heir could sense something troubled her. Though sequestered from Gottfried and the peerage, Rufus was not ignorant to their thinly veiled disapproval.

"Are you alright?" he asked.

"I'm fine."

Rufus finished his shot in silence, not daring to pry.

"It's just," she began, "I don't feel like I belong here."

"Don't be absurd, you're my mistress."

"That's not what I mean."

"Does it have to do with Cronenberg?"

Sophia did not meet his gaze. "No, but—"

"A word," Gottfried called, "your lordship?"

Rufus flinched at the sound of his voice. The heir glanced over his shoulder. The burgomeister was a tall silhouette in the shadows, leaning against a lamppost by the Rathaus.

The heir pushed in his chair, much to Sophia's discomfort. "I won't be long." Joining his confidant and aide, Rufus braced himself for the tongue-lashing. The Rathaus loomed as a crippling reminder of the grim duty of office. "Listen," he began. "I—"

"What the Devil are you doing?" the burgomeister snapped.

"I'm sorry?"

"Don't you, 'I'm sorry,' me. Do you have any idea what the implications of this are? Even your grandfather wouldn't dream of it. Do you really think this is appropriate? To bring a working girl as your consort. In front of the other nobles, nonetheless."

"Gottfried," Rufus whispered. "Keep it down."

"No. I will not be silenced after such a breach of etiquette. I've done everything I can to keep up appearances with your day drinking and whoremongering, but this is absurd."

"Oh, please. Like you're straight as an arrow. Who I court is my business."

"And it's the estate's business, which makes it my business."

"Frankly," Rufus said. "I don't care."

"What? Do you think denying the issue will make it go

away?"

Rufus felt the veins squirm under his brow. "The issue is you speaking to me as a child."

"Well, it wouldn't be a problem if you acted your role—"

"Enough," Rufus shouted, possessed by rage not entirely his own. "I am Baron Grünewald. I may not be my grandfather, but if it's one thing we have in common, it's our disdain for petty etiquette. And," he grabbed the burgomeister by the collar, seething with the livid fever of the wound, "if you're willing to overlook atrocities for my house," he hissed, "then turn a blind eye." At that moment, Rufus saw fear in Gottfried's eyes. Shuddering with shame, he released the burgomeister. "I'm sorry...."

"Perhaps," Gottfried managed, "now isn't the time."

Rufus did not reply, trying to extinguish his rage.

"Altstadt is a lonely place," the burgomeister admitted, "but did it ever occur to you what she sees in you? Did you ever ask yourself, what you see in her?"

"You're right," Rufus shook his head, "now isn't the time."

When the heir returned to the banquet, most of the peasantry had departed. Sophia was nowhere to be seen. Regret lingered in his heart. With a forlorn sigh, he resigned for the night. The Hofbräuhaus was crowded with travelers, and many had taken to the common room. Fortunately, Rufus's suite was vacant. He collapsed onto the bed, holding the medallion in his palm, massaging its bas-relief as the moon shimmered bright through the latticed window.

Gottfried's words did not leave him.

It was true, Sophia was beautiful in body and spirit, but he hardly knew her. They had only spent three nights together. Then she offered herself as his mistress. In retrospect, it was absurd. Perhaps she was after his fortune or a witch in her own right. No, it couldn't be. Rufus clawed at the bedsheets, lest he slap himself across the face in a fit of self-loathing. The true absurdity lay in the burgomeister's presumptions. Sophia had given him no reason to doubt her affections. It was the seed of rural prejudice. Nothing more.

Slowly, Rufus began to drift into dreams.

Sweating and shaking, the fever worsened as his thoughts wandered into dark corners of memory. He found himself in the labyrinthine trails of the weald, somewhere he swore to never return, wandering aimlessly in the moonlight. Spores and spiderwebs greeted the heir in a tangle of sickly flora, and untold eyes peered out of the woods. Every crossroads seemed to spirit him deeper into the wilderness—until he came upon the clearing where the Ladies of the Moon had gathered amidst the ring of sarsen standing stones, perhaps a henge of antediluvian origin.

"So returns the princeling," they mocked in unison.

"Come, come," said the eldest, "join us for this most auspicious of evenings."

Rufus did so reluctantly. "To what do I owe the pleasure?"

As he caressed one of the monoliths, the heir watched its shadow shift in the moonlight, as if the monument was a massive dial meant to align with the solstice—a calendar of antiquity.

"We celebrate your victory against a great evil," said the middle sister, raising a pair of black branches in druidic prayer. "Under the light of the Hidden Moon, all shall be revealed. So it has always been. So it shall always be. Such is what portended our first meeting."

In dreams, the moon was like a bonfire raging in blackest night. Under its gaze, the lithic idols brimmed with carven runes, though as Rufus caressed one of the depressions, he noticed its luster began to fade. It took him a moment to understand.

"The Thing in the Pit is strongest when the Moon is at its fullest," said the youngest. "And its servants dance in kind. Only then do the generals of darkness reveal themselves."

Though Rufus knew little of occultism, he recognized the faded rune from many of the piled tomes in the catacombs. "Like the Necromancer," he said.

"On those most dreadful of nights, you must vanquish whatever terror emerges."

"And if I don't? I mean, should I fail?"

"Then doom comes for us all."

The wilderness seemed to twist at the moon's mercy, fettered by its motherly presence.

Rufus endured warty hands, placing a laurel atop his head. "Charming," he said, "but I must ask. Why are you helping me? What is your stake in all this?"

The Ladies of the Moon murmured in laughter. "We have no desire to see the world fall to darkness," they said, dismissively. "We, too, are fools who live in it."

"However," added the youngest. "You have been touched by one who walks our same path. The medallion you bear carries a power. Through it, we were able to call upon your spirit."

"Wait," Rufus's heart sank, "Sophia's—?"

When his eyes jerked open, dawn had crept over the river and the easterly ridge. A raven took flight from the sill, cawing, though Rufus didn't remember leaving the window open. Wiping the sweat from his brow, he shuddered not merely at the vision but the revelation it entailed. The medallion still hung from his neck, dancing on a chain as a talisman of fate. Tucking the pendant behind his satin shirt, Rufus stood and left for the Rathaus. The joyous decorations of All Saints' Day had been torn down overnight, and Altstadt was its bitter self again. There was much work to be done.

"Sophia," he muttered to himself, "what are you?"

CHAPTER EIGHT

Though he dreaded the notion, Rufus rode out to the Narrenturm to pay Cronenberg an unhappy visit. The Old Road skirted the Grünewald's edge and cut through low peat moors, split by crossings and weather-worn signage. He slowed to a canter at the gallows and averted his eyes to rows of unmarked graves. Slowly, the Fool's Tower crept into sight, emerging from the fog. Dismounting before the gardens, Rufus took the liberty of knocking on the front door—only for Cronenberg to wheel from the neighboring bushes, a basket of botanical samples in his lap.

"Well then," the doctor said, "I wasn't sure you'd show up."

"Indeed," Rufus said. "How's the specimen?"

The doctor grinned. "Oh, I'm working wonders and I'm eager to share."

Cronenberg led the way down the entry hall to the lower ring of cells. The ceaseless wailing of the mad and misbegotten echoed within rows of padded cells. To the left curved the block proper, and to the right was a stone enclosure centered on a fortified guard tower—a panopticon of primitive science. Cronenberg was utterly unfazed by patients slamming their heads against iron-barred doors, let alone the stench of bodily fluids. Rufus paused to eye soiled graffiti inside a cell, one of sigils and scripture, able to read a single passage.

That play is the tragedy, 'Man,' and its hero, the Conqueror Worm.

"Your lordship," Cronenberg called, "this way, if you

please."

Rufus quickened his pace. "Not the cleanest folk, are they?"

"Decidedly not, but we keep up appearances as best we can."

"I'll take your word for it."

The laboratory was darker than Rufus remembered, illuminated by livid limelight and oil lamps, its high windows barred and shut. He was led to the autopsy table where the nine-eyed eel lay stretched and strewn with pins and hooks, organs throbbing yet sedated with laudanum.

"Vivisecting the thing took no small effort," Cronenberg said.

Rufus gagged at the sight. Horrible as the serpents were, the idea of slicing one open as it squirmed was more than he could stomach. To his horror, Cronenberg reached into its entrails and carefully unwound them like a ball of yarn—long and elastic, pulsating with raw viscosity.

"Forgive me," the doctor said, smirking. "I should've warned you."

"What is the purpose of this? I mean, why?"

Cronenberg plucked the intestines like the strings of a cello. "If we are to understand the neunauge, we need to learn what makes it tick." He injected the specimen with a small syringe as it began to stir. "Do you know why its organs are so springy?"

"Oh, do tell…."

"The neunauge, or nine-eyed eel," Cronenberg began, "is an exoparasite. Much like the louse or the leech. But smarter. Indeed, it can think in a fashion. It latches onto the host, applies suction from its lips, and rasps into its flesh with a tongue-like appendage. Think of it like a cheese grater. Of course, this is only part of its feeding habits. When the neunauge selects a suitable host, the parasite, well, allow me to demonstrate...." The doctor raised a steel rod, perhaps a defibrillator, and pressed the tip against its heart. The specimen shivered and expelled its entire digestive tract through its jawless maw. "We call the process, 'evisceration,'" the doctor paused, as if sensing the heir's confusion. "Ever seen a sea slug?"

"No," Rufus admitted.

"Well," Cronenberg said, "like a sea slug, the nine-eyed eel can expel its own entrails. But our little parasite takes it to another level." He raised a suckered intestine with a pair of tongs. "It mingles its own viscera with the host's, wrenching control of bodily functions like a highwayman to a carriage."

"And it can mingle with dead flesh as well. How?"

"I suspect that lies in the hunter's organ which conducts electricity through the host's blood like water. A low-power battery, if you will, able to animate the living and the dead through specific shocks to the muscular and nervous system, contracting the muscles."

"That doesn't explain how the thing can talk."

"Eh? Talk?"

"When I was in the catacombs," Rufus began to recount the delve, "the host, or hosts, it's difficult to tell, spoke for the parasites. As if they shared thoughts, as part of a whole."

"A colony organism," Cronenberg muttered. "Intriguing. What did it say?"

"It called itself the Conqueror Worm."

Cronenberg shifted in his wheelchair. "I see."

"Does that mean anything to you?"

"No."

Rufus knew the doctor was lying, about to inquire further—when a number of iron bells rang throughout the asylum, throbbing in his ears. The alarm had been sounded. Cronenberg tore a knife switch, and the portcullises throughout the facility came cleaving down like guillotines, preventing escape by any and every means. The rallying footsteps of orderlies and paid guards filled the upper floors, followed by the sounds of violent struggle.

Cronenberg sighed. "Give them a moment. Apparently, we have a break."

"Sounds more like a riot."

"It will be quelled soon enough."

Shouts and blood-curdling screams filled the upper floor. Judging by the sound of snapping limbs, the guards were armed with wooden cudgels and little else. Eventually, the escapee was subdued, and the nagging bells began to cease. A moment's silence passed. The heir stood, about to take his leave, when Cronenberg raised a gloved hand, as if to address something which troubled them both.

"I understand you're acquainted with Sophia," said the doctor.

"More than acquainted, I hope. How do you know her?"

"Oh, she's one of my former assistants. And a higher functioning patient."

That caught Rufus off guard. "What do you mean?"

"Does the term, nymphomania, mean anything to you?" The lamps cast Cronenberg in an unflattering light. "Oh, don't get me started. Sophia has quite the track record, if you take my meaning. Charming woman, but driven by insatiable desire. She served as my assistant, but I've been studying her for some time."

"What has she done to warrant treatment?"

"Chronic masturbation and excessive fantasies—"

"Hardly a crime."

"I'm a doctor, not a judge."

The thought of Sophia in a straitjacket, locked amidst the lunatics, was sickening. Rufus felt himself tower over the doctor, casting a long shadow. How many of these folk were genuinely ill? How many were simply undesirables and poor things discarded by decency? Cronenberg was unintimidated by the heir's impudence—if anything, he was angered by it.

"You may as well be an executioner," Rufus said.

Cronenberg sighed and wheeled back to the autopsy table. "With all due respect, your lordship, you haven't the faintest idea of what you're talking about. I've devoted my entire life to such pathology, and you're an eligible bachelor infatuated with the town whore." He glanced at the heir from over his shoulder. "Perhaps you should seek some treatment yourself."

"We're done here."

"Oh," Cronenberg called, "I suppose then you don't wish to know the rest of my findings? How, say, you are succumbing to infection?"

Rufus halted in his tracks before he could take a step, but did not reply.

"You may want to cover up that little hickey of yours," Cronenberg tapped at his neck, "or at least manage your symptoms. Moody as you are, I can help. Laudanum and cocaine may be in order." He paused. "The bouts of anger are getting worse, aren't they?"

"There's more, isn't there?"

"I'm afraid so," Cronenberg said.

Rufus allowed the doctor to prick his finger and examine a sample of blood under the brass microscope. "As I suspected," he muttered. "Take a look, if you wish."

Rufus did so with grave reluctance. He peered into the piece only to spy little white worms, smaller than the smallest maggot, writhing in crimson fluid. The heir gagged and felt a case of the vapors wash over him, shuddering at the evil lurking beneath his very skin.

"The larval stage of neunauge," Cronenberg explained, "bloodworms."

"What does this—?"

"You will be sensitive to the phases of the moon. As it waxes, the disease progresses. As it wanes, your suffering will abate. Make no mistake, you will succumb to your lower instincts sooner rather than later. With every cycle, the severity will increase. Until...."

"Until what?"

"You lose yourself entirely."

Rufus laughed in morbid defeat. The irony did not escape him. Evil in the blood haunted him since his arrival in the Grünewald, only to be made manifest. It seemed he was doomed by his line's atrocities, condemned to pay for the sins of the father. The heir's face flushed with scarlet rage at the sheer injustice. From the moment he set foot on the Old Road, he had done nothing except attempt to do the right thing. And this was his reward. Before he knew it, Rufus rode back to Altstadt. No one was there to greet him, save the bottle at the Hofbräu.

The following days seemed to blur together, and the moon began to wane.

Rufus began a strict regimen to prevent further infection, though he put little stock in folk remedies. Mincemeat's penchant for licking his wound seemed to curb the fever better than myrrh and bile salts. It would scab but hardly scar. Enduring a collar of linen bandages, he preferred to administer treatment himself and kept an eye on his varicose veins. Languishing on the upper floor of the inn, Rufus was careful to not exert himself lest he take a turn for the worse.

There was a delicate knock on the door.

"Dammit, Gottfried," he muttered. "It's too late for this." He jerked open the door, only to be greeted by his mistress. "I," he choked, "uh, hello."

Sophia stepped into the room with a woven basket in hand.

"How's the wound?" she asked, briskly. "You should be resting."

"I rarely sleep well these days."

Sophia rummaged through a basket full of tinctures and tonics, some of questionable content, and drew a poultice wrapped in a wet rag. "Gottfried said you were doing a little worse."

"I'm fine," he lied.

"Uh-huh," Sophia sat him down on the bed, "hold still." She examined the wound with firm care and probed about the weeping tissue. "It's a little inflamed." Her words did not reach Rufus's ears, who sat on the bed, picking at his cuticles. "Are you sure you're alright?"

Rufus did not reply for a long while.

"You know. I didn't expect you to be so versed in medicine."

"Midwives and cunning women aren't unheard of in these parts."

"Even with the witch-hunts?"

"Well," she said, "if they haven't hung me for my other profession...."

"Fair enough," Rufus said. "Where did you find these remedies?"

"Oh," Sophia said, "I made most of them myself, but I'm no stranger to the Narrenturm. Cronenberg was willing to part with a few ingredients."

"I see," Rufus did not dare to pry, "I appreciate the concern, but—"

"Stop talking," Sophia pressed the rag against his neck, "you'll just agitate it."

Rufus felt the wound weep, and soreness began to abate.

He smiled sheepishly as his physician tended to his injury for a quiet hour. He wanted to tell Sophia everything—his frustrations and fears. It wasn't a matter of distrust; rather, a desire to not trouble her further. She'd already done so much. She'd proven her care.

And yet, somehow, Rufus felt more alone than ever before.

"I'm surprised you didn't apply the leeches," he managed.

"Left those at home." Sophia wrapped Rufus's neck with firm care and caressed his ear with a lover's touch. "There. That should help a bit. Let me know if it gets any worse."

"Thank you," Rufus said.

"Now try to get some rest."

Before he could reach or speak out, Sophia had already left downstairs. Once more, Rufus was alone in silence, save for the creaking murmurs of the rafters. He took a nightcap out of boredom. The world began to darken as his thoughts drifted to his agenda for the estate. Regardless of his own weakness, Altstadt would not defend herself. Rousing himself from bed, Rufus returned to the bar to brood and plan once more. Gottfried was already nursing a brandy and joined him in bitter silence, not bothering to pry. Instead, he silently slid an opened letter addressed to the heir. Rufus recognized the seal from the festivities of All Saints' Day, the boar's head of Westerham. Its cursive read, simply,

Hurry to Westerham, a day's ride west of Schloss Fleischburg. I implore you to prepare accordingly and bring ample men. The Swine are rising. They bear the worms.

Rufus folded the letter neatly, recalling the cryptic words of the Weird Sisters. That he must confront "whatever terror emerged" whenever the moon was full. Only then would the way be opened. As to what exactly that entailed, Rufus did not know, but hoped it would lead to the truth he so craved—or, at the very least, quell the evil in his blood. Regardless, he gazed out the window upon dawn's first light. Time was short. He'd rested for too long.

CHAPTER NINE

The Hofbräu housed no surplus of fresh recruits. Few had arrived by coach in recent weeks, let alone signed the roster or pledged themselves to House Grünewald's cause. The ongoing agenda was a mercy mission to Westerham as organized by Gottfried in response to the urgent plea for aid. Wilhelm accompanied the heir as he checked the trading post for provisions and supplies. Prices had tripled even from the imperial standard due to wanton banditry on the Old Road, and Rufus weighed the cost of a spare shovel against a few more torches.

He didn't know what to expect west of the Narrenturm.

"Schweinemensch," Wilhelm repeated. "Of this I know little."

"I suspect Westerham's reports aren't exaggerations."

"Odd to be sure." The witch-hunter examined a tinderbox. "Of the neighboring estates, it is the closest to Altstadt. And its industry and exports of pork are one of the only things keeping the barony from bankruptcy. It's fitting that you defend such a lucrative region."

"You'd think Gottfried would've told me."

"I suspect your aide keeps many things from you."

That caught Rufus off guard, but he thought it best to hold his tongue. With packs laden with supplies and steeds mounted, they embarked to the west—unburdened by new recruits. Come midday, they stopped to rest in the shadow of the Fool's Tower. Rufus struggled to open his tinned delicacies. Wind brought with it the faint odor of blood and offal, suffocating his appetite. Within the hour, they had resumed the trek, regardless of the nearing stench. The low moors bled slowly into green hill country that would've been tranquil, if not for the empty acres of farmland. Entire homesteads were abandoned, left to mold and rot, pens robbed of livestock, and yet, cloven hoofprints led to and from many a tin-roofed barn—side by side, as if delivered by beasts on hind legs. Wilhelm knelt to investigate a set of tracks and muttered bitterly.

"Is something the matter?" Rufus called.

"Yes," the witch-hunter said. He touched the earth with a gloved hand, and a swarm of little white worms burrowed up from the soil. "Whatever made these tracks was infected."

Rufus shuddered. "Then we'd best get a move on."

Great plumes of smoke rose to blot out the setting sun in a miasma of smog, and the company reached the Scarlet Mill by the river. Rufus paused to examine the oddly metallic structure with its soot-stained chimney and red shingles, watching the waterwheel rotate with the flow of filth and sewage. It was unlike anything he'd seen, even in the city of Chimay.

Then Rufus beheld his destination.

The high stone walls of Westerham greeted them with a grim facade. Roofs and gables of townhouses peered over ringlets of barbed wire designed to keep something in—or out. A culvert allowed the slough of a river to pass onto the mill, while a pair of fortified gates stood stalwart in the muddy roadway. A monstrous stench pervaded every home and hovel in the Back of the Yards. Rufus raised a handkerchief to his nose, gagging at the odor. He turned to Wilhelm, expecting him to share in his shock, but the witch-hunter remained unfazed.

"What is this place?" he asked.

"A glimpse into the modern age."

The gates opened slowly for the strangers. Twilight bled upon shacks and shanties lining the road, where tenants choked out their lives with sixteen-hour shifts and fifths of gin. Peppered moths fluttered about the streetlamps. Webs of clotheslines hung from window to window, aprons flapping like soiled banners of war. Silence pervaded the slums, breached only by the steady hum of machinery. There, in the heart of the town square, loomed the Abattoir. Its triple smokestacks towered as the turrets of a prison, walls laced with barbed wire and lude graffiti, flanked by warehouses and stockyards—where workers paid their debts in blood. Rufus tried to avert his eyes, unable to meet the gazes of the impoverished, but the destitution was inescapable. Dressed in heavy boots and leather aprons, most were en route to a given shift or the shanties and shacks they called home, though homeless amputees sat by the road, hands as lumps of scar tissue, eyes milky white and robbed of the will to live.

As they took to a side street, on the way to the coaching inn, Rufus beheld a weatherworn man seated by the filth, bearing a sign salvaged from the lid of a crate.

SON'S A CHIMNEY SWEEP
NEED SCRIP FOR HIS BREAD

Wilhelm halted for a moment, eyed him sharply, and dismounted, boots splashing down in a black pool of water. He knelt to the beggar's side, seemingly to digest his surroundings. Though bitter and forlorn, the witch-hunter reached into his coin purse and offered a handful of silver shillings—no small fraction of reward for the delve into the Necromancer's lair. The beggar's eyes widened in shock and teared with wordless thanks. Wilhelm dropped the donation into his bowl yet said nothing, leading his horse on foot. A crowd had gathered.

Rufus followed in a canter, not wanting to dirty his shoes further.

"Didn't take you for the charitable sort," he muttered.

"You know little of me," Wilhelm said, "let alone what I stand for."

If Rufus didn't know better, he would've taken the witch-hunter for having sympathy for these folk—then again, perhaps he did. Wilhelm was silent and willful in his course, not bothering to hide his discomfort. Curious eyes were fixed upon them.

Whether they saw salvation or cuts of long pork, Rufus did not know.

Together, they crept through the smog and came to the Stuck Pig, a lopsided taphouse on the west end of town. A swaying sign depicted its namesake in uncanny detail. Dim and sagging under the weight of misery. The interior was vacant even the staff, it seemed, shared a shift at the Abattoir. Rufus felt the floorboards stick to his boots as he approached the lonely bar, when he noticed a tin bell by a bowl of fried pork rinds. The sole patron was a local vagrant surrounded by empty bottles. Rufus tapped the bell, delicately—no response.

"Hello?" he called. "Is anyone there?"

Bootsteps clomped down the stairs. A middle-aged woman with coarse black hair emerged from the upper floor. She eyed the heavily armed strangers up and down with a blend of annoyance and shock, only to shrug and come behind the bar. Silently, she poured a round of gin, much to the heir's disgust—even he had a hard time stomaching the stuff.

Wilhelm raised the glass to his lips and sniffed its contents with grave reluctance.

Rufus's eyes darted about the walls. Fliers were stuck to the corkboard by the empty hearth, most of them pamphlets and calls to action—particularly in relation to the Butcher's Guild. This confused him greatly. Westerham had spoken of a lack of security, and yet, the town seemed to have no shortage of serrated blades and able bodies.

"Cheery place," Rufus said. "I take it you don't get many travelers."

"That we don't," the barmaid replied in a hollow tone.

"Be that as it may," the heir continued, "your hospitality is most appreciated."

The town drunk stirred and met him with weary eyes. "The only things that leave Westerham are squealers and queers. Keep the chit-chat to a minimum. Don't know who might be listening." He slapped a hit of tin scrip on the countertop. "Agnes. Another."

As the barmaid refilled their glasses, Rufus noticed that she was missing several of her fingers, as if sliced off by machinery—or perhaps as punishment for some transgression.

"Ah," Rufus managed. "Charming." He turned to Wilhelm, who stifled his drink with a bitter gag. "We'd best get a move on. Especially if we're to meet with Lord Westerham?"

The bartender nearly dropped the bottle. "What do you say?"

"Uh," Rufus said, "we're—"

"Get out."

"Half a moment. There must be a misunderstanding."

The bartender reached for the hunter's musket propped atop the shelf. Rufus recoiled and raised his hands in an attempt to de-escalate the situation.

"It's all right," Rufus said. "We'll leave."

Wilhelm nodded in rare agreement, sliding a silver coin across the bar, and bade Rufus to follow him outside. Together, they took in a lungful of stale air.

"Well," he said. "I've had warmer welcomes."

Shouts and commotion echoed from the town square, where crowds of workmen had gathered—torches blazing bright against the silhouettes of signs and saw-toothed polearms. Half of the town seemed on strike, surrounding the Abattoir in a grizzled mob. Standing atop a stack of crates, a hulking man waved a banner to rally the proletariat, amidst the babble of demands and half-baked slogans. Trite though it was, Rufus felt a twinge of admiration for the workers—the gall to demand a better future from their betters. He kept his distance, content to watch the strike unfold from the courtyard's edge—a warning shot pierced the ranks. Fear spread like wildfire among the mob. The wrought-iron gates of the Abattoir creaked open, and a steam-powered tank rolled onto the roadway, armored with sheets of gunmetal, equipped with heavy mortars and primitive riflery, pipes billowing with exhaust. The Grand Panzer had come to put the masses in order. Before Rufus could process the ironclad behemoth, the Abattoir erupted with a shrill alarm, silencing the chants.

Rufus knelt and covered his ears.

The crowd showed no sign of calming—indeed, the flames of unrest had grown hotter. Before Rufus could process the implication of the machine, squads of men-at-arms clad in sallets and scarlet gambesons emerged with baton and blunderbuss at the ready.

"Move," they demanded, holding the masses at gunpoint.

Rufus was torn between horror and gratitude as Westerham's constabulary began to corral the townsfolk as chattel in their own right—a riot was about to erupt. The outsiders were ushered to safety as the local guard began their retreat, covered by the Grand Panzer, immune to the incendiary cocktails and cinder blocks hurled at its hull. Slowly, the magnitude of Westerham's tyranny dawned on Rufus. The burgomeister was a business magnate, as well as the lord of the manor—a lynchpin of order in the wake of open revolt. When the factory gates were shut, segregating Rufus from the masses, the heir found himself in the stockyard.

"Truly a marvel," he wondered aloud.

What amazed Rufus most of all was how compact Westerham seemed, little more than two square miles of densely packed slums, and yet, it housed over triple the population of Altstadt. It was truly a window to tomorrow. Then, from out of the smog, Lord Westerham emerged with a cane at hand, flanked by iron-masked officers, limping to greet his guests.

"Rufus," he exclaimed. "Pleasure to see you!"

Despite his discomfort, Rufus accepted the burgomeister's embrace, feeling the grease on his palms slide off his waistcoat. He patted Westerham lightly on the back.

"Welcome, welcome," the burgomeister said. "Thrice welcome to my humble abode."

"It's certainly," Rufus paused, "industrious."

"That it is. Your grandfather helped me get it off the ground, as it were. Full of brilliant ideas, he was. I must admit, though, I was expecting more men at your disposal."

"Wilhelm is my champion in matters of the occult," Rufus said. "He will prove most valuable in getting to the bottom of what ails your estate."

"Most capital. Well then, my manor awaits."

Rufus shot his companion an uncertain glance. The neighboring alleys were strewn with urban detritus and remnants of wooden crates, yet were somehow better kept than the slums proper. Within minutes, the company arrived at the Westerham House—the only building of splendor in the entire town, and the cleanest plot of land within miles. Sequestered from the slums by walls and delicate gardens, the manor was annexed by the factory grounds—a chateau in all but name, a baroque interpretation of the medieval ruins that peppered the moor, willfully ignorant to the weeping masses. Rufus walked past the neatly trimmed hedges and porcine sculptures along the aisle, coming to the doorstep and portico proper.

"Impressive," Rufus admitted.

"It was once a summer home of House Grünewald. Offered to me by your grandfather as a reward for military service." He turned to face his guests. "I have prepared quite the supper. This way, if you please. And don't stray into the west wing. It is undergoing renovation."

Past the gilded doors, the dining hall was opulent to say the least, with luscious pink and red cushions and a table overflowing with a banquet of fleshy delicacies—prime rib, mashed potatoes bathed in garlic, and all manner of sweet rolls and pastries filled with pork. Rufus should have been grateful for the hospitality—in truth, he found it nauseating.

Picking at his meal with a silver fork, the heir wondered what Westerham's motives truly were. If there was a point to the flaunting of wealth and prestige.

"Tell me," Rufus began, "what do you need of us?"

Westerham waved a hand. "Oh, there will be plenty of time to discuss such things. First, you must eat." He raised a buttery morsel to his lips. "Please, make yourself comfortable."

Rufus tried to do just that, but the trophies of wild boar heads made him more than a tad uneasy. Long silence passed as the heir indulged in red wine and a hand pie. As the crust dissolved like ash in his mouth, he wondered what the workers were eating, if anything at all.

"The sooner we've finished," Wilhelm muttered, "the sooner we move on."

Rufus nodded in agreement.

By the hour's end, Westerham had wiped his greasy hands clean with a cloth and announced, "Well then, I suppose you're wondering why I've summoned you."

Rufus shifted in his seat, intently.

"Regardless, the nature of my hardship is not limited to revolts. I assure you, my talk of 'schweinemensch' has a literal meaning." He stood to tap his cane hard against the floorboards. The rattling and rumbling of engines erupted beneath the dining hall. Rufus grasped the arms of his chair as the chandelier began to quiver with the fragile rafters. "I didn't build this wonder on sweat-soaked backs alone, mind you."

"What do you mean?" Wilhelm asked.

"I mean," Westerham said, "your grandfather played no small part in developing this wonder. He was its financier when no one else would understand my vision. However, the bowels of my industrial beauty, like any beast, are not immune to parasitic infection." He bid the company to follow him to the annex. "This way, if you please. I will tell you all."

Wilhelm was bid to wait in a drawing room while Rufus was to follow Westerham into the private study—lined with rows upon rows of bookshelves filled with leather-bound ledgers and tomes, an archive of documents tracing to recent years with schematics and patents of industrial marvels, none of which were Westerham's own. Rufus lingered by the windowsill, watching the gas lamps flicker to life, one by one, as curfew was announced by town criers.

"You certainly put no small stock in security," Rufus said.

"One has to sleep somehow," Westerham said. "Times are hard, as you're well aware, and I need to keep the barony afloat. If only in honor of your grandfather—my friend."

"With all due respect," Rufus said, "I believe you owe me a bit of an explanation."

Westerham nodded, reluctantly. "So I do."

"You seem hesitant to speak of it."

There was a long pause. Despite Westerham's efforts to sequester himself from the surrounding filth, a sluggish draft ushered the stench of smoke and burnt tripe into the manor. "You must have concerns," the burgomeister said. "Not all of them founded, but concerns nonetheless." He caressed his scabbing scalp. "The years have not been kind to us, I'm afraid."

"Most certainly," Rufus uttered.

Westerham shot the heir a grim aside.

"It is truly a marvel." Rufus attempted to recover from the faux pas. "What you have built." He eyed the copper pipes and pneumatic tubes tangled amidst the wooden rafters. "All to revolutionize how we process meat. But, well, what does the Abattoir do, exactly?"

The engines beneath the floorboards seemed to tremble at his inquiry.

Westerham pulled a nondescript tome at an angle from the shelf and revealed a hidden passage into a darkened corridor. "There is much to show you," he said. "If you are to help me salvage the Abattoir, you must first understand the nature of the beast, as it were."

Following his host down the staircase in a sheer descent, Rufus listened to the drones of machinery as vapor hissed through pipeage, linking the manor to the Abattoir. The air grew hot, and the way was lit by sizzling lamps. Round windows stared out into the factory. Far above the toiling workers, Rufus gazed upon the disassembly line where pork luggers and butchers sliced into carcasses of questionable origin, steam pulleys hoisted product by the leg, and drums of brine served to pickle cuts of flesh. Pacesetters swiped sweat from their brows, and overseers shouted orders muffled by panes of glass. The floor was bathed in blood and puddles of half-dried scum. Even from the lofty corridor, Rufus gagged at the stench of bad meat and body odor. With little ventilation, flies swarmed about heaps of tripe and lard, while rats and other vermin scuttled in the shadows.

"All this for the processing of pork?" asked the heir.

"Profit is ten times that of traditional farming."

"Forgive me," Rufus said, "that it seems a bit…excessive."

"The future will be excessive," Westerham sighed. "Feudalism, farms and fields, these will be replaced by machinery that can meet the demand of urban appetites. Pastoral hardships will be supplanted by industry, and man will reach new heights in the age of steam."

"To what end?"

"I would see the hardships of peasantry as a passing thing. Do not think me ignorant of their suffering. However, the wheels of industry cannot turn without workflow."

Rufus saw the morbid vacancy in the workers' eyes—men, women, and children shackled to their stations with no hope of a better life under serfdom. He didn't believe a word of Westerham's rhetoric. If the burgomeister truly cared for his subjects' welfare, then he'd at least foster a poorhouse for those he so callously discarded. In his naivety, Rufus thought not even profit could justify that, at least, not to any moral mind. There had to be something else.

"It seems a bleak existence. To work in this house—"

The machinery began to sputter and whine, filling the pigline with smoke. Pot-bellied furnaces flared with impossible flame and blowback in the chimneys, casting smoldering coals about the flammable floor. Rufus ducked as a cast-iron gear ricocheted against the wall and collided with the window. The screams of the injured blared in Rufus's ears as he narrowly dodged a barrage of broken glass. His eyes and lungs began to sting. He caught glimpses of melting flesh and faceless silhouettes trampling each other in a blind effort to escape the factory.

Westerham took the heir by the arm, bolting to the hall's end, and isolated the segmented corridor with the slam of an iron door.

"Damn," the burgomeister sighed, "that'll put a damper on output."

Moments blurred together, and the smoke began to clear. Dead workers lay strewn about the carcasses in puddles of blended blood, maimed and mangled, nigh indistinguishable save for scraps of cloth and leather. Rufus stifled a gag in a fit of numbness, unsure as to whether he felt pity or revulsion, if this was a mere accident or something more insidious.

"Saboteurs," Westerham said, "from below."

"Disgruntled employees?"

"Nothing of the sort. Those I can manage."

Something skittered in the ductworks above, cloven hooves against hollow bronze. Rufus reached for his letter opener but knew it would do little against the perpetrator, regardless of its bestial nature. The rumbling faded into the far ducts and into the depths.

"The Swine," the burgomeister muttered.

"What are they?"

Westerham neither replied nor seemed to pay his subjects any heed. Swift as the clearing of corrosive gas, maintenance workers had arrived to repair the damaged machines and haul off the dead. The gears were unyielding. The Abattoir would be operational soon enough.

Such was the burgomeister's design.

"You wrote in your letter," Rufus mustered the will to speak, "that they 'bear the worms.'" Every second served to deepen his distrust of Westerham, slippery as he was. "If you're going to ask me to risk the lives of my men, I need to know more than you're letting on."

"I," Westerham said, "am in no position to confess at the moment. However, I will say this much: if you truly wish to rid this land of evil, you must cleanse the Swine as well."

Rufus postured, sharply. "Frankly, your lordship, I do not trust you and have ample reason to retract my offer of aid. Business ethics aside, your definition of cooperation is loose."

Westerham puffed his chest. "I beg your pardon?"

"I'll grant you my pardon if you don't start talking."

Silence stung the air. Westerham's face bloomed with rage yet was fettered by embarrassment. "We'll talk about this tomorrow. Only a fool would take to the streets at this hour. Give it some thought," he paused, "won't you?"

Rufus eyed him with bitter distrust. "I don't plan on

sleeping tonight."

True to his word, the heir locked himself in the guest room and barred the windows. He would not risk another knife in the dark, be it wight or swine. Laying on the bed, staring at the quivering ceiling, he waited for a degree of quiet to befall the town. He remembered Westerham's request to avoid certain rooms of the mansion. Such a comment inspired his own investigation. Rufus reached for his blackthorn shillelagh and crept about the mezzanine encircling the foyer. To his surprise, the door to the west wing was unlocked.

Rufus ventured into a lightless corridor caked in dust and grime, left unattended by servants or staff for months on end. Floorboards creaked with every step. He raised a hooded lantern to illuminate the hall, flanked by faded wallpaper and stretches of wainscoting. Most of the doors had swollen shut, and few led to rooms of note. With shillelagh at hand, Rufus tread lightly, hearing nothing save his own shallow breaths. Weirder still were the brass placards naming the rooms and their purposes.

One in particular stood out.

Astronomical Observatory

Rufus entered with care. Motes of dust trickled from holes in the ceiling, as if the roof had been struck by lightning repeatedly. A telescope stood by the window, pointed at the starless sky, though slivers of moonlight pierced the blackest smog, shining upon a desk covered in charts of parchment and open tomes. Rufus examined the charts closely, uncertain as to what the cycles meant, for the lettering was archaic at best. Only the annotations in the common tongue shed light on its purpose, alluding to celestial phenomenon and outer spheres.

A loathsome squeal carried from the streets. Rufus shuddered, not daring to guess what manner of beast made the sound. A certain wrongness pervaded the room, as if tainted by the same evil that lurked in the foundations of Schloss Fleischburg.

Next to the charts stood a phonograph.

Out of curiosity, Rufus turned the handle, slowly, and listened to the recording.

"You don't mind if I record this, do you?" said a slightly younger Westerham, his voice distorted by the static of wax and steel. "I find it most useful."

"Not at all." Rufus almost dropped his cane upon hearing the second voice, recognizing it all too well as Matthias Grünewald—the late baron. "I trust this will remain confidential."

"Of course, my dear friend."

Rufus was shocked to hear his grandfather after these long years. Wading against the tide of memory, he sat before the desk, listening as a voyeur of voices past. Something crept past the window, but the heir did not notice. Among the technical babble of taxes and the flaws of welfare, Rufus waited for the conversation to turn darker—and so it did.

"To answer your question," Matthias said, "it is quite possible to fuse man and pig, seeing as their flesh is most similar. The problem arises in what you'd use as an adhesive."

"Indeed," Westerham replied, "I figure those marvelous eels of yours—"

"The neunauge are not playthings." The baron paused, as if to emphasize the seriousness of the matter. "You must treat them with due respect. They have minds of their own. However, the notion of creating a host from multiple sources is most intriguing, I must admit. It never occurred to me to stitch them to create a workforce. With the eel as the source of locomotion."

"Though it would take surgical precision to produce such a host."

"Doctor Cronenberg is a miracle worker in that regard. I'm sure he'd donate a few patients for a modest fee. Perhaps he'd construct a prototype for you."

"Capital, most capital. I've ample stock at my disposal. If you take my meaning."

They shared in posh laughter.

"Be that as it may," Matthias said. "Once you have designated the host, you simply apply the exoparasite to the epidermis and force an evisceration. Expelled tissue will then mingle with dead flesh, reanimating it within moments. The process is extraordinary, really."

"Yes, but how does one tame an eel?"

"You will see soon enough. But tell me, why create these swine-things when men will suffice? Forgive me, but it seems counterintuitive."

"Oh, my dear Matthias, does an artist need to justify his inspiration? Or is it better to run with the fantasies that come to us in dreams? It is a vision of the future."

"Your whimsy is most endearing. More tea?"

"If you please."

There was a brief pause until Matthias began to speak again.

"I am grateful for your assistance in my research. However, there is also the notion of these creatures, these children, if you will, as beings in their own right. Amalgams of flesh and sinew, true, but still beings of cognition, though…primitive."

"What do you mean?"

"As I said, the eels are not mindless beasts. They carry a will of their own. And, in time, they will adapt to their new forms, their new lives—"

"Oh, if pigs could rise like the masses, they'd govern farms by now."

"Be careful what you say, my friend. You may just find yourself the prophet."

The recording ground to a halt. Rufus did not rise from

his seat, stupefied by the extent of the late baron's schemes. How far did his influence reach? How many had been roped into his monstrous plots? To what end did he commit to these practices? All this and more harrowed the heir's heart. Hearing his grandfather's voice, once a fleeting memory, sent chills down his spine—to know that a voice so soft and gentle could inspire such evil.

That he shared in a legacy of darkness.

CHAPTER TEN

Despite its gilded delights, the Westerham House was a shade of nobility, a shawl cast over a rotting carcass of a manor. Somewhere in those upper halls, Rufus crept along its dust-choked corridors with a lantern at hand, dabbing his brow with a handkerchief. He had stolen a number of texts and charts from the observatory, eager to share his findings—when the floor erupted with mechanical rattling, shaking the mansion to its foundations, stronger than before. He stumbled back and tore at a sconce blindly, pulling it down with weight alone.

A metallic clunk echoed from under the wainscoting.

Slowly, the wall slid aside, revealing a hidden route into corridors between corridors. Rufus peered into the unknown hall, braced with dry wood and stained with oil and pitch. Only his lantern lit the narrow passage. With a deep shuddering breath, he crept down the way and wandered its many junctions. Amidst the storage rooms filled with wooden crates and iron cages, he peered past one-way windows into bathrooms and bedrooms, some of which had seen recent use. A steely click punctuated the silence. Hollow footsteps drew near. Rufus doused his lamp and retreated past the corner, peering at the shadow cast upon the far wall. He did not recognize the figure on first glance, but a bitter sigh revealed its identity.

"Wilhelm?" the heir whispered.

The witch-hunter stepped forward and lowered his pistol's aim. "Forgive me," he sighed with relief. "I thought you were...one of them."

"One of what?"

"Our quarry," Wilhelm said. "The Swine."

"Ah, yes," Rufus looked away, "I'm afraid matters are a tad more complicated than we first thought." He divulged his findings in a voice barely above a whisper. "Our host is not what he seems. He has collaborated with my grandfather and shares in his sorcery."

"You are sure of this?"

"Regrettably so."

"I see." Wilhelm looked away. "A workforce of stitched flesh, animated by the worms. It certainly explains the tracks we uncovered on the Old Road. What do you propose we do?"

"I don't know," Rufus admitted.

"Clearly, we cannot stay here. At the very least, we must return with a greater force."

"Are the streets any safer?"

"Not likely, but I might have an idea."

Navigating the manor was no simple task, but Wilhelm retraced his steps with astute care, leading the heir to the foyer and factory grounds. The streets of Westerham were bathed in darkness, with a meager number of streetlamps lining the roads. His course seemed clear until Rufus realized the Abattoir was enclosed with fortified masonry, its gates chained shut.

"Now what?" he hissed.

"Half a moment," Wilhelm said.

Wandering the stockyards, Wilhelm remained undeterred and examined the perimeter, fingers never far from his twin pistols. The Abattoir still rumbled with bone-shredding force, the lights of its furnaces flickering behind grimy windows. For a moment, the clouds of smog above parted, revealing the waxing moon and all it portended.

"We're running out of time," Rufus muttered.

Past the stench of the sties, he caught a whiff of pipeweed wafting from a warehouse. Languishing by a wheelbarrow of filth and gong, a number of youths passed a smoke back and forth, no doubt violating a dozen policies. Other shapes stirred in the shadows—fists clenched, clutching knives and lengths of chain. A gang of sickly and swarthy workmen emerged, staring at the strangers with bloodshot eyes. Rufus felt as if he'd wandered into a prison yard. He was about to step forward when Wilhelm pressed a hand against his chest.

"If I may," said the witch-hunter.

Rufus bristled yet conceded. "Be my guest."

"Gentlemen." Wilhelm laid a hand over his holstered pistol and spoke words Rufus never thought he'd hear from a witch-hunter. "What's happened here is an atrocity," his tone was calm yet commanding. "How can we help? Tell us. What evil has befallen your parish?"

As the workers exchanged uncertain glances, a butcher of a man pushed past them, sporting a heavy leather apron, wielding a saw-cleaver the size of Rufus's torso. He stared at the strangers with sagging eyes and spat a wad of bloody mucus into the mud.

"The question remains, what brings Baron Grünewald?" His voice was hoarse from an ailing cough. "We haven't seen noble stock in these parts since the war. Speak quickly."

Rufus was overcome with sheer numbness and, in his senseless stupor, spoke blindly. "With all due respect, I'd like assurance that you won't slaughter us beforehand." He stepped to Wilhelm's side—when the butcher pulled the makeshift trigger and snapped the cleaver wide, pressing its extended blade against the heir's throat. "Ah," he managed.

The witch-hunter cupped Rufus's shoulder. "I am Wilhelm Hexenjäger, Witchfinder General, at your service. This is, indeed, Baron Grünewald, but not the tyrant you knew. He is the successor of the estate. And a better man than most among the peerage." He eyed the butcher, sharply. "We were summoned by your lordship to provide aid to the estate."

"Westerham," the butcher snarled, "the man who holds

us by the chain."

"And a man he is," Wilhelm said. "Nothing more. Now, who are you?"

Slowly, the butcher lowered his guard. "Jim," he said, cautiously. "Jim Metzger."

"I take it you have some weight among the commonfolk, Jim Metzger?"

"You might say that."

Wilhelm forced a smile. "Our directive was limited, but… perhaps we'd best consult matters over a drink? I hear the Stuck Pig is quite the venue at this hour."

"Only if you're buying."

The next thing Rufus knew, he was surrounded by hushed voices and body odor. As the tavern door creaked shut behind him, the barmaid launched from her seat at the sight of the returning offender. Metzger raised a hand, wordlessly granting him passage. Together, in the dimness and dankness, the company approached a trapdoor in a shadowed corner of the taphouse. Metzger lifted the lid with care and bid the outsiders to follow him into the root cellar. Once all were present and accounted for, the butcher shut the way behind him and the lamps sizzled to life of their own accord—a lopsided table stood in the center of the cellar, surrounded by racks of pilfered weaponry and sacks of supplies, guns and grain enough to thrive in a famine.

"You people have been quite busy," Rufus managed. "Why the secrecy—?"

Wilhelm nudged the heir, sharply.

"Oh," Metzger sneered, "just taking 'precautions.'"

"I see," Rufus said. In truth, his obfuscating stupidity was a means to make himself seen as meek as possible, all the while he kept a firm hand over his little dagger.

"And," he said, "what is it you had in mind?"

"To make sure we understand one another." Metzger sat

at the head of the table, where it tilted the most, and clapped an empty stein against the lacquered surface like a gavel—commanding the attention of all. "For those unaware," he began, "Baron Grünewald and his lackey have come to 'aid' to our cause."

"Excuse me?" Rufus said, the color draining from his face.

"Am I mistaken?" Metzger stated.

"No," Wilhelm said, "he is not. I shall speak for the two of us, as representatives of Altstadt and its surrounds." He cleared his throat. "By decree of noble right, Rufus Grünewald's jurisdiction is greater than that of Lord Westerham. Indeed, he is the lord of your oppressor."

"You speak as if we don't know these things," Metzger said, curtly.

"Then I presume you know of what lurks beneath the Abattoir?" A pall of silence pervaded the throng of workers. Wilhelm did not take a seat, content to flaunt his presence and authority as a shepherd among sheep. "You know of what I speak," he said. "Though you feel powerless to confront it." His eyes drifted from man to man. "The Swine. Creatures of Westerham's design. Abominations that must be cleansed with fire, no?"

Metzger exchanged nervous glances with his subordinates. "True."

"Why were they created?" Wilhelm asked.

"Claimed it was to help with labor, but when he couldn't tame the brutes, he locked them in the old aqueducts that make up the bilge of the Abattoir. As if they'd never existed."

"And there they breed unchecked." Wilhelm nodded, as if feigning prior knowledge of these truths. "I, for one, am a servant of God. And answer to no master save justice herself. With your assistance, I offer steel and aid to infiltrate the Westerham House. I ask only that you do what must be done and burn out this evil."

Rufus was shocked to see flames of violence so easily stoked in the workmen. Wilhelm did not relent, rallying the swineherds with dreams of freedom and a brighter future—the words of an iconoclast. His voice rose to a commanding boom. "Westerham took your lands and shackled you to his machine as pigs to be slaughtered. Take back your livelihoods! Put the Abattoir to the torch!"

The crowd began to rouse in deafening obedience to this demagogue, only for Metzger to raise a hand, a wordless command for them to fetter their enthusiasm.

"And what of Baron Grünewald? What has he to say on the matter?"

Despite Wilhelm's promises, a tide of suspicion washed over the fickle crowd once more—eyes fell upon Rufus, scrutinizing him without mercy.

The heir shifted uncomfortably in his seat.

"You are content with this?" Metzger asked. "To lead a revolt against your own vassal?" He drummed his fingers against the table. "What will you do if we succeed, I wonder?"

"I," Rufus said, "do not approve of Westerham's treatment of you and your families. I had no knowledge of what had happened until today. To be frank, I took you all to be rural folk. Not…slaves." He stood, slowly. "Gentlemen, I am not my grandfather. That much is certain."

Metzger nodded in kind. "So it would seem."

"But," Rufus raised a hand, "my agenda is simple—to purge the estate of evil. Whatever form it may take. And I see no good is to come of Westerham's industry." He couldn't believe his own words, goaded by Wilhelm's gaze. "He must be held accountable for his crimes."

"Then it is settled," the witch-hunter said. "Let us march upon the manor. And hang Westerham for all to see. He is too dangerous to be allowed to live. Do you as well."

"Wait—!"

Rufus's words were swallowed by a choir of cheers and bleating shouts. As the mob took up arms, Wilhelm and Metzger shook hands—sealing their pact in blood.

Anger flared in the heir's heart, and he stormed up to the witch-hunter.

"You have no right. None. To supersede my authority."

Wilhelm raised a thin eyebrow, knowingly. "Is that so?"

The gears of revolution were already in motion. Rufus watched on helplessly as torches flared in the murky gloaming, and the workers took up muskets and billhooks—a flood of bodies gathering force at thunderous speed. Breaching the florid gates of the manor, they set dry hedges alight. A length of rope was drawn from an oak tree in a makeshift gallows. Shots were exchanged from the garden to the balcony. Many fell, but the flames blazed bright against the silhouette of the chateau. Metzger kicked in the front door and led a vanguard into the foyer.

Rufus followed the trail of blood yet kept his distance.

The manor had yet to burn, and his path was clear. The screams of maids and elderly staff carried throughout the servants' quarters, and he ushered the innocent to safety, making his way to the master bedroom. Scaling the stairs to the second floor, the heir knew he couldn't afford to see Westerham murdered. Not yet. He had questions. Questions that needed answering.

"W-what is the meaning of this? Get your paws off me—!"

"Stop!" The heir burst through the door—panting, on the brink of panic.

Westerham was perched atop his bed, dressed in a nightgown of silk and burgundy patterns, flanked by Metzger and his men, who held him at gunpoint. "Rufus! Oh, thank God you're here. The peasants are revolting! They'll see us hung, drawn, and quartered. Please, do something!" He paused, as his assailants turned to their attention in silence. "Rufus…?"

The heir's lips quivered, barely able to speak. "We can't kill him. Yet."

"Kill me?" Westerham gasped. "W-what on earth do you mean?"

"I know you created the Swine." Rufus stepped forward. "Also, I know my grandfather told you of the neunauge, 'those marvelous eels.'" His reluctance gave way to embers of rage. "You brought me here for a reason. Tell me. Now. Or I'll let the strikers do as they will."

Westerham's face contorted in a fit of indignation.

"Why did you summon me?" Rufus repeated.

"I," Westerham began, "very well." He raised his hands. "It is true that the Swine must be disposed of, but we were expecting you to be more…agreeable as baron. And I don't mean the royal we. I was to coax you into understanding and, well, given how well we'd gotten on during the festivities, I thought you'd reconsider your position. What with your heritage and all."

"Get to the point."

"Did it never occur to you? You've never seen what's become of your predecessor. And I don't mean a corpse. Matthias Grünewald. Your grandfather. He is alive."

A wave of nausea washed over Rufus in body and soul. "What did you say?"

"He is rather disturbed by your quest to undo his great work—"

"You're lying."

"I suppose some things are best shown. God's speed, Rufus."

At that moment, the burgomeister pulled a heavy silk tassel by the bedside. The floorboards collapsed where the heir stood. Sliding down a well-greased chute for what seemed an eternity, Rufus's coat narrowly shielded him from spikes and stakes smeared with filth. He screamed and, at last, landed with a crash in a sodden trough of carcasses—some pig, some men, others of less identifiable origin. He staggered upright and gagged at the stench, struggling to make sense of the situation. One thing was for certain.

Rufus was alone among the Swine.

CHAPTER ELEVEN

Far below the foundations of the Westerham House, and farther still from any help or hope, Rufus groped about the unhewn walls, footfalls light against slick, damp stone. The faint drip and trickle of water against rock echoed throughout the tunnel, broached by nothing save the heir's shallow breaths—and distant squealing in the depths. Rummaging through his pockets for a tinderbox, he lit and raised a lone match feebly against the darkness. Despite the natural formations of these caverns, wide pipes jutted and sprawled about the curving walls, leaking with all manner of liquid refuse and half-congealed sludge. The path split off in numerous directions, forming a maddening maze of warrens. And so, Rufus began yet another descent.

"I have to get out of here," he thought aloud.

Weaving about rubble sharp as caltrops, the heir's coat was snagged by stalagmites and rough edges, threatening to impede his flight from the hunter's chase. Ossuaries and larders of rotting corpses lined the walls. Portions of these warrens had been masoned in a primitive fashion, limited to post and lintel construction, but most of the labyrinth was untouched by any semblance of civilization. He waded through the murk and gloom, trying to ignore the maggots writhing in sewage, until he came to a swollen door to an unknown chamber.

He reached for the ringed handle, only to hear a scream within.

"Please don't," someone cried out. "No—!"

Such pleas were swallowed by monstrous squeals and punctuated by silence. A shiver ran down Rufus's spine as he fumbled for his sharpened letter opener. Nothing emerged.

He had no choice but to carry on.

Hours seemed to pass in silence, and Rufus questioned whether he was making any progress. He floundered deeper into the warrens. When a lukewarm draft snuffed out his last match, the heir sat on a slab of stone in defeat. It was not merely the lurking fear that haunted him, but the revelation that his grandfather yet lived.

Rufus could not—no, would not—believe it.

All this time, after everything he'd been through, Matthias Grünewald was not a phantom of past atrocities or an inherited sin. He was alive and sought to manipulate these dark forces to some unknown end. And the heir was but a pawn in such a scheme. It could not be so. Rufus caressed his shaking palms. The world seemed to spin around his pounding skull. Westerham was wrong. There had to be more. There had to be. Something writhed under the back of Rufus's hand. He shuddered in utter revulsion and leapt to his feet, hoping—praying that it was a trick of stress and not a symptom of worsening infection. Pressing into the depths, he salvaged the shards of his courage, and his sight cleared, somehow able to see silhouettes in the darkness.

None of it mattered now, save his own survival.

Against the colonnades and rancid slough, Rufus noticed that the old waterways had been repurposed into a sprawling network of sluices and ironclad cisterns, into a bilge for the Abattoir. Even now, the heir could hear the constant whine of machinery on the surface—drilling into his skull. He only hoped a way out was near. Ladders of rusted rungs lead up to bronze walkways and chambers, the latter housing boilers, walls of cogs, and all manner of machinery.

In one such room, Rufus noticed a hastily scrawled note on a desk.

Attention night crew,

It has come to my attention that some of you have reported weird sightings in the bilge. While I appreciate the thoroughness and concern, Lord Westerham has instructed us to remind you that such things are not to distract from daily tasks. Therefore, the night shift will be extended from fourteen to sixteen hours to compensate for maintenance in areas that have been recently neglected. I recommend you continue to work in groups of three to four and do not enter the "warrens" alone. I apologize for any inconvenience this may have caused you and your families.

Signed,
Management

Rufus scoffed at the polite sympathies of the overseer. He flipped the flimsy paper to find a map of the complex drawn in scarlet ink. Pocketing the memo, he followed the map to the best of his abilities. Eventually, he came to what seemed a tirage with a thick sheet of canvas separating it from the warrens. He slid the curtain aside, greeted by rows of stained cots with leather straps, and cabinets of tonics and tinctures along the walls. Flies swarmed, and the sight of bonesaws and surgical knives sent chills down his spine. Evidently, the hospital hadn't seen use in some time, but Rufus could almost hear the screams of its patients.

A journal sat on the desk, predating the overseer's note by months.

Per Lord Westerham's orders, I have been gathering the grievously injured and unclaimed dead for the "application process," as he so calls it. Most of the living are in critical condition and are ignorant of their surroundings. Those more coherent are to be sedated for amputation. His instructions are clear and to stitch the carcasses of man and pig together with surgical precision. As to what end, he has yet to divulge, but claims it is under Baron Grünewald's orders. I have my doubts on the truth of such claims. Last night, I approached the burgomeister during one of his hosted dinners and asked what good could come from such butchery. To that, he responded with a hypothesis on reanimating corpses through fringe science and "nine-eyed eels." The workers are not to know of these experiments. It is with skepticism that I carry out these orders. Tonight, I apply the eel to a new sequence of hosts and hope that—

The entry ended abruptly—whether interrupted by a patient's suffering or something else, Rufus did not know. Regardless, the heir flipped through the yellowed texts to various diagrams of human and porcine anatomy, scribbled with annotations and associations between the two species. Hesitantly, Rufus opened one of the desk's drawers—and found a collection of molars and spectacles. He shut it in disgust, the clatter of teeth louder than he'd intended.

A guttural snort echoed a stone's throw away.

Rufus's stomach sank, and he felt the color drain from his face. The shadow of a porcine hulk flickered along the wall, far too large to be confronted by strength of arms. Rufus crept to the corner. He held his breath and waited for the swine-thing to pass by, halting before his hiding place, sniffing the air, as if savoring a morsel of fear—only to lumber into darkness. With the swine-thing out of earshot, Rufus sprinted in the opposite direction.

It was not until he stumbled upon the remains of workers, judging by their overalls and flat caps, that he began to piece together the extent of these horrors—when one of the presumed dead grasped his ankle, face half-paralyzed by toxins delivered at spearpoint.

"Help," he slurred, "me."

Rufus stifled his revulsion and knelt to the cripple's side. He was hardly a year or two older than the heir—portly yet sickly pale, condemned to a lifetime of servitude.

"What're you doing here?" Rufus asked, stretching a linen bandage. "Hold still."

"My son," he managed, "didn't come home." Rufus wrapped the wound with care. It took a moment, but he recognized him as one of the beggars by the Stuck Pig. "He was sent to sweep the chimneys for overtime," the beggar coughed. "I went to look for him, but then—"

"Save your strength," Rufus paused, "Westerham sends… children down here?"

"The bastard owns the Abattoir—the whole damn town." The beggar shuddered and twitched—the toxin was taking its toll. "It's Westerham, always was, mark my words. He sent my boy into the pipes, knowing damn well what would happen. 'Cause we wouldn't stay quiet about wages more than pennies a day, I'd bet you anything. Still. Never thought those…."

Rufus felt little bones crunch under his boots. He eyed the earth, peppered with shattered skulls and fractured ribs. His breathing turned shallow as he reached to the wall for support.

"How often are they sent down here?" he asked.

"Often enough," the beggar said, tears in his eyes, "but people go missing all the bloody time. We're expendable. We won't be missed."

"Can you walk?"

"I can try."

Rufus helped the beggar to his feet, swinging a frail arm over his shoulder. Despite the attempt at kindness, the heir knew he couldn't rely on the poor soul if the Swine caught their scent, let alone save him from the cleaver. Step by step, they carried on.

"How can you see down here?" the beggar broke the long silence.

"Don't speak," Rufus whispered, "you'll just draw their attention."

Despite the evidence and insidious inventions, the heir

still did not know the true purpose of the Abattoir. Clearly, it was more than a slaughterhouse, a prison for the swine-things, but that did not explain its true nature. Every hatch was sealed, and the ladders led to nowhere—locked down, thanks to Wilhelm's revolt. Escape seemed impossible. The map was worn and frail in his hands, a touch away from dissipating into delicate shreds. One wing of the complex remained unexplored, one that he had made a point to avoid, simply labeled, "Restricted Zone."

"What do you know of this?" he asked.

"Not much," the beggar said. "Just the one place men don't go."

"Somehow I doubt that in practice."

"The only ways in and out of there are the chimneys," the beggar said. "To think I told him those stories were all made up. Oh God, I hope he's all right—"

A metallic moan echoed within the pipes overhead. The beggar's eyes widened and teared. He limped his way to the drain as swiftly as he could, clawing at the bars.

"There's him! That's my boy!"

Something stirred in the dark, scuttling within the ceiling. Rufus drew his letter opener in a flash of steel, brandishing its meager blade against the unknown.

"Don't just stand there," the beggar shouted. "Help me lift!"

Rufus humored his companion, weakened as he was. Together, they pried and lifted the grate loose, opening the way into the labyrinth of reeking ducts. The beggar crawled into the narrow route, leading the desperate search for his son. Hesitantly, the heir followed not far behind. The pipes were cramped and slick with fatty sludge. Moments of silence bled together seamlessly. Rufus slid along its length, knees slick with grime—when the tunnel caved under his weight. Screaming and tumbling along the broken pipe, the heir rolled flat on his back amidst a cloud of dust and debris. He coughed and wheezed, staggering to his feet.

The beggar was nowhere to be seen.

Rufus followed the desperate cries of the father searching for his boy—until the corridor yawned open to a chasm, flanked by sheer cliffs of rotten rock, and at the bottom lay a lake of bilgewater. Crags and crevasses were riddled with shantytowns of irregular design. Architecture was lost on its denizens. They sought to reverse-engineer bits of garbage, fusing shingles and shambles together with black resin and a disturbed talent for engineering, and yet, it was not without bits of finery adapted in their image of the good life. As if born of the hallucinations of rag-and-bone men, it was the bleeding heart of the warrens. Creeping in the shadows, Rufus listened to the snorts and squeals of swine-things, silhouettes rippling in smoke. He was careful not to touch the hook-ended chains, dangling with dismembered torsos and sides of man-flesh, while torn pieces of trousers and blouses lay strewn about the floorboards. Slowly, he knelt, spotting a wool cap among the scraps. Small enough to fit around a child's skull.

Before Rufus could comprehend this, squeals pierced his ears. A horde of swine-things galloped past the larder, armed with cleaver, club, and claw, bodies wrinkled and pale. The heir peered about the corner and watched them pile atop the beggar—beating and biting as blood pooled from under the porcine heap. They soon grew weary of such wanton brutality, skittering back for the victim to die, leaving as soon as they came. Rufus found himself clutching the cap with shaky hands and approached the broken man.

"Did you…find him?"

Eerie silence passed, breached by the clatter of wooden walkways and monstrous cries of the Swine. Though held captive by fear, Rufus uttered a whisper.

"Yes," he lied, "he made a break for it. You bought him

time. He's safe." He glanced over his shoulder as a low grunt carried not far away. "There's a tunnel to the surface." He pressed the hat firmly into the father's hands. "You did the right thing."

The father laughed, weakly. "I just wanted to hold him. Just...."

So the beggar breathed his last breath, and the swine-things closed in. Rufus stood, slowly, and found himself surrounded by Westerham's horrors. They were stitched together in leathery patchworks of man and sow, staring at him with milky eyes, deformed and ill-proportioned, living taxidermies, slaves to a will not their own. Some were fattened hogs, bloated with gas and intestinal tumors, while others were thin runts, barely able to hobble on their hind legs. Down there in the dark, they had built a barbarian state, and in that lay their malign intelligence. Even now, Rufus saw the sinew of eels squirm and contort beneath their discolored skin—animating the flesh and possessing the mind.

The heir gritted his teeth and clenched his fists.

They did not attack.

Slowly, Rufus softened his gaze and stepped to the swine-things, who trembled and quivered at his approach. In a way, he looked upon them with pity, as hounds left to starve in the rain. Grotesque as they were, the Swine had not chosen their fate, no more than the workers chose to be shackled to Westerham's machine.

"Why haven't you killed me?" he asked.

"Because you incubate the same power," said a baritone of a voice.

Rufus shuddered yet did not turn around, recognizing the presence from his unhappy youth. He shut his eyes, hoping it was merely a nightmare. That he would wake in Sophia's arms, caked in sweat, gasping for air, safe from whatever drew near.

"It's been a long time," the voice echoed throughout

the warrens, "my child." Rufus's thoughts were usurped by excruciating pain, as if his brain was about to burst within the confines of his skull. He slumped to his knees, and the pallid hands of the Swine grasped at his shoulders, ushering him into the source of his agony. "I am grateful that you are here."

Rufus did not understand.

Eventually, the agony lifted in the wake of candles and torches of human fat, and he was escorted to a temple hidden amongst the filth. At first, Rufus was awestruck, but its meaning soon dawned on him. Amidst towering pillars and high stone drains, the blood of the slaughtered flowed ever downward into fathomless pits, as if feeding some nameless horror therein. The walls were covered with pictograms and icons of annelid idols. Sanguine mists stung Rufus's watering eyes. In the center of the chamber was the colossus of the nine-tongued worm, coiled about a slab of crimson marble. The Abattoir was not a mere slaughterhouse—it was a sacrificial altar, reminiscent of the ziggurat from Rufus's fevered dreams.

"Dear God, what is this place?" he asked.

"Home."

Surrounded by the Swine, Rufus felt the bloodworms writhe along his flesh. He began to decipher the cuneiform along the walls and recognized the scripture as almanacs chiseled in stone—records of lunar cycles and the wisdom of the ancients. Upon the eastern wall was a most disturbing image—the rings of the Empyrean and outer spheres, lights breaching the dark tapestry. The stars were right, aligned in perfection with the earth at its core. Drawn to the image like a moth to the flame, Rufus raised a hand and touched the image of the earth—only to be bombarded with visions of perdition. The flame did not stop at the barony, nor at the borders of the Empire. The sea ran red, and continents fractured like dry bone. The heavens were bathed in blackest night, save the eclipse of moon and man. The world began to crack under the weight of titans, fragile as a robin's egg, an incubator for the Thing in the Pit. And there, between heaven and earth, under a beam of hideous light, stood its herald, its avatar.

Matthias Grünewald.

"You," Rufus choked, "you're not real...."

"Am I?"

"Gottfried told me. You died in the Pit."

"Did they find my corpse?"

Rufus mustered what strength remained, raising his head in feeble defiance. He shut his eyes, blinded by light, not daring to humor the illusion any longer. He could not speak, knowing well that he stood before his grandfather, or rather, what he'd become.

"You understand more than you admit," said the image of Matthias, "but are still ignorant of the truth. Despite the gifts I've bestowed upon you."

"I'd hardly call your failed estate a gift."

"That's not what I refer to."

"Then what—?" Agony returned, and Rufus slumped to his knees, the worms feeding upon his every thought. Mouthing a scream, he felt the vessels bulge in his eyes—deep infection mingling with his own viscera. "No," he gasped, "stop it...!"

The worms showed a moment's mercy, retracting their venomous grips.

"The power of the Conqueror Worm," said the image. "This is as it should be. I will not harm you, Rufus, but you must understand. Why I sent the letter. Why you are here. In part, what Gottfried told you was true. My obsession led to the excavation of that which stirs beneath our estate. Such an undertaking was no trifling matter. We dug for months, years, an eternity, but in the end, I alone made the descent to be chosen."

"Chosen?"

"Yes. At that moment, I ceased to be a man and became one with the nine-tongued worm. I set these events in motion and, in turn, chose you. You have strayed from that vision."

"What vision," Rufus spat, "to usher the End Times?"

"End? No, it will not end here. We live in a dark age, a bloody age. An age of devastation, an apocalypse born of man. And so it will always be, so long as we allow the world to continue down the path to ruin. I would see mankind spared from the breaking wheel of history. You live in ignorance of the horrors I have seen."

"But clearly not the horrors you have wrought."

"I would see you as my seed and successor, at my side. Not opposing the nature of your lineage. Of the gift in your blood."

"You would see me as a puppet on the strings of parasites."

Rufus clenched his fists, eyes dry and raw with fury. He knew it was noble wording and a coat of glamor over countless atrocities—the will to blame everything save oneself. He saw a daemon in the guise of family. A temptation whose sole power was the threat of pain.

"Think carefully, my child," the image said, as if reading his very thoughts. "I have achieved immortality—the mastery over life and death. Short of your potential, you are weak and will not be mourned. Ask the people of Altstadt." He offered a wraith of a hand, ash and smoke. "I offer you a way to achieve greatness. If only for a small sacrifice."

"You mean, my humanity?"

"Humanity," the image scoffed, "the root of suffering. Man is blinded by the light of his own potential, as are you. What you see are shadows on the cave wall, illusions of the true nature of things, as did I, once upon a time. Here, let me show you."

The hold of the worms began to falter. In lieu of pain, they slid into unknown corners of his body and mind, and Rufus felt their morbid absence. He was naked in the dark, as if stripped of purpose. No longer did he feel rage or a will to do good, but felt as he did upon his outset—the memories of his bonds and deeds seemingly a dream.

"Do you feel it? The weakness of your 'better nature'?"

Rufus stammered, unable to speak, raising a clammy hand, only for the image to dissipate into nothingness—the shadow of an incubus burned into his tearing eyes.

"This is what you are without my gift."

The holocaust reduced the land to scorched earth, leaving him cold, naked, and afraid, and yet, Rufus did not succumb. Not yet. Somewhere, resisting the power's absence, there was an ember of the self, that which fed the flame to carry on—to whatever end.

"Maybe so," he admitted, "but what of Altstadt? What we've built?"

Warmth filled his hollow chest as someone had touched him from afar. Though Rufus did not realize it at that time, the medallion, that lover's charm, shimmered against the hunger of the nine-tongued worm—a shield of radiance against the darkness in his own heart.

For a moment, Rufus saw her.

"Sophia," was all the heir could manage.

Suddenly, he snapped to the present. The swine-things squealed at an unwelcome intervention. Rufus was in the temple once more. Torches and gunshots pierced the darkness. Several of the wretched fell dead. Deafened by the rising noise of battle, Rufus collapsed, utterly dazed, but felt gloved hands hoist his ailing body upright. In a fit of delirium, he groped and rasped, desperate to feel something, anything, only to fall into himself—into the nothingness left by the gnawing wake of worms. Where not even lovers' light could reach.

"Come the Eclipse," Matthias spoke, "we will be one."

CHAPTER TWELVE

Astride a great black horse, Wilhelm watched the flames spread across the slums of Westerham as the riotous masses took what was rightfully theirs. Such a conflagration was mesmerizing to his eyes, ensnaring his soul in a tangle of memories perhaps best left forgotten. The burgomeister hung from a tree before his manor, and the serfs swept through office and bank alike, celebrating their liberation as the streets flowed with the blood of collaborators. Corporate guards lay in the streets, skulls cracked open by cinder blocks, gore and gray matter splattered about the cobbles. He felt no remorse for those who fell to violence, be they slave or oppressor, content to brood aloft his saddle—solemn in his conviction. Westerham had proven a cancer upon the land and his precision a lance to drain its foul humors. Even now, coattails whisked by hot, dry wind, clothes stained with smoke, Wilhelm rode in a deliberate canter, every hoofbeat a hollow clop against the road. It had been long since he'd seen such judgment.

Westerham had been cleansed.

Then it occurred to him. Rufus had mysteriously vanished after plunging headfirst into the manor. Was the heir cowering amidst the secret passages? No, he wasn't the sort. Knowing the idle youth, he likely ran inside to either save or question the burgomeister himself. If so, what happened to him? Wilhelm quickened his pace and approached the manor grounds once more, when he saw Jim Metzger hoisting a body from the rancid river.

"Metzger," he called.

The butcher did not reply, laying the drenched casualty on the shore—pale, wracked with convulsions. Wilhelm dismounted and strode across the pebbles, recognizing the heir as he approached the water. He knelt to Rufus's side and laid a hand against his clammy brow.

"His fever is worsening. What happened?"

As Metzger babbled about what he had witnessed beneath the Abattoir, Wilhelm watched the heir stir in delirium, as if suffering the throes of nightmares, much like a creature in his own right. Then, the witch-hunter noticed a strange medallion resting against his naked chest. Wilhelm examined the necklace with care—minted long ago, belonging to no saint or fable that he recognized, a lunar emblem of ambiguous nature.

Under the eerie pall of night, Sophia walked the lanes of gravestones and gardens blooming from corpse-rich soil. Picking nettles and cloves of garlic, she harvested ingredients for yet another batch of herbal remedies. Though a working girl, her trade was not limited to carnal deeds—men paid a deal more for those than her service as a midwife. In these uncertain times, she had to act the vapid waif to avoid unwanted attention. Sophia had learned the hard way. She wasn't always confined to this backwater. Once, she was a student of medicine, trained in the humors and methods of surgery—an artist with a knife. How she missed the Athenaeum and long hours spent in the Great Library of Lumiere, surrounded by centuries of philosophy and insight. And yet, she too remembered the conversation that led to her transfer.

"Sophia," the dean raised his voice, "this is a song you've sung to more than once."

It was more of a court procedure than a disciplinary meeting. Sophia was surrounded by faculty, livid with rage. "With all due respect," she managed, "I feel that dissecting a specimen is hardly a crime. The dead have no use for their cadavers."

"It's obscene," a counselor hissed. "Professor Tate's

remains deserved to rest in peace. Not to be butchered in some… extracurricular study.'"

Sophia eyed the dusty tomes lining the shelves—volumes of anatomy and dissertations on esoteric science, left to rot and remain unread. Her audience was a troupe of faux intellectuals. They knew nothing of the bond between professor and pupil, of classroom repartee and long hours spent after lecture—duels of the mind and the salacious touch of flesh.

"I'm sure he would've donated his body given the circumstances." She stood, running her fingers through her auburn hair. "Gentlemen, if I may…."

The dean rolled his eyes.

"The antidote which I've developed required a cadaver for testing," Sophia continued. "Seeing as no one has survived the infection of a nine-eyed eel, I felt a fresh corpse was the next best thing. Lawrence was in perfect health prior to his death. You must understand—"

"No. You must understand." The dean leaned across the desk. "Grave robbery is a serious offense. And this is the first incident in our most prestigious academy."

"Somehow I doubt that…."

Murmurs of indignation and outrage filled the chamber, though such whispers were tantalizing, only strengthening Sophia's conviction in her studies. The dean raised a hand, and a hush fell over the thinly veiled jury. "I have half a mind to expel you; however, given your standing and undeniable talent, I believe a different course should be taken." He cleared his throat. "If you have indeed developed an antidote to the venom of the nine-eyed eel, it must be approved before we can distribute it to the populace. You see, we follow the rules here at the Athenaeum. Consider it a 'field study.' Deliver your experimental tonic to Doctor Isidore Cronenberg in the Barony of Grünewald for review, and perhaps we can overlook this egregious incident."

His lips curled into a sneer. "Should you return, that is."

Sophia felt the color drain from her face. "And if I refuse?"

"Then you leave me little choice."

Months had passed. Sophia found herself volunteering in the Narrenturm, where Cronenberg treated the mad without consent or regard for his subjects—a far cry from her mentor. Worse still was that she learned from him. Most of his treatments were backwards and barbaric, but a few yielded results and manageable side effects. They had a cerebral understanding, though it did nothing to stop the doctor's leering and licentious passes. Dismissing her thesis, Cronenberg did not care for her questions and perceived insolence. Never before had she felt so alone. Until she met him, Matthias Grünewald.

He was handsome, tall, and brooding, a gentleman in a burgundy tailcoat, aged like a cask of brandy. Unkempt yet debonair, the baron seemed to glide about the asylum and spoke in a slow yet deliberate manner, commanding the audience of all who heard his voice. Sophia remembered when their eyes met and he kissed her hand, lips supple yet chapped. She made it a point to make repeated calls to the manor and attended his soirées, invited or not.

"Your presence is unexpected but a pleasure nevertheless," he said.

"I'm surprised the valet let me through."

"Well, I may have had something to do with that." He took her by the hand, those spectral blue eyes gleaming down at her. "Come, I have heard of your research."

The union of their minds was as supple as their touching lips.

"Tell me," he said, peering atop the balcony of Schloss Fleischburg, overlooking the decorated gardens and drunken aristocrats. "What is your interest in the nine-eyed eel?"

"My mentor held an interest in toxicology and the nature

of parasites," she said. "He invented the microscope and wrote many works on humors and infection."

"Professor Tate. Yes, I am familiar with his work."

"How did you—?"

"Oh, Cronenberg and I are—or were—among his classmates." He eyed her in an almost predatory manner. "Of course, my studies are more 'anthropological' in nature." He inhaled, sharply. "I am willing to facilitate your research, should you wish to collaborate. The good doctor is talented but does not share my vision."

Sophia felt her eyes widen on their own accord. "I would be honored."

"Very good. Come to the laboratorium tomorrow. You're welcome to spend the night." He smiled coyly. "I look forward to collaborating with you, Sophia."

In the following months, Sophia dabbled in occult sciences at the behest of Matthias and his generous sponsorship. Among the archives and wine cellars, she spent long hours peering at the worms from under a microscope, and humored weird methods that the baron insisted upon. Leechcraft and bloodletting were key in his science, and he held a keen knowledge of the outer spheres. Matthias would make frequent trips to the weald, where he would "consult those older and wiser" than he, though she found it hard to believe. Then, one night, under the light of the gibbous moon, she yielded to test her antidote on a living host.

"I assure you," Matthias said, "this is the only way to see if we can cure the afflicted."

Sophia stared at the lunatic bound to the table.

"I just wish that we had an alternative."

"Be that as it may," Matthias snapped his surgical gloves, "we must not let petty morality get in the way of our great research. Nor let word of our methods reach the public. Now then," he consulted an open text of anatomical charts, "the larvae are maturing as we speak."

Sophia injected the patient with her serum. A moment's silence passed. Thin forms writhing under his skin began to slow—until moonlight shimmered upon pallid flesh. Twitching and convulsing, the patient's eyes rolled over as strands of red sinew snaked from their sockets. Sophia staggered back in horror as the patient lurched and tore at the leather straps. What escaped his throat was not human—vocal cords contorted by parasites, reduced to a terrified screech. Before the worms could free and flee, Matthias drew a pistol and fired a point-blank shot into the patient's brow. As blood splattered the cold stone floor, the baron sighed deeply and returned to his desk, muttering in disappointment under his breath.

"W-why did you," Sophia stuttered, "what?"

"We learned one thing for certain," Matthias said. "The worms will flee a host injected with the serum. It is a cure, I suppose. And I must take note of that...."

Sophia did not mention the incident, though it troubled her for many a sleepless night. It was not until she sat down for a dinner of venison that she dared to speak her mind.

"I must ask," her voice quivered, "what is your interest in the nine-eyed eel?"

"Oh," Matthias wiped his face with a cloth napkin, "you need not worry about that."

"Then why did you...?"

"Kill the patient?" Matthias asked. "I saw what needed to be seen and couldn't risk him running his mouth if his condition improved. I can only do so much with the deranged. Besides, we yielded wondrous results that night. You should be proud of yourself."

Sophia picked at her meal with a silver fork. The longer she stayed with the baron, the more she thought her situation was but a gilded cage. "Excuse me—"

Matthias raised a soft hand. "You must understand, Sophia. I have put a great deal of trust in you. Whatever it is you're thinking, I advise you not to betray that trust."

Sophia locked herself in her chambers and began to plan her escape. Schloss Fleischburg was a stone's throw away from Altstadt, though the estate itself was isolated by miles of woodland and wilderness. Matthias had countless spies in his service. The servants of the castle were always hooded and cloaked, skulking in the shadows as they did their master's bidding. There was but one way to the village, through the undercroft and into the catacombs. Gathering her belongings posthaste, Sophia noticed that someone had been through her books. Fear gave way to anger. Matthias had stolen the keystone of her work. She returned to the laboratory under the moonlit night, only to recognize her leatherbound masterpiece in the hearth, its pages curling into ash and absolute nothingness in her fingers. Try as she might to salvage the crackling tome, she knew it was too late. She would never receive credit for her work.

Tears of rage in her eyes, the escape from Schloss Fleischburg was not the ordeal she had anticipated, and yet, Sophia knew that Matthias had merely let her go, discarding her like a broken doll. Treading mud and dressed in her favorite gown, she ordered a stiff drink at the Hofbräuhaus, enduring the gawking stares and whistles of the drunk and desperate.

They served to kindle her wrath.

The opportunity to exact revenge never came. Matthias never made a public appearance since, and rumor soon spread of his descent into the Pit—something he never spoke of, even to her. Slowly, she began to piece together the extent of the baron's plot. And, if the change in wights and wiedergängers was as serious as portended, then perhaps he had succeeded. Sophia had been used. The days grew darker, and sightings became more frequent. Establishing herself as a cunning woman, she took to the weald to gather rare specimens to recreate her masterwork—though her efforts were in vain. Robbed of equipment and access to Matthias's libraries, she relied on rudimentary cures to emulate even a fraction of her success. Sophia endured whispers and gossip that she slept in the Devil's bed and seduced her clients in rituals of blood sacrifice, and knew her survival depended solely on the existence of greater threats.

Such as the Weird Sisters.

Here and now, Sophia heard the frail gates of Altstadt creak open as Wilhelm rode to the stables with a pale passenger. She gasped upon recognizing the sickly rider, wrapped in a cloak and hood, head bobbing and limp, utterly at the witch-hunter's mercy.

The excursion in Westerham had gone morbidly south.

Sophia rushed to the stables and helped Rufus from horseback. He was sweating profusely, eyes glazed over and milky, groping blindly for support. Whether he even recognized her touch, she could not say. She pushed back his lank hair and examined the festering wound on his neck—the symptoms were indeed worsening.

"What happened?" she asked.

Wilhelm still mounted his steed, glowering with grave suspicion. "We were separated during the riot in Westerham. Rufus attempted to fight the enemy yet succumbed."

"Riot?" Sophia asked, holding the heir in her arms.

"Complications arose upon the discovery of heresy."

"I can see that."

Wilhelm reached into his pocket and withdrew a familiar charm. "He was wearing this upon discovery. I recognize the mark from covens past, though I know little else."

Sophia felt the color drain from her face.

The witch-hunter raised a thin eyebrow. "I believe Rufus was cursed by something. Or someone. Claimed by dark powers.

Do you have any insight as to what?"

Sophia was not ignorant to the reputation of witch-hunters. His was a soft accusation, yet he clearly had greater matters to attend to—for now.

"No idea," she lied.

"Indeed," Wilhelm said. "The people of Westerham told me otherwise. 'Queer magic, that,' they said. They haven't seen the image since the children went missing."

"Excuse me?"

Wilhelm nodded, solemnly. "Forgive me. Not long ago, 'unpleasantries' swept Westerham and her sister villages. Witches, they were. Women who appealed to outlying farmers and simple folk, promising them protection from the ravages of war, in exchange for a tithe of blood." He paused. "What manner of tithe, I wonder?"

Sophia did not reply, unwilling to divulge the incriminating truth. She knew of covens, licking the blood from their lips and ladles, as to summon the Devil for black rites, though she hadn't seen it firsthand. Evidence was plenty in hamlets across the Empire. She knew Wilhelm had dealt with many executions, just as he had in Westerham. Even so, the witch-hunter knew little of her walks in the weald, her charting of paths that yielded the most potent fungi and horticultural oddities. Those sleepless nights seemed to awaken something within her, a maternal instinct that she never thought she possessed. Matthias had betrayed the Weird Sisters and her own trust all the same, and Sophia had sought out their guidance more than once.

"Children," Wilhelm continued, "firstborn children. The coven met in the weald. Under the light of the moon," he scoffed, "sacrificing the future to preserve the present." He eyed Sophia, sharply. "We cannot suffer such an evil."

"First time I've heard of it."

"Heresy soaks the very soil of the estate. And I will not

falter." Wilhelm clutched the medallion, eying its warm bronze in his hand. "However, I do wonder how your lover came about this...charm." He began to ride in a canter. "See to it that he lives."

"Where are you going?" Sophia asked.

"I was a fool to think I alone could root out this evil. I will seek out capable men."

"What kind of men, I wonder," she muttered.

"Men of God," Wilhelm glanced over his shoulder, "a jury of righteousness. All will be questioned. Those with nothing to hide need not fear the flame." His eyes gleamed like drawn blades in torchlight, alluding to an ember he took pains to douse and fetter. If Sophia didn't know better—she would've called it lust. "Rest assured, I will return."

When the witch-hunter had gone, Sophia sighed with relief. She ushered Rufus to his quarters in the Hofbräu and dabbed his brow with wet linen. Treading the line between science and sorcery, she began to trace his bulging veins with her finger, to discern where the worms had latched. Even now, sickly as he was, Sophia found beauty in the heir's potential. That, perhaps one day, he would achieve the same prestige as his forebears.

Rufus began to stir, eyes fluttering open, and grasped Sophia by the wrist.

"You," he said, "you're here?"

"Yes," she caressed his cheek, "I'm right here."

Tears trickled down the heir's face as he began to hyperventilate. "I'm," he managed, "I'm losing myself. Help me. Please. I don't want to hurt anyone...."

Slowly, his eyes drifted shut as he fell into deep catatonia. Sophia lingered upon the bedside, unsure what to think or how to feel. Once upon a time, she too thought of leaving Altstadt. It was not until she heard word of Matthias's next of kin arriving that she made the decision to stay. Now, like Rufus, she was a part of this place.

CHAPTER THIRTEEN

Wilhelm rode his steed through the Grünewald, through the hinterlands between the hamlets, down the Old Road which few had traveled in recent years, digging his spurs deep into the side of his great black horse. The ancient pitted cobbles were hardly a match for his determination to cover leagues with haste—the longer he delayed, the more souls were at stake. Under a canopy of slender branches, dangling with twig effigies and charms, Wilhelm kept to the route skirting the border of civilization, lest he earn the ire of those he hunted. Even now, herds of beasts seemed to eye him with morbid suspicion before fleeing at his approach. Such eeriness did not faze the rider, until something caught his eye—a clump of cloth laying in the middle of the muddy roadway. He dismounted and knelt to examine the curio.

A rag doll.

Wilhelm raised it to his nose and sniffed. Pine of the deepest reaches of the weald. Horsehair from the stables of Waldesrand. He knew the scents. Judging by the tracks leading off the trail, whatever girl called the toy her own had vanished—days ago, it seemed. Wilhelm delicately placed the trinket beside an unmarked grave.

He carried on, fists clenched about the reins.

Rain began to patter upon Wilhelm's shoulders and, in the distance, he heard the toll of a church bell. When at last he breached the murk of the weald, the witch-hunter halted upon the hills of the westward ridge, overlooking the farms and fields of Waldesrand.

Such was the parish of witches.

Wilhelm came to the pastoral stretch, where trellised hops

rose from tilled black soil, peasants toiled as steadily as autumn's march, reaping bundles of wheat and hauling their bounties to wheelbarrows. The witch-hunter thought it odd how verdant the common land seemed, and yet, there was something amiss among the tight-lipped populace. They looked upon him with fear and suspicion, yet knew better than to challenge his authority. Even in the haze of smoke, a throng of militiamen emerged, recognizing Wilhelm as the Witchfinder General.

"So," said the eldest among them, "how goes the investigation?"

"You were right," Wilhelm said. "Evil soaks the very soil of the estate. And I'd be loath to burn it alone. The heir has succumbed to a poison of a daemonical nature. Things are far worse than I'd ever imagined." He eyed the militia, sharply. "Where is our constable?"

"Sentencing a few crones, sir, but—"

"Take me to him," Wilhelm said. "My business is most urgent."

Isolated and insular, Waldesrand was hardly a village square lined with tall stakes amidst bundles of tinder and branches, ever in the shadow of the Drudenhaus. Among the lanes of half-timbered houses and shuttered windows, he dismounted before the Hag's Cauldron and allowed himself a moment to bask in the scent of hunter's stew.

Warily, Wilhelm began his approach.

The Drudenhaus was built upon the bones of an old monastery, clinging to some vestige of medieval prestige with a fortified facade and bastioned corners. High roofs of burgundy slate sloped starkly against the limestone walls lined with iron-barred windows—stacked upon one another as portals of stained glass. Angled from the manor proper was the east wing, an annex of sorts. No doubt picturesque in its prime, it had been left to sink into the moor, and yet seemed to float amid the smoke as a tabula. So he marched to the grounds that dominated the village. Already, he could hear the strike of the lash and screams of the imprisoned—heretics all. Converted into a gaol and torture cellar, the Drudenhaus had earned its name as a prison of witches. Wilhelm took no pride in the pain he inflicted, but knew it was only through suffering that the wicked would find mercy in the Kingdom of Ends.

So he followed the murmured accusations.

Thrusting open the heavy wooden doors, Wilhelm came to the courthouse. The constable loomed over a jury of hysterical peasantry, slamming a gavel upon the podium, wordlessly demanding order. He was a gruff man with a mustache befitting his rural office. He spoke with authority over the shouts and jeers of the maddened mob. Before the court, a midwife in a scold's bridle stood, unable to speak, flanked by a pair of deputies with missing teeth.

Wilhelm stood at the rear in reverence before the law.

"Although it is ever my wish to uphold justice with mercy," the constable recited, "your practice of witchcraft is an abomination before God and man. I therefore sentence you to burn at the stake, and may the Lord have mercy on your soul."

When the court had cleared to witness the execution, Wilhelm approached the podium as the constable collected his ledgers and lawbooks—a copy of *Daemonologie* among them.

"Ah," he said, "Wilhelm. Ever the faithful, though your report is overdue."

"You speak as if I am under your jurisdiction."

"My apologies." The constable snapped his book shut. "Things have been far from pleasant. You must understand, I have my hands full with accusations."

"More ale-wives?" Wilhelm asked.

The constable nodded, as if hesitant to admit the truth. Wilhelm heard the screams and slurs of the rallying mob. Though he'd seen such a sentence done time and time again, he had no desire to witness the burning out of zealous sadism alone.

"Was she guilty?" he asked.

"She bore the mark and confessed," the constable said. "That's guilt enough."

Wilhelm nodded, solemnly. "Under duress, I imagine."

"Come, we have much to discuss."

They walked the halls of the Drudenhaus, past the libraries and offices of deputies and civil servants, willfully ignorant to the cries in the cellars beneath their feet.

Wilhelm divulged in his many encounters.

"And why not rally the people of Westerham to your cause?" asked the constable. "If the lord of the land was so easily disposed—"

"Metzger's folk have need to rebuild and root out evils of their own. I'd be loath to ask them for aid. The evils of Schloss Fleischburg are not so simple. Moreover, I will call upon them in due time. To aid us in confronting the champion of eternal darkness."

The constable sighed, deeply. "What is it you wish to accomplish?"

Wilhelm paused, deliberating over his choice of words, and yet, should the constable resist, then he would exact justice as he saw fit. He did not speak for a long while.

Though the witch-hunter did not make his agenda known, he passed the empty cells in search of cruel implements and inquisitive men. As a bastard child of the church, he commanded a sense of authority like no other. Hysterical screams filled the undercroft as those suspected of witchcraft were condemned to strappado and twisting screws all the same.

Anything to extract a confession.

"If we are to truly liberate ourselves of sin," Wilhelm began, "we must not tolerate those who succumb to darkness."

He fiddled with the medallion recovered from Rufus's person, examining its copper in the torchlight. "I suspect the heir apparent has already fallen," he towered over the constable, a stout man in his own right, but his strength was one of secular law. He did not share the witch-hunter's righteousness. "Rufus cannot be allowed to live."

"Isn't that a bit much?"

"Hardly," Wilhelm said. "He is no different than his predecessor and has all but inherited the baron's sin. You would be a fool to put stock in him."

"The son of House Grünewald is hardly trustworthy," the constable admitted.

"We will begin by putting the forest to the torch," Wilhelm said. "Corruption must be purged. We will slay the crones and besiege the castle from out of the ashes."

Murders of crows announced their departure out the high window, cawing into the twilight. Wilhelm knew that they were spies and servants of dark powers.

"The Ladies won't take kindly to that," said the constable.

Wilhelm raised a thin eyebrow. "You would allow them to continue the black mass and feast on the flesh of the innocent? We cannot suffer this any longer."

"Yes, but our missing children…."

A moment's silence passed. Truth be told, Wilhelm hadn't considered the possibility that they were still alive. The Ladies of the Moon were not midwives or cunning women. They were monstrous beings, old as the woods themselves. There would be no homecoming for the children of Waldesrand, and yet, denial and despair would not serve his cause.

"Yes," he conceded, "I will assist in the search."

Wilhelm wondered if the militia had even walked the trails of the deep weald—if they understood the severity of these heresies. He would lead them to true horror. Where tiny bones hung from branches, spores and slime molds festered in gardens of fungal malignancy, and the air was sweeter than molten caramel. He would show them the black cauldron where the coven brewed elixirs from the juices of the dying. Wilhelm knew the crones would not reveal themselves, fickle as they were, but a doomed search would serve to ignite the flames of rage in their hearts—to raze the Grünewald to the ground. When their tears had dried and the shattered skulls were buried, they would be fools to deny themselves vengeance.

They would serve him without question.

CHAPTER FOURTEEN

Darkness crept from the battlements of Schloss Fleischburg, bringing with it whispers of revenants and restless spirits. Sophia did not take any clients that night, nor for many nights to come. Not out of any pretense of monogamy, though Rufus had since taken her as his mistress, but out of genuine care for the ailing heir. He'd seen that she would live comfortably. She would honor the arrangement as best she could. Weeks bled together, and Rufus showed no sign of recovery. Seated on her paramour's favorite stool at the bar, Sophia ordered a brandy and nursed her snifter in crushing solitude, fettering her grief with shackles of indifference.

"How is he?" Gottfried said, raising his own glass across the bar.

"Not good," she admitted. "He's stable but…." She looked away, overwhelmed by the welling words in her throat. "It's getting worse. I don't know how much more I can do."

"Do? Or take?" The burgomeister raised a thin eyebrow. "You're a physician, but this has taken a toll on you. As it has us all."

Sophia rolled her eyes. "This isn't a contest of misery, Gottfried."

"True enough, but a little perspective may help." Grueling silence stung the smoky air, as the hearth's light began to flicker and wane. It was not until Gottfried regained the courage to speak that he earned Sophia's attention. "He is very fond of you."

"I know."

"I'm not sure you do," the burgomeister said. "Rufus is a sweet soul and in that lies his weakness." He sighed, deeply, as if on the brink of apology. "I may not approve of your mercenary attitude when it comes to the house, but he does care for you. If it wasn't for you, I'm not sure he'd still be here, managing the estate." He raised his glass in a rare moment of respect. "You are his reason for fighting. Even now. Especially now."

Sophia raised her glass in kind. "I'm not the temptress you think."

"And I hope you're right."

With the bottle of brandy finished by the hour's end, Sophia's thoughts shifted through a catalog of every possible concoction and folk remedy that she knew how to brew. Nothing could stop the infection outright. Not since her recipe for a cure was destroyed. And she lacked the equipment to even attempt to recreate it. Then a thought occurred to her.

"Gottfried," she said.

"What is it?" the burgomeister muttered into his stein.

"Are the laboratories of the castle intact?"

"What do you mean?"

Sophia lowered her snifter. "What I mean is," she paused, "if we're going to save Rufus, I'll need better equipment to recreate what Matthias destroyed, or better yet, find a sample of my serum. One that hasn't been lost." She watched the burgomeister's eyes nearly bulge out of their skull. "What? You didn't think I was just a concubine, did you?"

"I knew you were gifted in herbalism…."

"Oh," Sophia shot him a wink, "you have no idea." She divulged her academic history with Gottfried, if only to let the mask slip, revealing her capabilities and credentials. "I'm not a fighter," she said, "but if we're going to save him, you'll need my expertise."

"Well," Gottfried massaged his balding scalp, "it's certainly an option."

"It's our only option."

The burgomeister finished his ale and conceded with a sigh. Even now, the spires of Schloss Fleischburg loomed over Altstadt from its loathsome perch. Wind howled throughout its forlorn halls, whistling into the valley below, as if tempting them with the promise of arcane secrets and forgotten lore—the means to bring Rufus back from the brink.

"What would you need?"

Within the hour, preparations for the expedition were underway. Sophia rummaged through her wardrobe and retrieved an old leather coat—stained with chemical spills and reeking fluids. Donning her surgical gloves and stuffing a raven-beaked mask with all manner of fumigants, she selected a number of knives and sheathed them to her belt. Her satchel was lined with corrosive charges and grenades pilfered from Cronenberg's supply. Eyes obscured by deep green lenses, her lungs were safe from foul vapors that undoubtedly infested the castle grounds. Sophia examined her form in the tall mirror—it had been long since she'd worn such a uniform. Pride churned with fear as she recalled her studies in plague-stricken slums, cutting through bone and the gangrenous foot with saws and heavy draughts, peddling in tinctures and tonics to pay for tuition. Even those amputations, grisly as they were, would serve little reference against the horror which awaited her. A sharp caw carried from the windowsill.

Sophia glanced over her shoulder and spied a crow staring back at her—a servant of the Weird Sisters. Though she knew little of sorcery, Sophia had nevertheless dabbled in their council in her darker hours. As if sensing her despondence, perhaps they had come to offer her aid—for a price. With hesitation in her heart, Sophia opened the window and bid the crow inside.

The bird pranced about the floor, eying her with wizened intent.

"You seek the means to bring him back," a feminine

voice ran inside her skull. "However," the words began to shift, "darkness encroaches once more, its embrace far greater than any we've encountered before. The Thing in the Pit stirs yet."

"I know," Sophia knelt and whispered, "that's why I'm doing it. We're running out of time." It didn't take a philosopher to know the implications of the moon, let alone its impact of the parasitic growth of eels. "If we don't do this by the next cycle…."

"He will die, yes," the voice chuckled, darkly, "as do we all."

Sophia stood, slowly. "The worms are maturing, but that's not all." She averted her eyes, not daring to speak of what truly troubled her, lest she make an unwitting bargain. "Never mind."

"Speak, child. Our threads are already tied in a knot of fate."

She took a deep breath and began. "There's a witch-hunter under Rufus's payroll, Wilhelm." She winced as the crow fluttered and cawed in alarm. "Do you know him?"

"The Witchfinder General," the voice called. "Yes. A man of conviction, blinded by hate. He has thankfully put few of our sisterhood to the torch, but murdered many he deemed to be unworthy of life. Beware and trust him not. He serves no one save his own judgment."

"I gathered," Sophia paused. "Why've you come?"

"To ask why you care for the boy so?" A shrill cackle reverberated throughout her racing thoughts. "He is of the same blood that used you and condemned us to the weald. Are you certain of your feelings? That he will not cast you aside when the time comes?"

Sophia's heart sank into her chest. "He's not like that."

"Do not be so certain," the crow began to take flight, "his blood is fickle. And men say many things on their deathbeds. Deceitful in their curtness, bludgeons in the dark—"

There was a sudden knock on the door.

"Sophia," Gottfried called. "Are you ready?"

She turned to shoo the familiar, only to find that it had already gone.

"One moment," Sophia said, gritting her teeth, and opened the door, greeted by the burgomeister and the purring mascot of the estate.

Gottfried eyed her up and down in studious surprise.

"I didn't take you for a plague doctor."

"Haven't worn this for a while."

Mincemeat rubbed against her leg and sneezed.

Downstairs, Sophia was greeted by a meager number of soldiers to choose from—mostly aspiring sellswords and landsknechts. She would have to make do.

"Gentlemen," she said. "We need to infiltrate Schloss Fleischburg once more. Our purpose is not to slay any particular fiend, but to investigate and recover an artifact that may change the course of this campaign. I will need the lot of you to accompany me." The men shifted uncomfortably where they stood, some reaching for liquid courage—the reputation of the castle and its denizens was well known among them. "Any questions?"

Little more was said.

The briefing proved short and clear enough. The miserable party escorted her into the dark of the night. Guided by the lantern's light, Sophia led the trek up the trail to the castle grounds. Wind howled through the brittle trees, and the swollen moon shimmered eerily through billowing clouds, bathing the woods in a livid glow. A flash of lightning shattered the silence, and rain began to patter in sharp torrents against the battlements. Its indomitable gates were left ajar by expeditions past and seemed to beckon the party into darkness. Even Sophia's lamp seemed fragile against the malaise, thick and unnatural, wafting from the black soil in low wisps of fog. The men drew their swords with slow deliberation.

She led the vanguard into the upper halls.

Sophia's thoughts were as bleak as the surrounding stonework. Retracing her lonely steps, she wandered corridors of thought, recalling the masquerade balls and canapes of happier days, as well as long hours spent in study, toiling over archaic manuscripts and applying the esoteric to fringe science. These halls aged as bitterly as her feelings of betrayal—a shadowed complex of spires and annexed wings.

"This wind cuts to the bone," said one of the swordsmen, words aquiver, "and you're not even shaking. Sophia, are you alright?"

She did not reply. In the courtyard, rain merely slipped off her waxen robes, and petrichor did not reach her. Her surgeon's mantle was armor enough against an onslaught of infectious memories. The Great Tower loomed from the far side of the yard, where the north and east walls met, and had served as the seat of House Grünewald throughout the ages. Stark and stout, and crowned with conical rooftops, the keep wafted with a cold indifference to its charge as warden of Altstadt and the surrounding woods. Sophia approached the front door and pressed an ear against the wooden panels, laying a finger to her lips.

Silence passed until she slowly pushed open the door.

If memory served, the laboratory lay somewhere adjacent to the entrance hall. One by one, the company crossed the threshold and entered the Great Tower. The ground floor was largely a kitchen with pantries and stores off to the side—slabs of graying meat dangled from hook-ended chandeliers, cast-iron cauldrons buzzed with vermin, and all manner of unclean cleavers lined the walls. Sophia did not dare to guess the ingredients of whatever stew had been festering for months. It seemed even servants had abandoned their duties in the baron's absence.

"Nothing to be found here," she said to herself.

The spiral staircase took them to the second floor. Under a heavy oak ceiling, the hall was devoted to entertaining guests and delegates, as demonstrated by tapestries of flora and fauna, and trophies of woodland beasts mounted upon the walls. And yet, for all these moth-eaten displays of wealth, wilting bouquets, and silver spoons, Sophia's eyes fell upon a painting above the hearth—oil on oak, a hamlet burning in chiaroscuro, a scene of vivid, violent motion.

"Men," a soldier called, "I think I've found something."

Following the hoarse voice, Sophia was greeted by a chill draft, following the footsteps of her unscrupulous companions. The hall was lined with suits of gothic armor with an assortment of sallets and frog-mouthed helms—an armory with crossed halberds and pikes, and miniature cannons. Banners of black livery hung from the rafters, bearing the heraldry of House Grünewald and its neighboring allies. Sophia recognized the corridor as adjacent to the laboratory. They were close now, and success seemed promising, should their presence continue to go unnoticed. She thrust open a set of iron-banded doors and was greeted by a wooden balcony overlooking the "laboratorium," as Matthias once called it.

Where her work had been destroyed.

Sophia descended the rotting wooden steps and came to the ground floor of the tower. Surrounded by strange instruments long abandoned by servant and master alike, she examined the operating table and black, labyrinthine cables reaching high towards the open ceiling, where lightning flashed and shed scant light upon the interior. Spanning nearly the entire floor was a vast grate of rusted iron, reminiscent of the brig of a seaworthy vessel—tarnished by ill weather and other elements. As to where the drainage led, Sophia never dared to guess. She rummaged through the cabinets and side rooms, desperate to find any trace of her masterpiece, yet found nothing save empty bottles and the remnants of failed experiments.

Someone had been here recently.

"Keep looking," she ordered. "There has to be something."

"And what exactly are we looking for?" sighed a swordsman.

Sophia did not reply, investigating every stray tome and discolored stone, until at last she leaned against the wall in defeat—and heard a faint clicking within the wall. A bookshelf slid aside, its heavy wooden weight grinding against the flagstone floor, revealing a hidden route into the antechamber—a secret room. Hope sprang in her heart. As she stepped into the chamber, a ring of electric lamps sizzled to life, shedding white light upon a stone table and a syringe seemingly floating in midair. She recognized the sickly fluid almost instantly, reminiscent of briny water or formaldehyde—it was her serum, possibly the last dose to exist.

The syringe shifted unnaturally in the light as Sophia moved about the room, as if encased in polished glass or perhaps a viscous material. She knew better than to grope blindly. Rummaging through her leather satchel, Sophia drew a polearm from her inventory, little more than a telescoping extension of the hand, ending in a clawlike appendage. It slipped through the translucent membrane with a chemical sizzle, like a pair of greedy fingers in a jar of molasses, and stretched open to grasp the elixir. Though Sophia removed the syringe from its prison, she refrained from allowing herself a moment's joy. Her suspicion proved fair as deep rumbling filled the tower. At first, she mistook it for a peal of thunder, until the screams of her companions breached her ears—followed by an unforeseen presence.

"I thought I told you," said a low baritone, "not to betray my trust."

Sophia pocketed the syringe and fled to the tower, only to gasp in horror. Nine crimson tentacles, dozens of feet in length, had torn and burst through the grates, tangling and flinging her comrades about like broken dolls. Lightning struck the rods upon the ceiling, sending shivers of electricity through the cables and wires overhead. Seeing men torn limb from limb by sucker and barb, she felt the color fade from her face as nausea washed over her, as blood splattered her mask. The tentacles groped about the tower—searching for her.

"You cannot hide from us," said the voice. "Nor can you save him."

In a fit of desperation, Sophia skirted the perimeter of the tower, dodging crates and contraptions as they were hurled across the hall. A heap of rubble collided with the door to the entrance hall—collapsing the way out. One route remained—the stairwell to the second floor. Racing up the wooden steps, she was confronted by one of the heaving tentacles, which slammed its entire girth against the high walkway, shattering it effortlessly.

She was trapped.

"This is as it should be," the voice carried from the depths of the estate. "My heir will succumb to the true nature of things and will be our champion. You, my dear, will die alone and unremembered." It uttered a mocking laugh. "You should've never returned."

Lowering her gaze into the pit, Sophia saw a host of cephalopodan eyes glisten and shift in the darkness below. Alien as they were, they reflected a familiar evil.

Slowly, the truth dawned on her.

"Matthias?" she gasped. "Is that…?"

"Not anymore."

Before Sophia could so much as scream, what remained of the walkway collapsed under her. Plummeting into darkness along with timber and debris, she was greeted by a yawning maw ringed with rotten teeth. Slipping down the gullet, she tumbled into a reeking abyss and slammed her skull against something. She mouthed a scream, only to be swallowed whole.

Into the belly of the beast.

CHAPTER FIFTEEN

Tossing in his sheets, Rufus drifted in and out of coherent thought, lost in a limbo of sweat and shadows along the walls. Images of cruelty flashed through his mind's eye, woodprints of war crimes as though sliced into blocks of his own will—things that he'd never seen, nor wanted to comprehend. He was helpless to parasites in the blood. Coughing weakly, he gripped the sheets, desperate to cling to some semblance of reality. Even in maddened dreams, he saw the silhouettes of little worms writhing under his eyelids.

Wake up….

Rending himself to the present, Rufus bit into his own wrist, eager to feel the proof of pain or to dismiss a false awakening. His head swirled in a stupor of color and half-remembered nightmares. Dressed in a sweat-stained nightgown, he staggered down the stairs, clutching his shillelagh—nearly slipping down the steps, crippled by fatigue, as something pulsed within his very skull. Rufus all but laughed at his pitiable state—a prisoner in his own body.

There was only one thing left to do.

Rufus crept behind the empty bar and helped himself to a pour of local reserve—feeling a strange craving for raw meat—when something slithered under his skin. Something spoke to him within his own thoughts, though not in any language known to man. Nor was it his grandfather's will. A wave of discomfort washed over him, but ebbed like the tide, followed by a lurking annoyance as it receded throughout his very blood. Rufus jolted out of his seat and reached for a kitchen knife, inches from carving into his own flesh, when aches flooded his body.

I would not do that….

"Who's there?" Rufus gasped.

The knife clattered on the floor. The invasive presence hissed, and he involuntarily covered his ears. Something was puppeteering him from the inside, like a marionette on strings.

That would be me….

"You?" Rufus wiped the sweat from his brow. "No, no," he paced about the tavern, "this isn't—this can't be. You're just the fever, a bit of cheese, or—"

Are you always this neurotic…?

"No," Rufus stuttered, "I mean, well, y-yes, but I fail to see…why that's relevant."

Something hissed in the back of his skull, and his stomach growled on its own accord.

Your muscle tone is abhorrent. You need to eat….

"What—?"

Eat….

Rufus found himself pillaging the larders—moldy bread, cheese, whatever he could find. The heir lunged and snatched a rat, snapping its neck with brutal efficiency, and began to flay it with a dull knife. Crouched over a pile of refuse, he was disgusted by the illusory flavor, as if the thing had altered his palette to that of a deranged barbarian.

"Why does this taste so good…?"

Because man cannot live on whiskey alone….

Suddenly, Rufus noticed lamplight flicker down the steps as the innkeeper shed light upon his crouched form. "I, uh, it's not what it looks like," he belched.

He'll make fine eating….

"No!" Rufus screamed and lunged to his feet. "We are not eating him."

The innkeeper stared at him with wide eyes, trembling in horror.

"M-my apologies," Rufus wiped the blood from his mouth,

forcing a laugh, "but do you have anything else in the kitchen? I'm," he managed, "very hungry."

If he alerts the town guard, we eat him....

"I'd like to keep this between us," Rufus slapped the nape of his neck, "if you please. Also," he whispered to the thing inside, "there is no town guard."

Enough with the niceties....

"Shut up," Rufus hissed.

"I didn't say anything," the innkeeper managed.

Rufus rolled his eyes. "I wasn't talking to you." He gestured to the kitchen, his patience running thin, as the thing growled along his thoughts. "Just throw whatever you have together.

Please," he all but begged, "I need to eat something."

The heir lurched to the nearest table and reached for the whiskey bottle—a double was in order. He caught himself salivating and reached for his pocket handkerchief, as if to salvage the remnants of his dignity. "What in the hell are you?" he murmured into the cloth.

An entity from the outer spheres who stumbled upon a wretch of a host. One with an unhealthy dependence on spirits. To think you are of his bloodline....

Rufus's stomach dropped. "You mean, Matthias, I presume."

Yes. That is what we call the Chosen. This intrigues you?

The innkeeper arrived with a bowl of beef pottage from the hunter's pot, stale bread, and a fistful of figs. He slid the meal wearily before the ravenous heir and kept his distance. Rufus raised a wooden spoon to his lips. "What can you tell me of him?"

Matthias Grünewald. Yes. He sought to call upon us. I am but a strand of what he sought to tame. He was able to "live" with the hunger of the Conqueror Worm....

Before he knew it, Rufus had devoured the entire meal—the thing hissed with satisfaction as its hunger was finally sated.

"Do you have a name?" he asked.

Not one that you can pronounce. No....

Rufus dropped the spoon, fingers wracked with tremors. Flexing his wrists, he struggled to maintain control of his own musculature, his efforts faltering with every twitch.

"You are the Conqueror Worm?" he whispered.

In a manner of speaking, yes. Strands separate from the whole yet bound to its indomitable will. In time, you will understand. Power over the flesh....

"Power over me, you mean."

That remains to be seen....

Rufus staggered to his feet, dabbing sweat from his brow, and uttered a mad laugh. "What am I doing? This is crazy. I'm talking to a bloody parasite."

Yes. You are. And I suggest you cease your prattle, lest the people grow suspicious....

Rufus's eyes darted to the door on their own accord—the innkeeper had crept to the open street, leaving the heir to his own devices, perhaps to call upon Gottfried or worse. Rufus's thoughts raced to the incident in the undercroft when the militia failed to assassinate him.

He could not afford for such a thing to happen again.

Follow him....

"Excuse me," he called.

Not like that....

The innkeeper halted his tracks. "My lord?"

"Where are you going?"

"I," the innkeeper paused, "was going to inform Gottfried on your recovery."

"I see." Rufus nodded in an attempt to feign understanding. "Well then, I suppose you don't mind if I come with you?" Despite his fatigue, strength returned to his limbs in a tide of adrenaline. "We've, I mean, I've been out of commission for some time."

"Yes, you…certainly have."

Together, Rufus and the innkeeper approached the Rathaus, where Gottfried made his office and oversaw daily affairs. Despite his desire for discretion, Rufus thrust open the doors and marched to the burgomeister's desk. The heir forced a toothy smile.

"Rufus?" Gottfried gasped. "Good lord. What are you doing up and about?"

"A speedy recovery, I assure you," Rufus said.

They suspect something. Tread lightly.

The heir pinched his underarm to silence the worm's nagging. "Well then," he began. "I'm pleased to inform you that Westerham has been…dealt with."

"Murdered by an angry mob. Yes, I've heard."

Rufus pulled up a seat before the desk. "I'm afraid it's not so simple," he said. "Westerham was in league with Matthias Grünewald and proved a danger to the cause and myself. Regrettable it may be, he had to be pacified. Wilhelm saw to that."

Gottfried's eyes widened over his spectacles. "What're you implying?"

Rufus confided in Gottfried on every detail of the expedition sans that his grandfather yet lived. The heir watched a pall of dread and shame wash over the burgomeister's face until it became clear that he knew nothing of Westerham's schemes.

"Good sir," he addressed the innkeeper, "a moment, if you please."

Alone at last, Rufus felt the parasite lessen its grip on his spine, allowing him to heave and sigh in recovery. Gottfried eyed the heir with grave concern.

"Rufus," he began. "What happened?"

I know this one. Yes, we can trust him. Speak freely….

The heir rested his rigid face in his hands. "Yes," he said. "The worms are maturing and, well, Matthias. He's alive."

"That's not possible—"

"Dammit, Gottfried!" Rufus slammed his palms against the desktop. "I saw him! He's one with the Conqueror Worm. He has power over the neunauge." He gestured madly out the window. "Everything we thought we knew was a lie." He felt tears of panic flow down his numbed cheeks. "Matthias brought me to be his successor, a puppet on his strings, and so far, he's succeeding. He showed me what will happen. And…it's in my head," he clutched his skull, eyes bulging out of his skull, "the worms, they're getting stronger. I'm not sure how long I have left or what to expect. Please," he all but begged, "help me. There has to be a way to stop this. Before the Thing in the Pit breaks free! I'm," he began to sob, "I'm losing myself."

Quite pathetic, aren't you…?

"Shut up…."

Gottfried stood, slowly, and approached the heir with care and caution, laying a hand on his shoulder. "The worm… talks to you?" his tone was tinged with hope. "What does it say?"

Rufus raised his head. "Well, it's very sarcastic."

Only to those deserving of scorn….

"And you can only hear the one voice?" Gottfried asked, managing a grin.

"I think so?"

"Have you considered the possibility that—"

Sudden lights flared out the window—torches burned bright, wielded by roughly a dozen silhouettes in the open street. Rufus reached to the drawer for the wheellock pistol, veins bulging and varicose under the skin of his hands.

"Oh no," he snarled, "no, not this again!"

You were far too obvious….

"I hate this." Rufus's eyes jerked towards Gottfried. "You need to hide."

"You need to leave," the burgomeister said. "I'll let you

handle it."

Rufus had a fleeting hunch that Gottfried didn't mean the heir per se. Fury rose in his heart, igniting a furnace of feverish wrath and ravenous hunger.

"Just let me talk to them first," he pleaded.

The next thing he knew, Rufus thrust open the doors and approached the rallying mob, his legs shaking. Armed with pitchforks and repurposed farming implements, they formed a thin phalanx about the grounds of the Rathaus, trembling in their boots.

Well? Let's see the politician at work....

"Gentlemen," he raised a sweat-soaked hand, "I don't know what you've heard, but rest assured, I am of perfect health and spirits—!" A surge of nausea overcame him, and he wretched a pool of black ichor onto the open green. "I'm fine," he gagged. "This is fine."

"He's been turned," said the innkeeper.

"Turned? W-wait a minute." Steely clicks punctuated the eerie shroud of night as poachers among the mob took aim. The clock tower struck the witching hour. Slivers of pale moonlight shone upon Rufus and his black veins. "I don't want to do this."

I do....

Rufus wrapped his arms about his chest. A tremendous surge of adrenaline eclipsed his vision and thoughts. He was a passenger in his own flesh, eyes rolling over white yet able to see clearer than in brightest day, his gaze piercing the pounding hearts of those who'd oppose him. The heir's spine began to hatch in violent demonstration, tentacles of crimson sinew erupted from his back—lashing, barbed with spikes and teeth.

"Come at me if you wish," the worms spoke through him, "but know I shall rip you apart and feast on the marrow of your bones." Tears welled in his eyes—not of fear or remorse, but in awe of the intoxicating power. "I am not Matthias Grünewald."

Hunters among the mob opened fire. Shots pierced his rippling flesh. Rufus felt no pain. Tearing his thoughts free of bloodlust, he cried out in mortal anguish and wrenched control of his corpus, leaping up the tower, scaling its masonry with unnatural grace.

Coward….

"I don't want to hurt them," Rufus snapped.

Really? They certainly feel otherwise….

Rufus leapt from rooftop to rooftop, skittering across shingles and thatch in a lunatic high. Crouching atop the belfry of the abbey, he paused to collect his thoughts and debate the beast within, shuddering in the autumn breeze. Sickly darkness seemed to ebb and flow about his body, enshrouded by a waistcoat of black ichor and miasma. Rufus stared at his own damp hands, realizing that the entity he carried was unlike anything he'd ever encountered.

"You're not like the other worms, are you?"

How astute of you. No, I am not. Nor are you like other hosts. Despite your timidness, you carry his bloodline and are…different. As demonstrated by your will….

"Glad to hear it."

Not only that, but you seek to defy the Conqueror Worm. Your own nature. This is futile, but I can feel your resolve. What's more, you want to…usurp him?

"What? That's—"

Don't bother denying it, Rufus. I have come to know you well as I gestated within your flesh. Soon, you will understand. I have been a passenger for some time. I will merely take the reins now and again. And you, well, you will grow to appreciate what I have to offer….

"And you don't feel any loyalty to my ancestor?"

In a word. No….

Rufus crept about the buttresses and balustrades, clinging to the gargoyles as they leered over search parties and their meager lights. The parasite seemed to smirk inside his mind, laughing behind his eyes, and Rufus harkened to its black speech.

Listen carefully, Rufus. I believe we have potential. You and I....

Head bowed and hands deep in his pockets, Rufus brooded upon the lip of the parapet. He smirked to himself and his newfound ally, tempted by the notion of a second wind—a chance to rid the estate of evil with its own venom. When at last the mob had split off into the farms and fields surrounding Altstadt, he descended upon Main Street and returned to the Rathaus.

"What happened?" Gottfried asked, lamp at hand.

"I think," Rufus managed, "we have a new variable in the equation of our quest."

"May I suggest laying low for a bit, my lord? Gossip spreads like wildfire among the common people. I'll be surprised if they don't see us hanged together."

He's right....

"You're right," Rufus admitted, "but where should I go?"

Gottfried opened the study window and leaned against the sill. "I believe you have the means to combat the evil of the estate. Now more than ever."

The worm purred with inhuman hunger.

"And of what these...appetites?"

"Try not to eat too many villagers."

Rufus was unsure if the burgomeister meant that in jest. Gottfried had assisted with countless misdeeds and atrocities as a household bureaucrat. Slowly, it dawned on the heir that his most trusted confidant was loyal to nothing save House Grünewald itself, regardless of master, and given that his predecessor yet lived, Rufus had his doubts.

"Who am I, Gottfried?"

The burgomeister paused, as if unsure what to say. "You are Rufus, the rightful heir and baron of the Grünewald Estate and all its people and holdings."

"And what are you?"

"I am your most devoted servant, just as I have been to your father and his father before him." He cupped the heir's shoulder. "What're you trying to say, my lord?"

"If Matthias is out here. Beneath the estate," he could not bear to look at his venerable aid, "what does that make me? In the line of succession? Of your loyalties?"

Gottfried opened his mouth, as if to speak, but not a word escaped his lips.

"You have been my dearest friend," Rufus said, "but I need to know, when the time comes, will you stand with me against my own ancestor?"

"Well," Gottfried laughed, nervously, "I don't have much of a choice, do I?"

"No," Rufus said, "I suppose not."

His suspicions were shackled by that which lurked within his body.

You're wiser than you let on, but there's something else that troubles you....

"Where is Sophia?" he asked.

Your heart is racing –

Rufus slapped the nape of his neck to silence the thing along his spine, cheeks red with indignation. "I didn't see her at the Hofbräu," he said. "Is she alright?"

"She," Gottfried paused, "departed to the castle."

Rufus's eyes widened in horror. "What?"

"Your condition was worsening, and she went to recover certain medicines," Gottfried said. "I provided her with ample men. She couldn't be talked out of it."

Panic flared in Rufus's heart, overshadowing the mental leash of the worm. Before he knew it, his will exceeded even the persistent tremors and fetters of the parasite. Summoning this newfound strength and taming it as a stallion, Rufus was deaf to opposition as he departed the hamlet and set his course to Schloss Fleischburg.

You care for her. I see. But I know that I will not be tranquilized by some midwife and herbal remedies. It is far too late for that. We cannot allow her to meddle in our growth….

"I know," Rufus said, sprinting down the trail with inhuman speed.

What's more, you wish to usurp your ancestor. Impossible. Matthias has already proven to be the Conqueror Worm's chosen. You'd be a fool to defy this….

"Then why are you helping me?" he asked.

I'm merely along for the ride, as it were….

So Rufus came to the courtyard of Schloss Fleischburg. With a crunch and crack of his wrist, he summoned a fistful of claws, slicing through his fingertips as daggers of bone. His eyes were sharp even in absolute darkness. He caught the scent of sweat and terror within those walls.

His purpose was clear.

When at last the heir had reached the Great Tower, he was greeted by signs of struggle and carnage. Equipment of wood and steel lay strewn and obliterated by blunt force, as if caught in a hurricane. The odor of salty things was palpable in the stagnant air. Something had burst through the iron grate upon the floor, something massive, only to retreat into the darkness of the unknown. Even with his terrible gifts, Rufus was uneasy.

She's in there. I can taste her fear….

Standing upon the brink of the abyss, he peered into its sheer depths. Monstrous purrs wafted with the wind of foul breath. Rufus knew what was happening. He felt Matthias's taunting presence emanate from within, wordlessly goading him to slip into madness.

Are you sure of this? She will attempt to "cure" you….

The parasite churned under his flesh. He scraped at his nails, bleeding a black fluid, stunned at his own hesitation. Nothing was holding him back.

"She wouldn't do that," Rufus lied to himself. "She'll understand."

Will she now…?

Rufus lingered and deliberated, though no rational thought was to be heard, for shock and numbness silenced any internal monologue. He took a step back.

"What's wrong with me?"

CHAPTER SIXTEEN

Sophia woke to utter blackness. She groped blindly, her leather mask breached by the overpowering stench of acidic bile and corpses. Slowly, she managed to stand. Half-digested bones squished and flukes squirmed under her boots. Her lamp was broken. Not even shards of jagged glass could pierce the pliant thickness of those fleshy walls.

"This is the price you pay," a deep baritone, an echo of Matthias, reverberated throughout the digestive tract, as if spoken from within. "A shame, really. We could've shared in this."

"You're disgusting," Sophia hissed.

The voice chuckled, darkly, and said no more. Though she pressed on, Sophia was ensnared in the rotten bowels of the Conqueror Worm. Panic pounded in her chest as she realized the severity of her situation. Lighting a mucus-caked match, she was greeted by cysts and white polyps, festering along the crimson depths, and looked down to behold the mangled remains of her companions. Her hand slipped against a yellowish web, and she gasped and recoiled in disgust—stuck to adhesive strands. In a surge of frightened strength, Sophia tore herself free and nearly stumbled backwards among the tumors. Though her match was extinguished by filth, living lights flickered ahead, as fireflies in the mire, illuminating clusters of bulbous silhouettes.

A chittering purr carried from behind. Sophia was not alone.

Sprinting as fast as she could, she ran aimlessly into the intestinal labyrinth, lured by an irregular heartbeat. Sophia outpaced whatever creeping thing might have caught her scent. Slipping upon a puddle of congealed slime, she fell prone in the gloom, when something skittered along her gloved hands. Sophia brushed the tiny chitinous things away, though she could not see them, but more skittered along her legs. In a fit of desperation, she reached for a flare and struck the match with a tinderbox—sputtering sparks almost swallowed by the humidity, but not before those pale isopods fled into hives of holes.

"Oh God...."

Huddling in a grotto of flesh, Sophia felt panic take hold. Heart palpitating and hands shaking, she felt something slip from her coat and roll down the throbbing floor—the syringe of crimson fluid. Grasping the instrument, she rallied her thoughts to Rufus and his ailing state. Without her, he would succumb to infection—or worse.

This was not the time to falter. She had to get out of here.

To administer the cure.

At that moment, as if in response to her fleeting resolve, something crept out of the hollow sphincter, snapping in ravenous hunger. Raising her flare, Sophia was greeted by the sight of unimaginable horror. Twin claws lunged as bludgeons from the nesting orifice, like the clubs of a translucent lobster, and a thousand spindly legs carried the bulk of a parasitic predator. Antennae twitched in the air, and its brittle armor, blotched with carbuncles and tubercles, was a cloudy window into black viscera and gave forth a stench. Revealing its loathsome girth in full, half of its face had been warped in the shape of a skull—its right eye blue and bloodshot, human in its paralysis, though its mandibles clicked and snipped with scissor-like precision. Perhaps it was once a simple beast, overtaken by corrupting will, and in that lay its malignancy, as a puppet of Matthias and a guardian of the Conqueror Worm.

Sophia ran. It gave chase.

Snarls and screams distorted by Matthias's will, the Millipede lunged with claws outstretched, slamming against walls of red flesh. Sophia reached for her dagger and sliced through thick webs of mucus, ignorant to the thing gaining on her. She slipped through the malformed tunnels—when the Millipede tore at her leg and cut into her arteries, grinding barbs deep into her calf. Shrieking in agony, she stabbed, desperate to pierce its shell, only for the guardian to drag her away, snapping its mandibles all the while, eager to rip into her supple flesh. Boots kicking against its clicking maw, she dug her knife deep into its black eye.

The Millipede uttered an all too human howl and, in a moment's folly, let its prey limp away to where she prayed it could not follow.

"You cannot escape us," called the baritone. "He's not coming to save you." Glancing behind to see if the Millipede followed, Sophia stumbled into a vast webbing of bile—perhaps residue—and found herself suspended in its drooping strands. "You will trouble me no more." As terror swept over Sophia, she swore Matthias's silhouette lingered in the farthest shadows, taunting her with a hallucinatory presence. "Rufus has accepted the gift. What? Did you really think that you could turn my own flesh and blood against me?" It gave a cruel laugh. "My dear, you cannot save him. Nor would he let you even if you could…."

Sophia felt the Millipede's hot breath upon her neck, as if savoring a morsel of fear. By all accounts, she should've surrendered then, accepting her fate, but in lieu of despair, embers of rage smoldered in her heart and gave way to flames of blind fury. Gripping the hilt of her dagger, she began to carve through her bonds—the shadow vanished in a wisp of foul vapor.

It was no longer a matter of saving him. It was a matter of vengeance.

When at last Sophia broke free, she scaled what she hoped was the gullet and saw a light ahead and far above. Her climb began to slip. The Millipede opened its mandibles wide, its toothy mill rolling like a meat grinder, and a tremendous force slammed shut upon her thighs, seconds tearing her legs from her pelvis as she clung to a ropy strand. Matthias's malice shone in the Millipede's remaining eye. Sophia felt her ligaments begin to tear, when—

"Let her go, you filth."

In a moment's shock, the Millipede seemed to obey. A cold, clammy hand grasped Sophia's wrist with inhuman strength, hoisting her to relative safety. She did not recognize the man looming above her, coattails aflutter like tattered banners against the beast's breath. The Millipede hissed and recoiled, pacing about the steep esophagus, fidgeting its claws. To Sophia's awe and horror, her savior, the man in black, bore no weapons. Though his face was hidden, his eyes shone with hate unrivaled, surpassing the beast's own.

Matthias was oddly silent.

Leaping into the abyss, the man in black tackled the Millipede with inhuman strength, wrestling as they fell together into darkness. Though wracked with fatigue and excoriating pain, Sophia heard the squeals of isopods and nameless things. Perched above the scene, she gasped as her cure clattered with them. She could only watch the desperate duel.

Pinned against the stomach wall, the stranger's throat was all but crushed by a great pincher. He struggled and wheezed when his knuckles split open into a fistful of bone claws. He impaled the creature through the maw and stabbed upward, piercing through its carapace and mouth—those mandibles clamped upon his forearm. Shaking its head like a rabid hound, the Millipede flung him across the chamber. It trembled and chittered, oozing a sickly blue substance from its wounds, before charging to finish off its prey.

The man in black leapt to his feet, but to Sophia's horror, he began to writhe and contort. His "waistcoat" was in truth a shroud of leathery flesh. The stranger's back contorted into scarlet tentacles, not dissimilar to the tongues of the Conqueror Worm.

As if goading the Millipede, the man in black paced about the stomach floor as if he were dancing with bulls, lost and leering. Then, with a cry no sane soul would summon, he struck the monstrosity's left claw, tearing it open with a crack of shell and white gore. The Millipede howled as if dismembered, but the stranger did not relent, stabbing its malformed face—again and again—until it swung with its rightmost limb, knocking him across the skull.

Whimpering in fury, the Millipede paced about the red organic arena, seething as an enraged toddler, and reared its segmented tail with a barbed stinger, like a scorpion imagined by a syphilitic madman. It stabbed the calloused floor in a tantrum, and the Conqueror Worm quivered as if tickled, narrowly missing its prey with each strike. The man in black rolled aside, dodging every swipe and stabbing step, until he slipped underneath the Millipede's soft belly and stabbed upward with a cry of mutual lunacy. The Millipede screamed and began to retreat.

"Back, back," the stranger yelled in triumph, as if ignorant to his own injuries.

The Millepede obeyed, creeping into a corridor of cancerous flesh. Whether to tend to its mortifying wounds or simply die, Sophia would never see the thousand-year fiend again.

Mustering will against pain, she slipped down to her savior's side.

"Who," she managed, "who are—?"

As the stranger knelt to retrieve the cure, he turned to face her with a broken smile.

Sophia felt many things then—anger, joy, and, most of all, dread.

"Rufus?" she managed.

"Yes," he said. "I'm...yes."

Wiping the blood from his sweat-soaked brow, Rufus moved past her, as if she were a mere mirage. Perhaps it was the throes of panic and battle, but Sophia couldn't help but feel resentment boil in her heart. The way Rufus twitched and clutched the culmination of her life's work—it was as if he truly were the stranger she'd previously imagined.

"Are you okay?" she asked.

"Never better," Rufus managed, pocketing the syringe.

"You were bedridden. I went to find that. To help ease...."

Rufus did not turn around. "I'm fine." Sophia did not know what to say or what to think—his face was grey, veins black, writhing about his neck, and his eyes were sallow with a deep sickness. "Anyway," he said at last, "I'm glad you're alive."

"Anyway?" Something in Sophia snapped—fear gave way to frothing rage, and her voice rose to a scream. "What do you mean, 'anyway?!' I was almost killed, Rufus. The only reason I went down here was to save you. Because," tears welled in her eyes, "you're changing. You're not yourself. I've seen what'll happen and...you couldn't care less."

Rufus stared at her in stunned silence. "No," he began, "I just—"

"Give me the cure," she demanded.

The heir reached into his pocket—and drew the syringe with a shaking hand. His eyes were damp with guilt and remorse, and yet, something held him back.

"Rufus," she repeated. "Give me the cure."

In a snap of fleeting sanity, he seemed to listen. The yellow tinge in the whites of his eyes began to fade. "Y-you're right," he stuttered, as if stifling a low torrent of pain. "I'm sorry."

Sophia held him tightly, wrapping her arms around his rigid frame, barely recognizing his touch in kind, as if he was but a corpse—cold and remote. As he shuddered, Rufus parted with care and began to climb the slick gullet of the Conqueror Worm.

"We have to go," he said.

Hand in hand, they scaled the innards, mockingly allowed to leave, though Sophia remembered little of the trek to Altstadt—its scenery lost in the gathering fog.

Neither of them slept easily that night.

CHAPTER SEVENTEEN

Rufus kept to the darkness beneath forlorn trees, stalking the muddy trail as a predator on a leash, and Sophia raised a dim torch against the pervading gloom. Few words were spoken on the long trek south, and the heir was lost in thought, muttering and hissing in debate.

The thing in his blood made its discomfort known.

You gave her the cure....

"She means well," Rufus's voice was scarcely above a whisper, "besides, it might not be a bad thing to have available. You never know—"

Given her way, she would kill me and castrate you of power....

Rufus paused and caught a dire scent in the air—smoke. Beyond the forest and the hills, torches blazed bright as the clamor of men drew near, punctuated by the odd bark and bay of a hunter's hound. Shadows moved near the low fieldstone walls of Altstadt. The people had not given up their pursuit of evil. Rufus crept about the trees, eyes gleaming with hunger and hate. To think these folk would take up arms against him, after everything he'd done for them. They deserved the monster they imagined. Soon, they would be the hunted.

You're learning quickly....

"I knew all along," Rufus said. "I just didn't want to admit it."

Clutching a thick black branch, the heir felt saliva trickle from his lower lip as he yearned to rip their sinew from bone. And yet, Rufus's better nature kept him fettered, or so he'd like to believe. In truth, it was Sophia who stayed his hand. Without her, he would've surely slaughtered them all without a moment's hesitation.

"Rufus?" she asked.

"Keep quiet," he said. "Patrols are still out."

"What did you do?"

"Nothing out of the ordinary," murmured a distant third.

From out of the shadows, Gottfried emerged and lifted his hood, raising a finger to his lips. "Pleasure to see you both in one piece. Although I wish for better circumstances."

"Gottfried," Rufus sighed with relief. "I don't suppose you can talk this rabble down?"

"Sadly, I'm not a miracle worker, but I do have a plan."

Rufus's eyes were fixed upon the nearing shades. "We can't just waltz back into Altstadt. They'll see us hanged, but," he turned to Sophia, "I don't want to hurt them."

"Want a medal for that?" she scoffed.

Gottfried raised a weathered hand. "Listen," he said, "I've prepared a coach to take us to Innsbruck. You'll be safer there."

"What about the investigation?" Rufus asked. "Every day, it gets stronger."

"Don't be a fool," Gottfried said. "You can't govern the estate in your current form. Nor should you try. Trust me, my lord. Take the coach. Consider it a holiday."

He is right about one thing. The villagers no longer trust you. And if they see you with Sophia, she will be in danger as well. If these are your priorities, think carefully….

Rufus shut his eyes. "Innsbruck it is."

"Wait," Sophia grasped his hand, "it doesn't have to be like this, Rufus. We have the serum. It'll take some time, sure, but," she paused, as if doubting her own research, "this isn't you. You know that. Please, give me more time."

"Time is something we have in short supply," Gottfried said. "He can't stay here."

"He's right," Rufus said. "Frankly, a change of scenery

wouldn't hurt my mental health." He laughed, bitterly. "Where's the coach?"

"Follow me."

Gottfried sped down a hunter's trail deep into the woods, careful not to trip on the stones peppering the narrow route. When they came to the coach by the Grünewald, the shouts of pursuers began to fade. Sitting across from Sophia, Rufus propped his coat's collar and huddled in the velvet seat, shuddering at the hunger gnawing in the back of his mind. Gottfried took to the driver's box and, with the crack of a riding crop, began the journey to Innsbruck.

Do not trust the woman. She will try to administer the cure. She's worked for Cronenberg in the past. You've seen her work. Malpractice is not above her....

"I know her better than you ever will," Rufus said.

Bold of you to assume I cannot feel what you feel. Recall everything you've ever known. Yes, her touch is alluring, and her charm is unrivaled in your eyes. And yet, you hold her as just that, an icon of lust to be put on a pedestal and worshipped....

"What do you know of love?" he muttered.

It is an illusion, a pall of glamour, cast over the desire to pass on one's seed....

Rufus couldn't bear to look Sophia in the eye. Stuttering and stupefied, he writhed in his seat, trying desperately to tune out the whispers of the worm.

Sophia grabbed him by the hand. "Are you alright?"

"Y-yes," Rufus lied, "I'm fine." He reached into his pocket and drew his pewter flask. Whiskey did not taste as he remembered, but it was enough to pacify the worm and his own doubts—for now. "How are you?" he asked, regaining a semblance of the self.

Sophia shot him a smirk of disbelief. "Oh, wonderful...."

"Listen, I'm sorry for the trouble I've caused," Rufus said, taking another sip of liquor. "And I appreciate your efforts to make things right, but it's not so simple."

"Isn't it?" Sophia sighed. "Sounds like you're making excuses."

Rufus did not respond. The coach's route led to a crossing, and Gottfried took the southwest road, where cattails and tall grasses rose from greasy black pools swarming with clouds of midges and croaking things. The country grew damper by the mile, blighted with fen and bog, its fogbound malaise pierced only by louse-infested woods and cairns.

"How far is it?" Rufus called.

"We'll be there within the hour," Gottfried replied from the driver's box. "I'll deposit us by the waterfront and we'll make our way to the Rathaus."

By this point, the stagecoach had already passed a sequence of toll gates, each shutting as soon as they had passed. "Seems awfully protected," Rufus said.

"Innsbruck is a queer place, my lord." Gottfried glanced over his shoulder. "The people there keep to their own and have little sense of hospitality. You'll find it a far cry from Altstadt."

"Charming," Rufus muttered.

"Proper trade hasn't come to the estate for many years. Our destination is no exception. However, folk claim to have means to 'look after their own.'"

Slowly, the sun rose over the brooding mountains, its golden rays piercing the mists, casting scant light upon the hinterlands. Then, as mud turned to sodden sand and pebbled shores, Rufus beheld the lakeside parish on the border of the estate.

"We're here," Gottfried sighed, slowing the coach to a halt.

Roofs and gables stark against shimmering water, the port encompassed the northern shore with boardwalks jutting far into Lake Bathory, supported by piles and algae-crusted piers, flanked by huts and lopsided shanties. Bits of ragged finery held the town together, from ornate rugs turned doormats to wooden architecture reminiscent of mercantile republics, alluding to a prosperous history at the crossing of three rivers. Little white crabs scuttled about the wharf, and the Rathaus, a waterlogged twin of Altstadt's own hall, loomed in the midst of an empty market where fishermen stared vacantly at the water, lures bobbing helplessly upon the heart of the lake. Though it should've been a breath of fresh air, the brackish water seemed fermented with all manner of ill life, perhaps a lair for worse than worms.

Lower your guard. It is safe here….

Rufus disembarked and took Sophia hesitantly by the hand, well aware of his shaky touch. Together, they crossed the long bridge leading to the market, passing by shuttered windows and locked doors—not even the cock's crow could stir the fisherfolk.

"Why are we here?" asked the heir. "Simply to lie low?"

"Yes, but there's more," Gottfried said. "There is someone who may help us. I trust you remember the burgomeister who shares the parish's name?"

The oysters were delicious….

"Yes, the oysters were delicious," Rufus echoed in agreement, eying the burly dockers as they hauled barrels of daily catches. "Especially raw."

Gottfried and Sophia exchanged an uncertain glance as Rufus took the lead, all but ignorant to their concern. Down the rickety lane, he passed the locals, noticing their moist complexions, damp wool clothing, and gumboots. There was a sluggishness in their affairs, as if lost in a dreamy haze, leaving trails of slime with every step. None of them said a word or paid the travelers any heed, as if possessed by apathy as stagnant as the cradling waters.

When at last they came to the Rathaus, Rufus knocked on the door and was greeted by a portly manservant with a high collar, eyes bulging like a toad's.

"Yes?" he croaked.

"I am Rufus Grünewald." The heir went about the usual niceties as was customary in these parts. "There has been civil unrest in the neighboring hamlets, and I, regrettably, must seek refuge with my vassal and your master, Lord Innsbruck."

"No can do, I'm afraid."

Rufus's stomach began to sink. "What do you mean?"

"He's not present at the moment. You'll have to see the Gilman House."

"The local inn, I imagine?"

The manservant nodded and pointed a bloated finger down the way. "Just across the water. Keep to the wharf on the right and pass the crab shacks. You'll find it in no time."

Before Rufus could inquire further or give thanks, the door had shut.

"Insular lot, aren't they?" he muttered.

"Few visit the waterfront these days," Gottfried said. "Ever since the late unpleasantries and the war." He laid a hand against the heir's back. "Come, my lord. If we're lucky, we'll catch Innsbruck in a sensible mood. I think you'll find him quite the character."

"More so than Westerham?"

Gottfried shrugged. "A different flavor of peerage."

Far from at ease, Rufus followed the manservant's instructions to the inn. The fisherfolk had begun to stir and realize the strangers in their midst. Wide-eyed and slow-witted, they formed a crowd around the trio, though they showed no sign of aggression, like curious children who'd stumbled upon a playground oddity. The Gilman House was a complex of two taverns linked by a dilapidated skyway—little more than a bridge over the southern docks. Only the click of clay mugs breached the stillness within. The hearth was dead. In its stead, a fishbone chandelier drooped low from the ceiling, caked in stalagmites of wax, rimmed with candles, and a collection of pikes and sturgeons lined the walls as testaments to the bounties of the lakebed. Huddled about a table, a troupe of off-duty dockhands played liar's dice in the corner. The tavern reeked of booze and brine, and a staircase led up to dismal lodgings.

Of this place I know little, but imagine you'll find a way to dull your wits....

Gottfried ordered a round of grog from the low-lipped barkeep who recited his order in a hollow tone. Rufus took a moment to soak in his surroundings, nearly slipping on slick floorboards, and took a seat at a table by the window, staring at the water. A snore punctuated the dimness. Rufus turned to spy Lord Innsbruck, slouched in the corner, much as he remembered the burgomeister—a willowy man in marine colors. His face was hidden by a cavalier hat, and his feet were propped on a barstool, displaying his lanky height. While the clatter of dice stirred him briefly, it was not until Rufus had joined him that Innsbruck woke.

"Oh," he yawned, "you're...."

After a moment's pleasantries, the rest of Rufus's company had joined the burgomeister, and the severity of the situation was made clear.

"My lord," Innsbruck said, "this is all news to me. And grievous news at that."

"Maybe if you bothered to leave your hamlet, you'd have caught on sooner," Sophia muttered into her grog. "Listen, we're running out of options. And time."

"Options for what?" Innsbruck asked, wearily. "The Conqueror Worm has long slept beneath the estate. It is no surprise that it tosses and turns, now and again."

"What makes you so certain?" Rufus asked.

Innsbruck's smile only widened. "First, I must ask, Baron Grünewald. What do you want of me? I understand that you seek asylum, which I can provide, but surely there must be more."

"I," Rufus nodded, "would like access to your archives. If what you say is true, or if I understand what you're implying, you have something I lack. Protection. Of a sort."

Innsbruck lifted his own greasy cup to his lips. "Your noble instincts serve you well," he said. "I will not lie to you, Rufus. Our ways are the old ways and, since our needs are met, we have no need of ambition." He nodded at Sophia and Gottfried, in a lazy bow of thanks. "Altstadt will need you now more than ever. We will see to Rufus's protection."

"Do you have an apothecary?" Sophia asked. "I—"

Innsbruck raised a damp hand. "I will not supply you with means to 'cure' Baron Grünewald. Matthias once told the peerage much of your work. And aspirations."

"Excuse me?" she snapped.

Gottfried stood, sharply, though clearly more than a tad disturbed. "Thank you for your time, Lord Innsbruck." He turned to the heir. "Take care, my lord."

"We're going to just up and leave?" Sophia spoke with thinly veiled disgust. "He's not going to get any better." She turned to the burgomeister. "I don't know what you're plotting—"

"Oh, but I do." Innsbruck was unmoved. "Do us both a favor and take your efforts elsewhere. I'll have no part in them. Such as they are."

A moment's silence passed until, at last, Sophia began to plead.

"This is what you want, Rufus?"

He wanted to feel many things then—misery, anger, and empathy most of all. He hoped they were numbed by the thing in his blood, yet knew the truth.

Rufus looked away, eyes tired and heavy. "I'm sorry," he lied.

With a shuddering sigh, Sophia mustered the will to speak. "I was wrong, Rufus," her words dripped with venom. "You're just like him."

Before the heir could so much as react, Sophia had already departed down the boardwalk—alone in her grief and heartbreak. The heir raised a soft hand, moments from giving chase in a half-hearted attempt to mend the bridge, yet remained seated.

"I'll talk to her," Gottfried offered.

"No," Rufus said. "She meant it. And she's right."

Gottfried stared in shock. "My lord?"

"This isn't the thing in my blood," Rufus told himself, left with a hollow satisfaction that they'd parted ways, a serpentine realization that she'd trouble him no more. If they truly were to defeat the Conqueror Worm, then Rufus would gaze into the abyss as long as he needed to. He did not fear the dark—not anymore. "She's absolutely right."

Innsbruck yawned and staggered to his feet. "To the archives, then?"

"We have work to do," Rufus said, coldly.

CHAPTER EIGHTEEN

In the confines of Innsbruck's town hall, Rufus kept to comfortable study and pored over oddly preserved texts. Though the pages were brittle, he examined the illustrations along the margins as much as the written word. Such pictures were a bestiary of piscine things, ranging from trout and pike to no shortage of snails—the latter caught the heir's interest, especially in the notable absence of nine-eyed eels. Nursing a cup of lukewarm grog, Rufus took frequent breaks to sate his appetites for citrus and oysters. The thing in his blood purred with approval, and he savored every slippery morsel. Though mute attendants saw to his creature comforts, Gottfried's absence was noted. Everything about the office seemed so familiar yet off-kilter, as though it were a mockery of the hamlet he'd invested so much effort into preserving.

Then there was Sophia.

Rufus shut the tome with a sigh. He paced about the upper halls, enduring an odd silence inside his mind. The thing in his blood had been placated with shellfish, and the heir was granted the privilege to be himself again. Slouched over the railing, he took a moment to gaze out the open window upon Lake Bathory and the black forest beyond. The days were growing darker, and yet, he felt little concern for the future. Perhaps it was the doldrums of Innsbruck, but he felt a nagging void since his arrival in the fishing hamlet—since Sophia's departure.

As the thing snored inside his skull, Rufus drew a pen and paper and began to scribble with all the authenticity he could muster, to transcribe what little he felt.

What is important to me? Truly, the comfort of my line is a thin barrier against the horror of its responsibility. Sophia. I know you cannot forgive me, but know I did not choose this path any more than I chose Matthias as a forebear. There comes a time when one must make amends with their nature – that evil exists in all of us. And while you may interpret my acceptance as weakness, know that it is with great humility that I accept the long shadow of our past. This is as it should be.

He dipped the quill in the well and continued his stream of consciousness.

Responsibility is not something to be cured. This thing, this creature inside me, is my cross to bear. And with that truth, I must make sacrifices. If what you said is true, then I am filled with a great sadness, but I understand why you feel and believe the way you do. It is time I faced evil within and without. To not become my grandfather, as you so rightly fear, but to surpass him.

All my love,

Rufus

With that, he turned to the hearth, folded the letter neatly – and cast it into the flames. He had made his choice. Sophia had made hers. It was a pity it came to this, but in this power lay a martyr's gift – the means to challenge the Conqueror Worm, whatever the cost.

"My lord?" Innsbruck repeated from the study's threshold.

"Oh," Rufus hadn't noticed the burgomeister, lost in thought, "yes, I'm quite alright."

"You've been at work for hours," Innsbruck stepped into the office, deaf to his assurance, "and there is something I wish to show you. Now, if you please."

Rufus cocked his head with quizzical hesitation. "What is

it?"

At that moment, a lonesome bell rang across wharf and harbor, rhythmic in its toll—a call to prayer. Rufus sighed, barely fettering his annoyance. He had no time to humor the local clergy, yet there was something odd in the way the bell rang, deeper than the belfry of the abbey. Then came the horns—pipes of shipwood and bone—blown in rising sequence.

The noise did not come from Innsbruck.

"What is it?" Rufus asked again.

"Come," Innsbruck beckoned, as if luring him like an angler. "Books can only enlighten so much. You must partake in what we have to offer. Think of it as a custom."

Though filled with morbid distrust, Rufus conceded with a nod. At the edge of the Rathaus, a dinghy was waiting for the baron and the burgomeister, helmed by a wool-capped bosun. "Salutations," he said, gruffly. "Better get a move on for mass."

"Mass?" Rufus wondered aloud.

"Just as a worm lures the fish," Innsbruck said, as if reciting a heathen gospel, staring at the billowing fog, "so too does a truth lure the man."

What did I miss…?

"Quite a bit," Rufus muttered.

Innsbruck laughed, hardly deterred by the heir's strange habits. If anything, he found it enduring, or worse, a sign of providence. Slowly, they boarded the skiff and the rowers began to row, guided by the lantern's light, deep into the fog. After an indiscernible amount of time, Rufus disembarked on the far side of the lake. The mist thickened as deeply as the water, obscuring the world save a few feet in any given direction. Rufus groped about the pier and made out stark silhouettes in the gloaming—incredible monoliths looming throughout the woods, reminiscent of sarsen stones from his visions of witches. This was a sacred place.

They were not alone.

Following a line of fisherfolk waving lamps and censors, Rufus took to the well-trodden trail. Eventually, they came to a cave deep in the karst-cracked hills at the foot of the massifs. Hewn as a post-and-lintel façade, the entrance was engraved with cuneiform scripture that Rufus could read as if it were the common tongue.

SEESCHRINE

Cerulean priests pushed open the damp stone doors and bid the congregation to follow in a single file. Rufus caressed the walls with care, eying the clergy in nine-eyed masks. He did not fear them. Step by step, he descended into the temple, down the spiraling stairs of an initiation well lined with classical mosaics. And in the depths, among baptismal pools and idols of lamprey-drakes, something stirred. Rufus's breathing was shallow and weird, as black smoke rose from sticks of rich incense, distorting the shadows along the cave wall. Amidst the snaps of eerie life, the heir came to the altar and gazed upon the Whelk of Innsbruck.

She was many things, yet human was hardly among them.

Lounging on slime-slick cushions, she rested somewhere between a gelatinous woman and a gastropod in blue, bloated in her majesty, adorned with gold and silver, tribute for the tide and tithe. Her shell was a glorious conch, an icon of truth, and her eyes, resting atop twin stalks, were white and blinded by prophecy. Her lips curled into an inscrutable expression, and she raised a hookah to her maw—rasping, puffing forth rings of hallucinogenic smoke.

Rufus was compelled to bow before the Whelk.

"Who seeks my counsel?" Her voice was a song. "You," she raised a jellied paw in peace, "you carry the blessing of the Conqueror Worm and—have been touched by the sisterhood."

He did not understand, nor did she seemingly expect him to. "Rise, Rufus Grünewald."

Rufus was compelled to obey.

In the light of delusion, he spied larva and serpentine strands writhing beneath her girth—perhaps she was the womb of the worms. Regardless, the voice inside his head was silent, and the thing he carried still in reverence. There were many things he did not understand.

"Your kin?" he asked.

"The Ladies of the Moon," she said, "and their chosen."

Such bewitchment faded as soon as it came. Rufus gritted his teeth and looked away, shoving his hands deep in his pockets. "Ah," he managed, "yes."

"Why do you feel such shame—?"

"I've made my decision regarding Sophia," he hissed. "I know what you are. What this is." He gestured widely about the Cult of the Conqueror Worm as they murmured in protest. "Make no mistake. I choose my own path, even with this…thing inside me."

"You are as bold as they say," the Whelk chuckled. "Why have you come? Surely not to sightsee and bask in our magnificence."

"I," Rufus began, "seek the means to protect the estate, to break this godforsaken cycle." He felt the thing purr alongside his own conviction. "What needs to be done?"

The Whelk coiled her sluggish tail around the pillows. "You seek the means to defy your predecessor? To atone for the sins of the father? Sins you did not commit?"

Words of defiance were caught in Rufus's throat.

"Your spirit is strong," she said, "but the Conqueror Worm is not to be challenged so simply as a dragon. We are something far more powerful. In time, you will understand."

"Matthias already has."

The Whelk smiled, knowingly. "Perhaps we've underestimated you. It is true that our champion has a black heart, and you have the potential to defy that lineage." She nodded in kind. "And with the 'thing in your blood,' as you put it, this deed may not be impossible."

"Really?" Rufus gasped, hope in his heart.

"If you are to know the truth," the Whelk lifted her skirt of flesh, revealing a crystalline dish of thick, tarrish fluid, "drink from my ichor. Embrace whatever may come."

Go on. Everything has led to this point….

The next thing he knew, Rufus stared at his own reflection in the black substance. Gagging at the salty stench, he lifted the dish to his lips and took a painful drink—only to find it flavorless and numbing, a faint drip at the back of his throat.

"I don't feel much—"

At that moment, the world as he knew it melted away like candlewax against the warming flow of time. Rufus fell into himself in a spiraling descent far exceeding any reason or sense. Plummeting into cosmic depths, he felt his flesh and form disintegrate until he was but a panicked haze of thoughts, dreams, and fantasies—bones rattled into oblivion.

The estate seemed a mote of dust on the annals of the world, and the world was deeper and more terrible than any would dare to fathom. Rufus had breached the Sea of Souls, witnessing the vastness of dawning epochs, diving ever into these impossible depths. From the Third Age, he descended to the distant time when the world was young. In a year he did not know, millennia upon millennia before the foundation of the first settlement and the settling of the fertile crescent, the world was one land in the primordial sea. Fecund and ripe, man did not know a garden of earthly delights, rather, a veldt of impossible violence. Rufus saw through the eyes of a terror bird, soaring over the vastness of this land of beasts, and swept upon a dying troglodyte, ripping out his lungs and eating his heart.

He was all too aware of the crimson star in twilight, inching ever closer to the earth, and knew only dread. Then came the Shattering—and with it, silence.

Rufus saw nothing as the world was engulfed in the First Darkness, feeling the chill of endless winter swallow his soul, hearing a constant gnawing from within the Northern Crater, at the Roof of the World, spreading like a cancer. Something had burrowed deep into the untouched ice, spreading its seed throughout land, sea, and sky, inspiring the fear of the world's end.

Death was its daughter, and the samsara of messiahs were its sons.

At the End of the First Age came the curse of sentience. Such inspiration birthed archetypes drawn in blood and soil on the cave wall. In a way, the Calamity From the Stars was responsible for civilization as Rufus knew it. Seasons changed and tyrants died, and men would endure each and every "end time," be it at the hands of Pestilence, Famine, or War, so sure of themselves yet addled by constant anxieties, all rooted in that original sin that inspired the fear of death—no, the unknown. Such is what fed the worms of the earth. Propagating in the deep places of the world, these nameless things were of one mind, one will—a mockery of the Symphonia Mundi, the Music of the Spheres, and what it evoked through the eternal fear.

Beneath the glamour of geists and daemons, it lurked as the world's parasite. Just as the ones that God, the Grand Conductor, had scattered as seeds of salvation throughout the fields of time, so too did the Conqueror Worm. Fickle as they were, the eels cared not what host they took, content to pervert and fornicate until the world's soul was a plaything ensnared in webs of mucus and bilesome viscera. Such was the duel of the fates—Heaven and Hell sharing the godhead of a coin, and the

Conqueror Worm devouring its own tail.

Matthias was not important. He never was. Nor was Rufus. They both were links in the great chain—aware of these shackles of manipulation. In that moment of insane realization, the Conqueror Worm would offer one of these historic hosts freedom from the mortal coil, freedom from the prison of eternal recurrence—the price was merely union with its will.

Come the future yet unwritten, the Conqueror Worm would hatch from the egg of the world, that fragile shell of earth and rock, and spread its loathsome seed. With a whimper, man would be whittled and hunted until the flame of life was snuffed out—forever. And yet, at the bottom of the unfathomable abyss, a piece of Rufus, an ember of hope, defied his purpose as dictated by ancestral sin. Try as the worm might to seduce the heir with cosmic truths, Rufus refused—he was not a slave to the thing in his blood, nor to the schemes of his forebears. In lieu of broken will, warmth flowed through his flesh and form. It wasn't Sophia.

Beyond the horrors of the void, Rufus beheld a cosmic silhouette in a cruciform pose, arms wide, holding back the Conqueror Worm from ensnaring his soul. It was the Great Seal, the Keeper and the Gate, and the Far Messiah—the last hope in a world of perdition.

"Let go," he said. "Let go. Let go of everything."

Rufus understood—and obeyed. Offering himself in prostration, perhaps the heir was worthy to be chosen. For the first time in eons, the Conqueror Worm was intrigued.

"I will run," he uttered, "no longer."

CHAPTER NINETEEN

The western sky grew dark, casting a pall of crimson misery over the battlements of Schloss Fleischburg—its spires clawing at the moon and sun. The hollow bastion loomed over Altstadt and its environs, seemingly moments from cracking under the weight of the heavens. Once again, the stars were right and the hamlet sat in the shade of cosmic unrest, though none but the lunatics in the Narrenturm knew it, howling and shaking in their cages.

Moment by moment, the Eclipse gathered strength.

Sophia was ignorant to these astrological portents. Though the opportunistic and licentious sought to purchase her affections, she kept to the red room of the Hofbräu, locked away and wallowing in misery. Her cure, little more than a vial of scarlet bile and a syringe, rested upon the desk, gathering dust. Evil ran deep in House Grünewald, and Rufus was no exception. He had forsaken his humanity for the sake of monstrous power. The naïve youth who once courted her was dead. Only the Conqueror Worm remained.

Hands over the hearth, Sophia scarcely felt the warmth against her fingers—numbed by lamentations. There was a knock on the door. With a sigh, she approached the threshold, words of rebuke already welling in her throat, when she was greeted by Gottfried and Mincemeat by his side. The purring ball of fur and fat brushed against her leg, as if sharing her sympathies. The burgomeister stepped inside of his own accord and offered a snifter to share.

"Any word?" Sophia asked.

"None," Gottfried said. "It's as if he simply vanished. The last mercenaries left this morning. I can't say I blame them.

Standing idle without pay."

Sophia was hardly surprised yet said nothing.

"I understand what you must be feeling," the burgomeister continued, "I didn't take Rufus to be so...callous at heart." He took a swig of dark liquor. "It pains me too."

"I should've known better," Sophia said. "I'm too old to make these kinds of mistakes."

Gottfried sighed, deeply. "We both saw something that made us want to believe in him. Perhaps the Rufus we thought was our friend never truly existed, and that decision betrayed us. Perhaps...we have only ourselves to blame."

Sophia began to weep. "I don't see how he can live like this." She grasped the syringe, knuckles white with rage. To think her life's work mattered so little in the end. "I don't know how to make things right, but I can't stand by and do nothing."

Mincemeat leapt atop the desk and cocked her head, curiously, sniffing the air—when Sophia too caught the whiff of woodsmoke. Gottfried turned to the window, eyes wide with horror. A livid glow spread from the Grünewald, and the sound of screams and crackling trees drew nearer by the second, as crows scattered and cawed in sudden alarm over the hamlet.

"What is it?" Sophia asked, dread in her heart.

"The weald," Gottfried managed, "is burning."

"That's not possible, the Ladies would never let...." As her words trailed into silence, Sophia remembered the one who sought to oppose heresy, whatever form it took, real or imagined. Sure enough, the rippling silhouettes of cavalry emerged from the forests of arson, with a familiar figure at the vanguard. "Wilhelm," she gasped.

Sure enough, the Witchfinder General dismounted in the town square, surrounded by a brigade of men-at-arms—the militias of Waldesrand and Westerham under his command. By his side rolled the Grand Panzer, an ironclad mortar, armored with shields and embossed steel, capable of firing shots not sixteen pounds of blackest iron. Between his artillery and entourage, Wilhelm was unopposed as the people shut their doors and windows in terror.

Before Sophia could so much as speak, Gottfried marched down the stairs and thrust open the tavern doors, footfalls heavy with rage.

"What is the meaning of this?" he shouted.

Wilhelm, a shadow against the rising flames, glanced over his shoulder to face the defiant voice. He cracked a smirk, as if amused by Gottfried's fuming indignation.

"Ah," said the witch-hunter, "glad to see you again, burgomeister."

"Watch your tone with me, Wilhelm." Gottfried pointed a frail finger at his chestplate. "You may be the Witchfinder General, but I am still the practicing lord of this estate."

"As if I could forget," Wilhelm said, voice oozing with sarcasm. "Word spreads swiftly in these parts. I received word that your master has succumbed to dark forces."

Color drained from Gottfried's face.

"Where is he?" the witch-hunter demanded.

Gottfried did not reply, lip aquiver.

"Very well," Wilhelm sighed, as if masking his rage with disappointment. "Search the hamlet," he ordered. "Find the Baron Grünewald."

Helpless and held at gunpoint, Gottfried watched as doors were shattered and townsfolk were dragged from their homes. The cacophony of breaking furniture and torn floorboards filled the hot, dry air. Jim Metzger, deputy to the Witchfinder General, oversaw the merciless intrusions as women were dragged by the hair and tossed to the cobblestones.

"I am willing to negotiate," Wilhelm spoke to the burgomeister. "Westerham's treasury was overflowing with all manner of ill-gotten profit. I am willing to part with ten percent for you and the hamlet, should you surrender Rufus's location."

Gottfried kept silent.

"Very well," Wilhelm strode to the captives, "what of you, good people?" He offered a fistful of silver. "A handsome reward awaits whoever speaks out."

Though Sophia held her breath, she knew these folk were ignorant as to Rufus's whereabouts. They jabbered and gibbered, desperately making excuses and weaving yarns as to why Rufus had left—how he fed on the blood of the innocent and prowled the graveyard at night. Wilhelm feigned understanding, and yet, his intuition was sharper than any sword.

"I see," he said. "Lock them up."

Despite their pleas, the people of Altstadt were forced to the abbey, one household at a time. Wilhelm was visibly vexed and whispered something to his lieutenant—a gang of men-at-arms was dispatched to the lumber mill. Gottfried alone opposed the witch-hunter.

Stakes were raised amidst bundles of dry kindling.

"Make no mistake," Wilhelm said, coldly. "If you have nothing to hide, you have nothing to fear." He glanced through the window of the Hofbräuhaus. "Come to think of it," he mused. "Where is Rufus's consort? She's been suspiciously absent...."

Sophia crouched beneath the windowsill, heart pounding, and scanned the tavern for bottles to break or chairs to barricade the door—not that any of it would save her should Wilhelm put the tavern to the torch. Desperate to defend herself, she crept to the bar and grabbed a knife from behind the counter. Heavy footsteps breached the silence as Wilhelm's men searched the tables and taproom. Holding her breath, she held the knife to her breast and waited for the muttering soldiers to return and report back.

"Still nothing, sir."

"Dammit," Wilhelm snarled. "You try my patience." Sophia heard a shift in the flame, imagining the witch-hunter raising a torch to Gottfried's face. "Where is he?"

No response.

"Very well," Wilhelm fettered his voice. "Burn it."

"Sir?" someone objected.

"The hamlet must be purged."

"Are you mad?" Gottfried spoke at last.

"No," Wilhelm said, "but that would alleviate my burden."

"Surely you don't expect me to—"

"I don't expect anything," Wilhelm admitted, "but it is my duty to deliver the wicked and punish the heretic. This is the only way." He spoke with cold conviction once reserved for the justly accused. "Unless, that is, you concede and cooperate."

Sophia's stomach sank with dread as she deliberated. The mob would almost certainly find her, assuming she wouldn't burn with the liquor-soaked inn. Even if she managed to escape, where would she go? Wilhelm's men would undoubtedly find her, for as the hounds barked and bayed, time was short. She wouldn't surrender Rufus; however, the least she could do was appeal to Wilhelm's reason and see the innocents spared from the flame.

"Wait!" she shouted.

To Gottfried's horror, Sophia had already emerged from the inn.

"Ah," Wilhelm said, "a pleasure to see you again, Lady Grünewald."

"No," mouthed the burgomeister.

"I won't let you do this," she said. "There's got to be another way."

"You're absolutely right, witch—"

"Witch?" Sophia repeated, the implications of the accusation slowly dawning on her. "Oh no," she managed, "no, it's not like that."

"You have consorted with the Baron Grünewald and shared his bed," Wilhelm recited. "The people speak of you as a cunning woman who dabbles in sorcery. Moreover," he raised a familiar medallion, dangling on a chain, "you have ensnared Rufus with this charm." He stalked to her side. "You are an accomplice to generations of evil." He gave the order. "Begin."

Without trial or torture, Wilhelm showed his mercy in a fashion.

As the roaring fire began to spread to the hamlet's edge, the witch-hunter had the Grand Panzer aimed at the Abbey of Saint Hildegarde—holding the populace hostage. Main Street was lined with unlit pyres as the men-at-arms shifted nervously in their boots, as uncertain of their role. Sophia was first and foremost among those to be sentenced to the flame.

Gottfried was forced to Wilhelm's side to oversee the mass execution.

"Why are you doing this?" the burgomeister asked.

"It is simple," Wilhelm said. "I have done my best to tolerate your local ways, but the nature of the Conqueror Worm is insidious. Until your hamlet smolders, it will continue to fester unchecked, a blight upon the land. I must cleanse Altstadt in its eternity. For the entire populace has served under Matthias and Rufus alike. And you are no exception."

"You speak of a massacre."

"And should I leave it be? Evil will spread like a plague."

Wilhelm raised his torch and approached Sophia with solemn intent. His eyes reflected neither sadism nor regret, rather, a singular duty to do what he judged to be right. To him, they were vermin to be exterminated, regardless of their sobbing pleas.

"The time has come," he said. "You stand upon the brink of the abyss. And yet, despite your mortal sin, it is not too late.

I take no…pleasure in your sentence, and there is greater evil at work. Tell me where Rufus is and I will spare you—and the hamlet."

Flames licked the air, inching ever closer to her face.

Sophia felt many things then—fear, regret, and shame among them. The injustice of it all coursed through her mind. Shaking and bound to the stake, she tried to shift away from the torch, dried sticks, and thatchery scratching her naked legs.

"Think carefully."

In her heart of hearts, Sophia knew Rufus would not do the same for her—perhaps he never would've. In the shadow of the Eclipse, she raised her gaze to the heavens, for even the sun had forsaken the Grünewald Estate, swallowed by the moon, when a familiar caw reached her ears. Wilhelm paid the omen no heed. In the wake of murder, crows began to gather upon the roofs and gables, as if spectating whatever was to come. Even now, the Ladies of the Moon were watching. In that alone, Sophia found her strength. She spat in Wilhelm's face.

His eyes burned with unholy wrath.

He dropped the torch into her pyre, igniting its kindling instantly—howls erupted from the burning woods. In response to a madman's justice, the crows began to swoop upon the militia, squawking and tearing eyes from their sockets. Wilhelm drew his sword and turned to face the Grünewald. Barks of hounds faded to whimpers, as nags and dogs of war sprinted in terror—fleeing into the fields. The fire rose. Sophia coughed as smoke filled her lungs, the sight of heathen intervention rippling through waves of sweltering heat. Drifting in and out of consciousness, the voices of the Ladies reverberated in her ears.

"Fear not, child," they spoke in unison.

Wind swept through the forest, casting embers and cinders into the hamlet—a swirling gust of fate caused the flames encroaching upon Sophia to part like broth churned by a ladle. Though bound and surrounded by screams and panic, she glowered at Wilhelm, knowing that the Ladies of the Moon would exact their vengeance. Helpless to do anything at all, Wilhelm watched the fire of his own making spread from cottage to cottage. Within moments, Altstadt was engulfed in a holocaust of mothers' perdition, sealing the men-at-arms in a massacre. Then came thunderous hoofbeats, gaining speed, nearing from the sea of trees.

"Come back, you cowards," Wilhelm roared at his routing men.

A stampede of deer and elk, bears and wolves, and all manner of woodland beasts breached the forest's edge, howling in a cacophony of roars and desperate shrieks, trampling any and all in their path—peasant or soldier—for nature gave no quarter, leaving the mangled dead in her wake. Then it dawned on Sophia, the beasts were not merely under the Ladies' thrall—they were running from something. When the herd had passed, nothing but silence remained.

Wilhelm's ranks were reduced to Metzger and scarcely a dozen men, most of whom were too stupefied with fear to move. "Steady," the witch-hunter told himself, "steady…."

The Ladies of the Moon seemed to cackle with the crackle of blackening wood. Sophia did not expect them to appear in full. They had already manifested their will.

Something else stirred in the weald.

"We can't face this," uttered a soldier

"What can men do against such—?"

"Silence!" Wilhelm's voice began to crack. "Stand fast. Do not relent." He raised a hand. "Metzger," he ordered. "Investigate the perimeter. Report back as soon as you can."

"Why don't you do it yourself?" snarled a third.

With a roll of his eyes, Wilhelm raised a pistol and shot into the air. The deafening bang of black powder was enough to quell his men—for a moment.

"I'll go," Metzger conceded with a sigh, heaving his saw-toothed cleaver over his shoulder. "It can't be anything worse than we've already seen. No one will follow."

The deputy marched into the weald.

Wilhelm nodded in morbid respect, as if he knew Metzger would not return—a sacrifice he was willing to make. As Sophia struggled in her bonds, desperate to escape, Gottfried emerged from the smoldering debris. Raising a finger to his lips, he began to undo the knots, glancing over his shoulder repeatedly to make certain the witch-hunter was occupied.

A bone-chilling scream erupted from the forest.

"Metzger!" Wilhelm cried.

To the company's horror, a severed head was flung out of the woods, only to bounce across the cobblestones like a child's ball, rolling to the witch-hunter's feet.

"What the hell are you?" he roared.

Wicked laughter echoed from nowhere and everywhere alike. Clusters of crimson eyes gleamed from the burning weald and faded into nothingness. A silhouette emerged, one that Sophia recognized at once—or so she thought. Perhaps the fumes were getting to her; however, the figure stepped through the flames, possessed by a force beyond comprehension, carrying with it malice that she had never felt before. It leapt out of the forest on all fours, wreathed in smoke, contorting into formless flesh. A mass of wan and scarlet limbs, weeping eyes and shrieking mouths of men and worms, it was an unspeakable blasphemy of biology, a perversion of the natural order. Slicing through the soldiers with barbed and bladed tentacles, dismembering them without remorse or hesitation, it sent limbless torsos soaring in a rain of gore, towering over Wilhelm on what could only be described as its hind legs.

"R-ready the Grand Panzer," he yelled.

The mortar team rallied and took aim at the abomination. With the strike of a match, the Grand Panzer erupted with a thunderous boom, reeling back as a black iron shot barreled from its wide bore. The cannonball collided with the contorting mass of sinew and bone—perhaps breaking four or five ribs. It shrieked towards the bloodstained heavens, rupturing the ears of those nearest and shattering panes of glass in a barrage of shards.

Wilhelm clutched the sides of his skull. "W-what the—?"

Roiling as a red tide, the abomination swatted the Grand Panzer aside, dismantling its wheels with a single strike. The witch-hunter dropped his pistol in shock.

To everyone's surprise, the abomination simply strode to Main Street, passing by the burning houses without regard for the hysterical populace, as if aware of its own grotesqueness. When Gottfried had undone Sophia's bonds and helped her from the dying bonfire, it halted before them, eyes seemingly fixed upon her. With a guttural purr, the abomination stared through her, piercing the very membrane of her soul—an apology.

With a gasp, Sophia began to understand. "Rufus?"

He kept walking without regard for her presence, crawling about the ruins of Altstadt, mewling in pitiable sorrow. By the time she realized where Rufus was going, it was too late. He had already vanished into the wooded trail to Schloss Fleischburg.

"He's trapped," she choked. "We have to save him!"

"What are you—?" Gottfried began.

Barging into the Hofbräu, she scaled the smoldering staircase and retrieved the cure, hot in her hands. Hoofbeats gained speed as Sophia glanced out the window. Wilhelm pursued his monstrous quarry into the unknown. The heavens seemed to bleed—scarlet rain began to douse the flames. When she returned to the scorched square, Gottfried approached her with Mincemeat in his arms, shaken by what he had witnessed. Survivors wept for the destruction of their homes and livelihoods.

In the wake of slaughter, only sorrow remained.

"So much death," Sophia choked, "I can't believe this."

When the flames began to wane, most had been burned amidst the carnage, reduced to blackened bones tied to stakes, staring heavenward. The smell of smoke and molten fat was nigh unbearable. The wrought-iron doors to the abbey had been unbarred, and the sobbing few began to salvage what remained, tossing their loved ones into mass graves that had yet to be dug.

"I never thought I'd witness such a thing," Gottfried said.

"We don't have time, though," Sophia said, "I saw where it went." She all but pleaded. "Gottfried, come with me. We need to stop him from whatever he's doing."

"What would you have me do?" Gottfried masked his despair with a maddened laugh. "Slay my own master? As if I ever could. And what of the witch-hunter? Do you think I could lift a finger against him? I couldn't do anything then. And I certainly can't do anything now." He raised his voice. "Get the wounded to the Narrenturm." He addressed the abbot. "Be sure to behead the dead, so they can't be…reanimated. Consecrate the graves, so that we may mourn in peace." He lowered his head, holding back tears of his own. "Don't be too hard on yourself, Sophia. You had nothing to do with this. Do what you must."

For the first time, Sophia felt a glint of genuine respect for the burgomeister. "I'll be back as soon as I can," she said. "If I'm back at all."

Gottfried couldn't bear to look at her. "I don't expect you to return."

"I plan not to."

Sophia took the Old Road, following Rufus's slithering trail through the brittle hinterlands, ever up the cliffside, in the shadow of Schloss Fleischburg—when she noticed the serpentine tracks give way to prints of bare feet, as if there was a glimmer of humanity in Rufus yet. Or perhaps it was the Conqueror Worm twisting into his form. There was something left. She'd seen it. There had to be. Regardless, the Eclipse had nearly reached its zenith.

The final hour was upon them all.

CHAPTER TWENTY

Sophia did not pay any heed to the scenery she once knew—bathed in monstrous twilight. She kept to the shadows along the trail until even its battlements seemed to wane to the wake of the Eclipse. As always, the front gates were left ajar, as if bidding her an unhappy welcome to its halls and whatever awaited those who dared trespass—it mattered not. She sprinted past the keep's threshold and into the chapel, knowing well its cellars and catacombs, those she once used to escape the clutches of Baron Grünewald, so long ago it seemed.

The suffering of Altstadt seemed to vanish far above.

Matthias once walked with her down those worm-eaten routes. She raised a torch pilfered from a sconce and harkened to the groaning evil therein. The dust had been disturbed, whether by Rufus or Wilhelm, she could not say. The earth began to quake. Something stirred in the stonework above. Sophia lifted her light and glanced over her shoulder, but saw nothing save the darkness from whence she came. Her mission was clear—to bring Rufus back from the brink.

"It'll be alright," she told herself, "it'll be alright."

It was not until Sophia came to a subterranean crossing that she felt her way along twisting tunnels. The bedrock had been eroded by waves of corrosive flow over the millennia—pockmarked, pitted with weird hollows—and the bottom was a smooth channel, alluding to a great girth that had festered its way like a fluke in the bowels of some beast. Warped as the Grünewalds' ambitions, the path was slick and steep, and Sophia raised her torch cautiously as she covered her nose and mouth—to mask the reek of halitosis and rotting flesh. At last, she came to the source of the stench. Halting before a sheer drop of unfathomable depth, Sophia found herself at the brink of the abyss—the Pit of Schloss Fleischburg.

It was cold and vast, a crater of unknown origin. Growths of crystalized mucus had formed like plaque around the steep perimeter, shimmering a pale yellow against her fleeting light. In lieu of magma or meteor, there lay the Maw of Madness. With row upon row of supernumerary fangs, its jawless width spanned the entirety of the caldera—snoring, breathing forth a miasma of black breath. The Thing in the Pit stirred in slumber, its nine rasping tongues limp and askew, exposing a sheer drop into its bottomless gullet.

"Rufus," she whispered.

Though Sophia had no reason to believe, she knew the heir had descended into the belly of the beast—one last time. Clutching the cure with shaky hands, she lingered upon the ledge, pondering the likelihood of breaking her legs upon the fall. Against all sense and reason, she leaned forward and let gravity take its course in a mock suicide.

Darkness swallowed her in body and soul.

When Sophia woke, she was somewhere in the intestinal labyrinth once more. Bioluminescent vermin shed scant light upon the pulsating walls, flickering like fireflies along red flesh, taunting her with the way forward. Step by step, the moistened floor sloshed under her boots. Far below, through vessel and vein, she listened to the irregular rhythm of a beating heart. Rufus's tracks led on due course. In the distance, Sophia heard a commanding voice, echoing off the walls in a fevered cry—a voice demanding retribution for the blood of the fallen.

"I should've known you'd risk your life to save that witch," Wilhelm's words faded into the unknown ahead. "Just as she tried to save you...."

Sophia peered around the bend, watching a maddened

shadow give chase.

"Now," he said, "I'm going to do what I should've done long ago!"

Sophia delicately drew her dagger and stalked the witch-hunter, eager to plunge the blade into his spine—to avenge Altstadt and her own dignity, but Wilhelm had already gone. The percussions of cancerous life were gaining speed. Forced to a crawl, she came upon a sagging sack of a chamber where the witch-hunter stood with a torch at hand, eying cysts and white polyps along the walls with disgust and abject horror.

"So, this is the womb of sin," he muttered. "Show yourself."

Sophia crept as quietly as she could, seconds from dealing a fatal blow—when Wilhelm spun around and grasped her wrist, twisting back, hate in his eyes.

"You," he snarled.

Sophia cried in pain, only for the witch-hunter to shove her back.

"You are truly a troublesome whore," he said.

"Rather be a whore than a murderer."

"You're words are as hollow as your love, witch." Wilhelm stepped forward. "You will not forestall my judgment any longer." In a flash of steel, the witch-hunter drew his own blade and lunged with somber conviction. "Die, and curse as you will!"

Sophia dodged his swings and recalled many a violent client. She'd dealt a pacifying punch more than once, but this was different—this was a duel. Reaching into her pocket, Sophia kept a pouch of pepper and dust for such an occasion and threw the powder into Wilhelm's face. He screamed and cupped his eyes, nearly dropping his sword. Sophia clenched her fist and dealt a blow to his gut—her dagger still lay on the fleshy floor.

"Clever witch," Wilhem spat. "How typical of your kind to—"

"It's pepper, you idiot."

Retrieving her blade, Sophia aimed to slit the witch-hunter's throat, only for Wilhelm to parry the strike as a blind duelist. Such an exchange of blows seemed to last for an eternity. Her every incision was calculated with surgical precision, aiming for arteries and veins, for she knew the anatomy of man better than himself—until she was knocked prone onto the fleshy floor.

Clattering against bony growths, the syringe rolled to Wilhelm's side.

The witch-hunter caught the glass under his boot. "So you believe you can 'cure' him?" he scoffed, pressing his heel against its cylindrical surface. "Haven't you done enough?"

Sophia stared on in terror, and yet, her fury did not yield.

"You're going to burn in hell," she said.

Wilhelm rolled his eyes. "You have no right to judge me. I know of your vile practice with Baron Grünewald—and Cronenberg. You've tortured those most vulnerable to sate your own ambitions. How many prongs through the eye, Sophia? How many to silence those you deemed unworthy of life? Dealing out lobotomies like pints at the bar." His face was shadowed by a hate unrivaled. "At least I am sincere in my conviction."

"I," Sophia paused, "that's...."

"Cruelty is a sad necessity in a world such as ours, but I will not be lectured by the likes of you." He raised a pistol with a steely click and took aim, pressing its barrel against her brow. "May the Lord have mercy on you, for I will not—"

Blood spewed from Wilhelm's mouth—eyes wide with sudden pain. Sophia gasped in shock. A spike of bone had pierced the witch-hunter's chest. There was a malicious gleam in the encroaching shadows. Clusters of eyes made themselves manifest. On a whim, the tentacle tossed his failing body aside like a rag doll, only to retreat into the depths.

The cure, though cracked, remained intact.

Sophia limped past her bludgeoned pain and spat upon

Wilhelm's corpse. Heaving and seething, she collected the cure, knowing well what had happened. Who had saved her? Moments from resuming her grievous pursuit, a glint of copper caught Sophia's eye. On Wilhelm's person was the moonlit medallion she had once given Rufus. She knelt and felt the cold metal against the palm of her hand. Gripping the charm, she knew the truth. It was not the Conqueror Worm that gave the heir his strength; rather, the bond they once shared.

"Rufus." She kissed the coin. "It'll be alright. I promise...."

In the depths of the abyss, Sophia treaded the sodden soil with grave hesitation. The throbbing of sickened organs was deafening, a concerto of drums, rattling, and pounding in her ears. Such was the innermost chamber of the Conqueror Worm. Faint laughter carried from vocal cords hidden far above, strumming and mocking her mortal resolve.

"So," it cooed, "you have come to accept the truth, just as the Conqueror Worm said you would. You're stronger than I thought. I am proud of you, my child."

"No," she wheezed.

Plumes of acidic gas all but blinded her, and yet, she could see, however faintly, the outline of that ultimate organ—hell was in the heart, an amalgam of shriveled tissue and worm-ridden filth, a living failure of flesh. And in its embrace, she saw a familiar form.

"Matthias Grünewald," she uttered.

"It seems we have an uninvited guest," said the ancestor.

Though she had noticed the figure before the heart, Sophia gasped upon seeing Rufus rise from a kneeling position, hands shaking and head bowed. She kept a cautious hand over the cure, almost hoping that he would charge and allow her to plunge that needle into his chest—to alleviate him of the evil she had dedicated a lifetime to studying.

"Sophia," his voice was numb and hollow.

"I," she choked, her voice caught between tears, "wanted to...."

"So, you would rid me of this," he paused, as if hesitant to finish the sentence, "gift?"

"I'd hardly call it a gift," Sophia said.

"You know so little," he said, "despite your studies."

"Rufus," she pleaded, "I came to save you from this. All of this. Come with me. It's not too late. We can go back to Chimay. Anywhere. Just leave all this behind."

Rufus remained silent, his back turned to her, brooding in imagined solitude. In lieu of the heir, Matthias spoke louder than ever. He smirked from within the heart.

"Even now, you would dare to stand against us?"

"No," Sophia stepped forward, "I'd stand against you."

"I see," Matthias's words reverberated throughout the chamber. "Listen well, girl. There are forces in this world. Forces you can scarcely comprehend, insidious as they are terrible, and we serve the greatest of them all."

"Do you?" Sophia scoffed. "You've been awfully quiet, Rufus." Her voice dripped with pain and spite all the same. "What do you think?"

"You do not understand," he said. "You do not know the weight of the worm."

"You're right," she stepped forward, "I don't, but—"

Tentacles of darkness sprouted from Rufus's spine, flailing in a seizure of madness. Terrible as they were, they served a mere demonstration to deter her from reaching a heart fractured by abandonment—or so she wanted to believe. The heir bowed his head, as if burdened by the blood of the fallen staining his hands, of those he did not save.

Despite her morbid fears and misgivings, Sophia did not relent. "I'm not going anywhere," she said. "I'm sorry. For all of it. I'm sorry I gave up on you. When you needed me the most. It doesn't have to be like this. Please, if you can still hear me, say something."

"He cannot," Matthias said, darkly. "Your words fall upon deaf ears, child. When will you understand? This isn't a fairy tale that can be salvaged by some kiss. Your insipid pursuit of his redemption means nothing. You have long exceeded your role."

Rufus straightened his posture, brooding.

"Come," Matthias raised his voice, "the Eclipse is upon us. Time is short. Return to me. Complete the circle. Release yourself from this prison of humanity."

Rufus obeyed and began his approach.

In a fit of blind fury, Sophia lunged with the syringe as a dagger of hope. As she charged down the visceral path, her voice rose to scream, desperate to stab the needle into Rufus's spine, to expel the parasite—the evil within. On instinct, he cracked the back of his hand against her cheek, sending her reeling with a chitinous blow. For a moment, he stared at his own palm, as if haunted by a wraith of regret. He loomed, but dared not touch her again.

"I," Rufus said, "will do what must be done."

Deaf to Sophia's weeping pleas, Rufus knelt and wordlessly swore fealty to the Conqueror Worm—a pact rooted in sin and horror. Though pains of despair impaled Sophia's soul, she raised that medallion, that charm of young love, and threw it to his feet.

"Remember who you are!" she cried.

Rufus paused and, for the first time, turned to face her, as if in shame. He knelt again to lift the medallion from the flesh, its chain jangling like a string of shackles.

"You are responsible for so much death," he said, "generations of pain. But that's all over now," he sneered. "You no longer need to posture and be tortured by the burden of our sins." He rose sharply, clutching the medallion, sizzling in his clenched fist. Sophia saw Rufus's sense of self shimmer brightly in his blue eyes, only to dim again. He tossed the charm aside and turned to Matthias, brandishing every eldritch weapon in his arsenal.

"I will take care," he said, "of everything."

At that moment, Rufus summoned a host of barbed and bladed tentacles, and the walls shivered in kind. He marched to the heart, gaining speed with murderous intent.

"What is this? What are you doing, my child?"

"Succeeding you, grandfather."

In a fit of horrific strength, Rufus plunged a host of tentacles into the weakened chambers of the heart. Matthias was torn asunder and cast aside as a fetid miscarriage upon the floor. Lording over the wounded thing, the heir ripped his ancestor's skull from its spine and stared into those hollow eyes. He smirked, as if contemplating a hint of irony, and crushed its cranium effortlessly. He approached the empty throne, his existential purpose, and crept inside the womb of sin as the Chosen of the Conqueror Worm. The earth began to quake in agony, corpse-lights shone from Rufus's every orifice, and a choir of suffering erupted throughout the Pit.

"Now," said the Prince of Worms, "we are one."

EPILOGUE

Sophia did not recall how she escaped the estate. Perhaps she was allowed to leave—whether an act of cruelty or twisted kindness, she could not say. Lost in dissociation, she wandered the blackened woods, wreathed in smoke and low mist. Hope had perished with the holocaust, which had brought Altstadt to its knees. Sophia was alone. Slowly, she scaled the hill, through the ashes and along the charred trees, basking in the sight of the dead barony.

The Eclipse had passed, as had Rufus.

Despair washed over Sophia in a tide of utter darkness. With the cure still in her trembling hands, she watched as murders of crows bowed their heads in mourning, singing a dirge for the innocents so senselessly slaughtered. Though she knew nothing of the coming centuries, so began the End of the World—man's gradual descent to his own demise. For as apocalyptic as the Thing in the Pit was, it merely plucked the soul as the string of a lyre, every note a scream. Such evil was not born of worms, but a distortion of man's instincts and lowest nature. Perhaps the world would heal once the flame of civilization was extinguished, when it emerged from its fragile shell. Perhaps in that lay true mercy.

And so, Sophia recalled a stanza smeared in nightsoil on the wall of the Narrenturm, written by one of her patients—one, it seemed, far wiser than she.

That play is the tragedy, 'Man,' and its hero, the Conqueror Worm.

THE END

Diagnosed with Asperger's Syndrome at a young age, Fallon O'Neill has been writing since his sophomore year of high school. These scribblings and vignettes would eventually become the earliest drafts of his debut novel, *Geist: Prelude*. Dedicated and passionate, Fallon has worked his novels with the Blue Moon Writers' Group for over seven years, culminating in winning second place at the *Will Albrecht Young Writers Competition* of 2012, and publication in the eighth issue of the *Blue Moon Art and Literary Review*. His favorite pastimes include grabbing a beer (or four) at the local bar, blasting soundtracks into his skull, and watching German movies from the '20s to keep the existential dread at bay.

www.ingramcontent.com/pod-product-compliance
Lightning Source LLC
LaVergne TN
LVHW090601110826
845146LV00001B/223
9798891264915